W9-CGL-783

CHÉRI *and* THE END OF CHÉRI

SIDONIE-GABRIELLE COLETTE (1873–1954) was born in the village of Saint-Sauveur-en-Puisaye, in Burgundy. She would recall her country childhood as an extended idyll. At the age of twenty, she married Henry Gauthier-Villars, better known as Willy—a Parisian rake fourteen years her senior. He pressed her into service as one of his many ghostwriters, and the autofictional Claudine novels—an erotically frank coming-of-age story—were originally published under his name. The series enjoyed a scandalous success. Separated from Willy in 1905, Colette supported herself as a music-hall mime before establishing her own reputation as a writer. In her old age, Colette, who published nearly eighty volumes of fiction, memoirs, journalism, and drama, among them classics of the twentieth century, would be celebrated as a national treasure, and she was the first Frenchwoman to be honored with a state funeral. In addition to *Chéri* and *The End of Chéri*, NYRB Classics publishes Colette's treatise on gender, *The Pure and the Impure*, translated by Herma Briffault.

PAUL EPRILE is a publisher, poet, and translator. He has translated three novels by Jean Giono for NYRB Classics: *Hill*, *The Open Road*, and *Melville*, for which he was awarded the 2018 Translation Prize of the French-American Foundation. He lives on the Niagara Escarpment in Ontario, Canada.

JUDITH THURMAN is the author of two prizewinning biographies: *Secrets of the Flesh: A Life of Colette* and *Isak Dinesen: The Life of a Storyteller*, which won the National Book Award. Her other work includes the essay collections *Cleopatra's Nose: 39 Varieties of Desire* and *A Left-Handed Woman*. She is a staff writer at *The New York* specializing in cultural criticism.

CHÉRI *and*
THE END OF CHÉRI

COLETTE

Translated from the French by
PAUL EPRILE

Introduction by
JUDITH THURMAN

NEW YORK REVIEW BOOKS

New York

THIS IS A NEW YORK REVIEW BOOK
PUBLISHED BY THE NEW YORK REVIEW OF BOOKS
435 Hudson Street, New York, NY 10014
www.nyrb.com

First published as a New York Review Books Classic in 2022.

Library of Congress Cataloging-in-Publication Data
Names: Colette, 1873–1954, author. | Eprile, Paul, translator. | Thurman, Judith, 1946– writer of introduction. | Colette, 1873–1954. Fin de Chéri. English.
Title: Chéri; and The end of the Chéri / by Colette; translated from the French by Paul Eprile; introduced by Judith Thurman.
Other titles: Chéri. English
Description: New York: New York Review Books, [2022] | Series: New York Review Books
Identifiers: LCCN 2022001010 (print) | LCCN 2022001011 (ebook) | ISBN 9781681376707 (paperback) | ISBN 9781681376714 (ebook)
Subjects: LCSH: Middle-aged women—Fiction. | Courtesans—Fiction. | Young men—Fiction. | France—Fiction. | LCGFT: Novels.
Classification: LCC PQ2605.O28 C513 2022b (print) | LCC PQ2605.O28 (ebook) | DDC 843/.912—dc23
LC record available at https://lccn.loc.gov/2022001010
LC ebook record available at https://lccn.loc.gov/2022001011

ISBN 978-1-68137-670-7
Available as an electronic book; ISBN 978-1-68137-671-4

Printed in the United States of America on acid-free paper.
10 9 8 7 6 5 4 3 2 1

CONTENTS

INTRODUCTION

I

SIDONIE-GABRIELLE Colette may be the most misunderstood of great writers. Her best work is revolutionary without seeming to be. Its subject is conventional in French literature: forbidden desire. But the desires that interest her aren't the seductions of a bedroom farce, or the passions that destroy a royal house or that ruin a provincial housewife. And they aren't illicit so much as inadmissible. They defy gender assignments that were once absolute, and mostly still are. "Men are terrible," Colette once remarked, hastening to add, "Women, too." They both have urges to dominate and devour; they both have yearnings for containment. The lovers in her fiction are slaves and masters who eroticize their primal bonds—faulty attachments from which they struggle to separate even as they refuse to. Incest, for Colette, is the taproot of love.

This charming writer, best known for *Gigi*, is, in other words, a dangerous heretic. So I'm always disheartened when a cool French girl enamored with Georges Bataille recalls Colette as someone whom "Nana read *sous le bonnet*"—under the hair dryer. Or when an old actor who once emoted *Phèdre* natters on about her cats. Or when Sido, the mythical earth mother of Colette's memoirs (from whose thrall none of her four children escaped), is mistaken for a Burgundian Martha Stewart. As for *Gigi*, let's pause to consider it. Colette was old and bedridden when she wrote that delicious bagatelle during the depths of the Nazi Occupation, and its happy ending—unique in her oeuvre—capitulates to a fantasy. "To receive happiness from someone," she reflects, more like herself, in *The Pure and the Impure*, "is it not to choose the sauce with which one wants to be eaten?"

Here, though, one should admit that Colette bears some responsibility for the category errors of her critics and devotees. She is one of the supreme stylists in French, yet she liked to claim she was "born *not* to write." Her first husband, the deplorable Willy, who discovered her talent and then exploited it, christened her "a child of nature," and for the next fifty years, she played up her paganism on stage and page. ("My monstrous innocence," she called it.) Her vitality was too truculent; her speech, as she said proudly, was too "familiar"; and her fiction too beloved by its female readers to be taken seriously by the prissy mandarins who scorned them and her. Colette got fat and kept eating. She wrote an advice column for a women's magazine. She opened a beauty salon and did makeovers in a lab coat. "I'm not worthy of politics," she told an interviewer. But what are politics? A devious scrimmage for the upper hand. Colette understands power as viscerally as Euripides.

2

Nature's children are generally too busy climbing trees to produce great literature. Writing, Colette told a friend, was that "vomitous task" to which she "hitched" herself over and over. *Chéri* was her first masterpiece, although she already had a distinguished backlist. The Great War had just ended when she sat down to write it, at forty-five, in her manor by the sea in Brittany—a gift from the Marquise de Morny, her transvestite lover. But the title character was conceived in a series of belle époque sketches that Colette had published in *Le Matin*, the Paris daily that paid her rent. (Had she never written a word of fiction, she would still be remembered as one of the most gifted and prolific French journalists of her time.) The first Chéri was an inconsequential little snot with acne and a coke habit who falls into the clutches of a decrepit courtesan. The ever-frugal Colette recycled that grotesque couple in *Chéri* as "old Lili" and her teenage princeling. They serve as a warning to the protagonists as to what their union might become.

The unspoken pact between incestuous lovers is that the master-parent will maintain her detachment while indulging the child's guiltless voracity. When the novel opens, in 1912, Léa de Lonval is forty-nine and her "bratty nursling" is twenty-four. Their liaison, which Léa "sometimes called . . . 'an adoption,'" has lasted for six years. We meet them in dishabille, in her pink bedroom. Neither knows they are about to be expelled from Eden. In the paradise they inhabit, time and age have no meaning, nor do shame or idleness. This menopausal Eve and her pubescent Adam feast, frolic, and fornicate as the gods do, which is how they quarrel—in sublime bad faith. Colette endows them with exquisitely attuned senses: her own. No writer evokes pleasure with more nuance, and none is more susceptible to revulsion.

Chéri's arranged marriage disrupts their idyll. But when he jilts his young bride and returns, at midnight, to Léa's bedroom ("Nounoune, darling! I've rejoined you," he cries, as he throws himself at her), she surrenders to "the most terrible joy of her life." In doing so, she betrays her mortality—a flaccid neck, a vulnerable heart—and there's no return from that revelation. But Colette commutes their grief with another revelation: that the dalliance they treated as a transaction was, for both of them, a true love.

3

Six staggeringly eventful years in Colette's life—1920 to 1926— separate *Chéri* and his *End*. A proprietary mother and an ensorcelled child figure in her work of that interregnum: her idealized memoir of Sido, *My Mother's House*; her inspired libretto for Ravel's opera, *L'Enfant et les sortilèges*; and *The Ripening Seed*, a luminous story of lost innocence. The innocent in question is a teenage boy deflowered by an older woman, and his character was based on the virginal apprentice whom Colette had been schooling *à sa manière*: her sixteen-year-old stepson, Bertrand de Jouvenel. She had imagined Chéri long before this wanton adventure, but, as Bertrand would reflect as an old man, not ungratefully: "Perhaps she wanted to live what she had written."

Colette decided to get rid of Chéri at a pivotal moment in her own life—one of those radical breaks with the past that she calls a rebirth. Her second marriage was ending, and the affair with Bertrand was its coup de grâce. She had just met the man who became her third husband, and while their ardor would dissipate, their devotion would last. *The End of Chéri* contemplates the fates she had managed to escape: of a grown child mourning a state of fusion, and of an aging woman who achieves self-mastery at the price of her sex. In that respect, Léa is a crueler caricature of Colette than any cartoonist had ever drawn.

Most of Colette's sequels (the Claudine franchise and others) were inferior in power and artistry to their originals. *The End of Chéri* is an exception: a bleak and ambitious social history disguised as the debacle of an antihero. The men in Colette's work tend to be shallow, yet however terribly they behave, she pities them as the weaker sex. "Feminine delicacy in literature," she wrote to a friend, is "one of those clichés that make me furious. Except for three or four female writers, their [women's] vulgarity, their sentimental brutality, has all that it takes to make any man whatsoever feel wounded and embarrassed."

That is Chéri's predicament as the hostage of a gynocracy. A decade has passed since he parted from Léa, and through his eyes, Colette captures the sea change in manners, the shift in sex roles, the breakdown of hierarchies, the speeding up of time, and the alternating currents of greed, euphoria, and despair that defined postwar Paris. He has returned from the front as one of those casualties whose fatal wounds are invisible. The meek sylph whom he married, a rich cocotte's daughter, now manages their household and fortune with an immodest competence that disgusts him. Despite Edmée's beauty, which he admires ("It's not fair."), their conjugal relations are fraternal. She tolerates his disdain partly because her affections are engaged elsewhere —with the maimed soldiers in the hospital she has endowed and the doctor who runs it.

"What would you like Chéri to do in life?" Colette asked a journalist. "He wasn't going to become an industrialist!" The gigolos and kept women of her fiction belong to an ancient nobility whose code of honor is vested in hedonism, and the subtlest among them practice it as an art. But Cheri's muse has deserted him. He can't find relief from his sensual and moral shell shock in any of his old vices, including malice. When his mother suggests that a fling might do him some good, he frightens her by admitting that women leave him cold. "Ma Peloux" then makes a phone call.

Chéri hasn't ceased to dream of Léa, but he also hasn't thought about her. Now he calculates that she must be nearly sixty and passes out. His horror fades though, and he represses it. When a maid admits him to the salon of a bourgeois apartment, he finds two old dames engaged in coarse banter. One is a massive figure with a thatch of gray hair. "The thick flesh on her upper arms, as fat as thighs, kept them from resting at her sides. The plain skirt and the long, nondescript jacket—half-unbuttoned to reveal a pleated jabot—proclaimed . . . a sort of sexless dignity." The haunting, familiar laugh resonating from her throat plunges Chéri into "a vortex of memories," but he wonders where Léa is. Slowly the truth dawns on him.

4

Colette holed up to write *The End of Chéri*. She didn't want any distractions. In a letter to her friend Margaret Moreno, she marveled at her style's "nudity" and at an "aversion to adornment which surprises even me." Her rejection of excess mirrors Chéri's repugnance for the enterprise of his former friends in the demimonde, and the smug philanthropizing of his wife and mother. Years later, she admitted that she'd killed him off because she couldn't bear the thought of his heroically pointless life needing to justify itself. "Yes, Chéri's purity!" she exclaimed with vehemence, as one might protest an unjust conviction. "I believed it existed."

An ideal of purity animates her prose. Consider this passage, in which Chéri has retreated from Lea's flat like a sleepwalker to find himself in a street that he no longer recognizes:

> *Il remarqua que le ciel rose se mirait dans le ruisseau, gorgé encore de pluie, sur le dos bleu des hirondelles volant à ras de terre, et parce que l'heure devenait fraîche, et que traîtreusement le souvenir qu'il importait se retirait au fond de lui-même pour y prendre sa force et sa dimension définitives, il crut qu'il avait tout oublié et il se sentit heureux.*

Now consider it in Paul Eprile's English:

> He did notice that the pink sky was being reflected by the stream in the gutter—which was still swollen with rain—and off the blue backs of the swallows that were swooping level with the ground; and, because the evening air was cooling down and the memory he'd taken away with him was shrinking, like a traitor, into the inmost depths of his being—there to assume its definitive power and scale—he believed he'd forgotten all about it, and he felt happy.

Colette's fiction is as daunting to translate as poetry. It demands an ideal of purity as ruthless as her own. Few French writers have a richer vocabulary, and few are as innately musical. Colette's sensuality generates an intoxication that the sting of her wit and the austerity of her gaze ground like a lightning rod. Her translator needs some of the traits she prized in a lover: selfless patience, undistracted prowess, a lithe imagination.

I have never wanted to read Colette in English because she has never sounded like Colette. Finally, in this volume, she does. Eprile inhabits her.

—JUDITH THURMAN

CHÉRI

"L é a! Let me have your pearl necklace! Can you hear me, Léa? Give me your string of pearls!"

No answer came from the big bedstead. The frame, of wrought iron and incised brass, shone in the darkness like armor.

"Why wouldn't you let me have it? It looks just as good on me as it does on you, even better!"

At the snap of the clasp, the lace bedcovers stirred. Two bare, sumptuous, slender-wristed arms lifted two lovely, lazy hands.

"Leave it alone, Chéri, you've played around enough with that necklace."

"I'm having fun . . . Are you afraid I'll steal it?"

In front of the rose-colored curtains suffused with sunlight, he was dancing, all black, like a graceful devil with an inferno at his back. When he drew away toward the bed, he turned all white again, from his silk pajamas to his doeskin *babouches*.

"I'm not afraid," answered the voice—soft and low—from the bed. "But you're putting too much strain on the string. Those pearls are heavy."

"Yes, they are," said Chéri appreciatively. "He didn't take you lightly, whoever gave you this piece."

He stood, facing a full-length mirror that was mounted on the wall between the two windows, and gazed at his image: that of a very beautiful, very young man, neither tall nor short, his hair tinged with blue like the plumage of a blackbird. He opened his pajama top to reveal an olive-hued, firmly muscled chest, rounded like a shield, and an identical pink spark played on his teeth, on the whites of his dark eyes, and on the pearls of the necklace.

"Take off that necklace," insisted the feminine voice. "Do you hear me?"

At a standstill before his image, the young man was chuckling.

"Yes, yes, I hear. I know very well you're afraid I might take it away from you."

"No. But if I did offer it to you, you'd be capable of accepting it."

He ran to the bed and threw himself down, indignant.

"You bet I would! Me—I'm above conventions. I, for one, think it's ridiculous that a man can accept one pearl for a tiepin from a woman, or two pearls for some cufflinks, but considers himself disgraced if she gives him fifty—"

"Forty-nine."

"Forty-nine, I know the number. So, are you saying it doesn't look good on me? Are you telling me I'm ugly?"

Leaning over her while she reclined, he gave a provocative laugh, baring his small teeth and the moist interior of his lips.

Léa sat up in bed. "No, I won't say that. In the first place, because you wouldn't believe it. But can't you laugh without wrinkling your nose that way? You'll be good and happy when you get a few creases in the corners, won't you?"

He immediately stopped laughing, smoothed his forehead, and tucked back the underside of his chin with the deftness of an old coquette. They were giving each other uncharitable looks: she, leaning on her elbows, in the midst of her lingerie and lace; he, sitting sidesaddle, like an Amazon, on the edge of the bed. He was thinking: "A fine one she is to talk about the wrinkles *I'll* get." And she: "Why is he so unappealing when he laughs, this boy who's the very essence of beauty?" She considered for a moment, then finished her thought out loud: "It's that you look so mean when you're in high spirits... You laugh only out of spite or mockery. It makes you ugly. You're often ugly."

"It's not true!" Chéri yelled in anger.

Rage was knitting his eyebrows above the bridge of his nose; widening his eyes, which were filled with a glare of disrespect and fringed with bristling lashes; and half opening the pure, disdainful arch of his mouth. Léa smiled to see him the way she loved him: rebellious, then submissive, loosely bound, incapable of taking flight. She placed a hand on the youthful head that was shaking the yoke impatiently. She murmured, the way you do to soothe an animal, "There ... there ... What is it ... what is it now ..."

He leaned down on the lovely, broad shoulder, nuzzling in with his forehead and his nose, hollowing out his usual place, already closing his eyes and seeking the security of his long morning nap. But Léa pushed him away.

"None of that, Chéri! You're having lunch with our National Harpy, and it's twenty to twelve."

"Really? I'm dining at the boss's? You too?"

Léa slid lazily back under the covers.

"Not me. I'm on holiday. I'll go for coffee at two thirty, or tea at six, or a cigarette at a quarter to eight ... Don't worry, she'll always see enough of me. Besides, she didn't invite me."

Chéri, on his feet now, still sulking, lit up with mischief. "I know! I know why! We're going to have extra-special company. We're going to have Marie-Laure and her horror of a daughter!"

Léa's big blue eyes, which had been wandering, came to a rest. "Ah! Yes? Charming, the young one. Less so than her mother, but charming ... Now, take off that necklace, once and for all."

"What a pity," sighed Chéri, as he unfastened it. "It would go well in the wedding basket."

Léa leaned forward on one elbow. "Whose basket?"

"Mine," said Chéri, with comical self-importance. "*My* basket and *my* jewelry for *my* wedding."

He leapt up, landed on his feet after a properly executed *entrechat-six*, parted the door-curtain headfirst, and vanished, shouting, "My bath, Rose! As quick as you can! I'm having lunch at the boss's!"

"There you go," Léa mused. "A lake in the bathroom, with eight towels swimming in it, and razor scum in the washbasin. If only I had two bathrooms..."

But she reminded herself, like many times before, that it would mean losing a wardrobe and scaling back the dressing room, and she concluded, like many times before: "I'll bide my time until Chéri's wedding."

She lay back and noticed that, yesterday, Chéri had thrown his socks on the mantelpiece, his underwear on the secretaire, and his tie around the neck of her portrait bust. She smiled, in spite of herself, at this hot-blooded, masculine messiness, and half closed her big, placid eyes. A youthful blue, they'd kept all their chestnut lashes. At forty-nine years of age, Léonie Vallon, commonly known as Léa de Lonval, was approaching the end of a successful career as a well-heeled courtesan, a good-hearted girl whom life had spared the flattering catastrophes and the exalted sorrows. She kept the year of her birth secret; but she freely admitted, while casting a look of voluptuous condescension on Chéri, that she was reaching the stage of allowing herself some little indulgences. She loved order, beautiful linens, aged wines, refined cuisine. As a young blond idol, and in her maturity as a rich demimondaine, she'd tolerated neither angry outbursts nor misunderstandings, and her friends recalled a race day at Auteuil, around 1895, when Léa replied to the sub-editor of *Gil Blas*, who'd addressed her as "my dear artiste":

"Artiste? Oh, really, dear friend, my lovers are awfully loose-tongued..."

Her contemporaries were jealous of her unshakably good health. And the young women—whose backsides and bellies the fashions of 1912 were already filling out—mocked Léa's generous bosom. In like manner, both young and old envied her Chéri.

"Well, my God," Léa used to say, "there's no reason for it. Let them take him. I don't keep him on a leash, and he goes out on his own."

She was half lying about this, proud of an affair—she sometimes called it "an adoption," as she tended to be candid—that had lasted for six years.

"The basket..." Léa said again. "To marry off Chéri...It's not possible, it's not...human...To give a young girl to Chéri...Why not throw her to the hounds? People don't know what Chéri is."

She rolled her necklace—it had been tossed on the bed—between her fingers, like a rosary. Nowadays she took it off at night, because Chéri, who adored the beautiful pearls and was wont to caress them in the morning, would have noticed too often that Léa's neck, grown fleshier, was losing its whiteness and exposing slackened muscles behind the skin. Still sitting, she fastened the clasp at her nape and picked up a mirror from the bedside table.

"I look like a farmwife," she judged, unsparingly. "A market gardener. A market gardener from Normandy who'd head off to the potato fields wearing a necklace. This suits me like an ostrich feather up my nose...and I'm being polite."

She shrugged her shoulders, harshly critical of everything she didn't like in herself anymore: a high complexion, healthy, a little flushed, an outdoor complexion ideal for deepening the pure blue of her irises encircled by a darker blue. Her proud nose still found favor in Léa's own eyes; "Marie Antoinette's nose!" maintained Chéri's mother, who never failed to add: "And in two more years, this lovely Léa will have the chin of Louis XVI." Léa's mouth, with its close-set teeth, almost never burst into laughter, but smiled frequently along with her large eyes, which blinked slowly and rarely; a smile a hundred times praised, celebrated in song, photographed; a meaningful and confiding smile, one that could never wear thin.

As for her body, "It's well known," Léa used to say, "that a sound body stands the test of time." She could still show it off: this large white body with its rosy blush, blessed with long legs, and the flat sort of back you see on the nymphs in Italian fountains. Her dimpled derrière, her high, upturned breasts, could hold out, said Léa, "until well after Chéri's wedding."

She got up, wrapped herself in a dressing gown, and opened the curtains herself. The midday sun entered the pink bedroom: cheerful, over-decorated in a style of dated luxury, with doubled lace curtains on the windows, ribbed fabric with a rose-leaf pattern on the walls, gilded woodwork, electric lights in pink and white shades, and antique furniture covered in modern silks. Léa wouldn't give up this cozy room, or her bed: an imposing masterpiece, indestructible, of brass and wrought iron, hard on the eyes and even harder on the shins.

"No, not at all, not at all," Chéri's mother used to protest, "it's not so bad as all that. Myself, I like it, that room. It's of a period. It has its style. It reminds you of Païva, a harlot's palace."

While she put up her disheveled hair, Léa smiled at this memory of the "National Harpy." When she heard two doors slam and a shoe crash against a piece of fragile furniture, she hastily powdered her face. Chéri was coming back in fighting mood, wearing shirt and trousers, his ears white with talc.

"Where is my tiepin? What a miserable dive! Are they filching jewelry now?"

"It was Marcel—he stuck it in his cravat to go and do the shopping," said Léa, straight-faced.

Chéri, devoid of humor, ricocheted off the jest. He stopped prowling, and could only come back with "That's delightful! And my ankle boots?"

"Which ones?"

"The buck!"

Léa, seated at her dressing table, raised excessively amorous eyes. "I didn't make you say it," she insinuated, with tenderness.

"The day a woman loves me for my intelligence, I'll be truly done in," Chéri shot back. "In the meantime, I want my pin and my boots."

"For what? You don't wear a pin with a jacket, and you already have your shoes on."

Chéri stamped his foot.

"I'm fed up. Nobody looks after me around here! I'm fed up!"

Léa set down her comb.

"All right, then! Clear out."

He shrugged his shoulders, rudely. "You don't really mean that!"

"Clear out. I've always had a horror of house guests who ransack the kitchen and smear cream cheese on the mirrors with their sticky fingers. Go back to your sainted mother, my child, and stay there."

He couldn't endure Léa's gaze, lowered his eyes, and protested like a schoolboy, "So, what, I don't have any say? At least you'll loan me the car to go to Neuilly?"

"No."

"Because?"

"Because I'm going out at two, and Philibert's having his lunch now."

"Where are you going at two?"

"To fulfill my religious duties. But did you want three francs for a taxi?... Silly boy," she resumed, gently, "maybe I'll come by for coffee at Mother Superior's at two. Doesn't that make you happy?"

He shook his forehead like a little ram.

"People abuse me, they won't do anything for me, they hide my things, they..."

"So, you'll never learn how to dress yourself?"

She took the tie out of Chéri's hands and knotted it for him.

"There! Oh, that purple tie!... In fact, it's just right for the lovely Marie-Laure and her offspring... And you wanted to add a pearl, on top of all of that? Little show-off... Why not some dangling earrings?"

He ceased to resist, blissful, slack, irresolute, in the grip again of a sluggishness and a delight that made his eyes close...

"Nounoune, darling..." he murmured.

She swept the talc from his ears, and straightened the fine bluish line that parted Chéri's hair. Then she dabbed his temples with a finger dipped in perfume and rapidly kissed—because she couldn't help herself—the enticing mouth that was breathing so close to her. Chéri opened his eyes, his lips, held out his hands... She drew away.

"No! A quarter to one! Off with you! And I never want to see you again!"

"Never?"

"Never!" she hurled at him, laughing with enraged tenderness.

Alone, she smiled with pride, let out a broken sigh of subdued lust, and listened to Chéri's footsteps in the courtyard. She saw him open and shut the gate, then set off with his winged stride, to be greeted right away by the rapture of three shopgirls walking arm in arm. "Oh me, oh my! . . . It's not possible, he must be fake! . . . Should we ask for a touch?"

But Chéri, indifferent, didn't even turn around.

"My bath, Rose! The manicurist can leave. It's too late. The blue tailored suit—the new one; the blue hat—the one with the white lining; and the little shoes with the straps . . . no, wait . . ."

Léa, her legs crossed, touched her bare ankle and shook her head. "No, the blue lace-up booties, the kid leather ones. My legs are a bit swollen today. It's the heat."

The lady's maid—elderly, coiffed in tulle—gave Léa an understanding look.

"It's . . . it's the heat," she repeated obediently, rounding her shoulders, as if to say: "We know . . . Everything has to wear out . . ."

With Chéri gone, Léa went back to being lively, determined, unburdened. In less than an hour she was bathed, rubbed with sandalwood cologne, her hair was done, her shoes were on. While the curling iron was heating up, she found time to examine the butler's account book and summon the manservant Émile to show him a misty blue patch on a mirror. She darted a confident eye—almost never deceived—around herself and ate her lunch in joyful solitude, smiling at the dry Vouvray and the June strawberries served, with their stems, on a faience dish the color of a wet green frog. Long ago, someone who loved to dine must have chosen, for this rectangular room, the large Louis XVI mirrors and the English furnishings of the same era; the airy sideboards; the tall wheeled trolley; and the slender, sturdy chairs; all of them made from wood almost black and decorated with delicate garlands. The mirrors and the massive pieces of silver plate caught the flood of daylight and reflected the green trees on avenue Bugeaud. While she ate, Léa closely examined a residue of rouge polishing powder in the engravings of a fork, and then shut one eye, the better to judge the sheen on the dark woodwork. The butler, standing behind her, dreaded these exercises.

"Marcel," Léa said, "your wax polish has clung to the silver for a week."

"Madame thinks so?"

"She thinks so. Use some mineral spirits and melt it away in the bain-marie, it will take no time to redo. You brought up the Vouvray a little too early. Close the shutters once you've cleared, we're in for some real heat."

"Very good, madame. Will Monsieur Ch—Monsieur Peloux be dining this evening?"

"I think so . . . No cream-filled desserts tonight, just make us some strawberry sorbets. Coffee now in my boudoir."

As she rose, tall and erect, her legs visible through the skirt wrapped tight against her thighs, she had the opportunity to read, in the butler's discreet glance, a "madame is beautiful" that did not displease her.

"Beautiful . . ." Léa said to herself as she climbed the stairs to her boudoir. "No. It's over now. At this point, I need white linen next to my face, and very pale pink for my undies and dressing gowns. Beautiful . . . bah . . . it hardly matters anymore."

Still, she didn't allow herself any siesta at all in her painted silk boudoir, after coffee and the daily papers. And it was with martial mien that she ordered her chauffeur: "To Madame Peloux's."

The arid tree-lined avenues of the Bois de Boulogne shaded by their new June greenery already fading in the wind; the tollgate; Neuilly; the boulevard d'Inkermann . . . "How many times have I made this trip?" Léa asked herself. She counted, then grew tired of counting, and paid close attention, while pausing in her tracks on Madame Peloux's gravel, to the sounds that were coming from the house.

"They're in the conservatory," she said.

She had freshened her powder before arriving and had drawn the blue veil—a gauze as fine as a mist—over her chin. To the servant who asked her to come through the house, she answered, "No, I'd rather go around through the garden."

A real garden—almost a park—enveloped the sprawling, all-white suburban Parisian villa. In the days when Neuilly was still on the outskirts of the city, Madame Peloux's villa was called "a country estate." The stables, now used as garages, and the outbuildings, with their kennels and washhouses, gave evidence of this, as did the scale of the billiards room, the conservatory, and the dining room.

"This place cost Madame Peloux a small fortune," devoutly repeated the old spongers who came, in exchange for dinner and a glass of brandy, to sit facing her for hands of bezique or poker. And these dowagers would add: "But where *doesn't* Madame Peloux have money?"

As she walked in the shade of the acacias, between the massed, flaming rhododendrons and rose-covered arbors, Léa could hear a murmur of voices pierced by Madame Peloux's nasal blasts and a burst of Chéri's humorless laughter.

"He laughs badly, that child," she mused. She paused for a moment to focus on a different, female tone—retiring, kind—that was quickly drowned out by the formidable blast.

"There, that's the girl," thought Léa.

She took a few quick steps and reached the threshold of a glass-walled conservatory. Madame Peloux sprang up, blaring, "Here she is, our lovely friend!"

Compact as a keg, Madame Peloux (in reality Mademoiselle Peloux) had been a dancer between the ages of ten and sixteen. Sometimes Léa would search, in Madame Peloux, for traces of the little blond and pudgy Eros of the past and the dimpled nymph who followed. She found only the big, unyielding eyes; the finely chiseled, forward-thrusting nose; and a coquettish way she still had of placing her feet in the fifth position, like the member of a ballet company.

Chéri, brought back to life from the depths of a rocking chair, kissed Léa's hand with unintentional grace, then spoiled his gesture with a "Damn it! You've worn a veil again, I hate that."

"Would you please leave her alone!" Madame Peloux intervened. "You don't ask a woman why she's put on a veil! We'll never make anything of him," she said, fondly, to Léa.

Two women had stood up in the pale yellow shadow of the straw blind. One of them, dressed in mauve, held her hand out, somewhat stiffly, to Léa, who assessed her from head to foot.

"My God, you're so beautiful, Marie-Laure! Nothing is as perfect as you are."

Marie-Laure condescended to smile. She was a young redhead with brown eyes, who dazzled without moving or speaking. As though she were flattering herself, she pointed to the other young woman. "But would you recognize my daughter Edmée?" she said.

Léa held out a hand toward the girl, who was slow to take it.

"I should have recognized you, my dear, but a schoolgirl your age changes quickly, and Marie-Laure changes only to disconcert us more every time we see her. Are you all done now with boarding school?"

"I should certainly hope so, I should certainly hope so!" blared Madame Peloux. "You can't hide it under a bushel forever, this charm, this grace, this marvel of nineteen springs!"

"Eighteen," Marie-Laure said, sweetly.

"Eighteen, eighteen! But, of course, eighteen! Léa, do you remember? This girl was taking her first communion the same year Chéri ran away from boarding school, isn't that right? Yes, you nasty brat, you ran off and frightened both of us out of our wits!"

"I remember very well," Léa said, and exchanged a little nod with Marie-Laure—something like the "touché" that honest fencers call out.

"She has to get married, she has to get married!" went on Madame Peloux, who never repeated a truism less than twice. "We'll all go to the wedding!"

She fluttered her short arms about, and the young woman looked at her with unaffected dread.

"She's the right sort of daughter for Marie-Laure," Léa reflected, observing the girl closely. "In every way that her mother is showy, she's subdued. Bushy hair, ash-blond like it's been powdered; eyes that are restless and secretive; a mouth that holds back from talking, from smiling...Just what Marie-Laure needed, but she must hate her all the same..."

Madame Peloux cast a maternal smile at Léa and the young woman. "How friendly they were already getting in the garden, these two children!"

She pointed toward Chéri, who was standing in front of the glass wall of the conservatory, smoking. He was clenching his cigarette holder between his teeth, with his head thrown back to avoid the smoke. The three women looked at the young man, who, even with his forehead leaning back, his lashes half-closed, and his feet together, still seemed like a winged figure soaring, motionless, in the air... Léa wasn't the least bit mistaken about the bewildered, defeated look in the eyes of the girl, and granted herself the pleasure of giving her a start by touching her arm. Edmée's whole body shivered. She pulled her arm back and spoke, fiercely, under her breath: "What?"

"Nothing," Léa answered. "My glove had dropped."

"Shall we go, Edmée?" Marie-Laure ordered breezily.

The young woman, mute and obedient, came up to Madame Peloux, who fluttered the tips of her wings. "Already? But no! We'll meet again soon! We'll meet again soon!"

"It's late," said Marie-Laure. "You expect a lot of guests on your Sunday afternoons. This child isn't used to society."

"Yes, yes!" Madame Peloux cried tenderly. "She's lived such a sheltered, solitary life!"

Marie-Laure smiled, and Léa gave her a look as if to say: "Now it's your turn!"

"But we'll be coming back soon."

"Thursday, Thursday! Léa, are you coming for lunch on Thursday too?"

"I'm coming," Léa replied.

Chéri had rejoined Edmée at the entrance to the conservatory. He stood close to her, disdaining any conversation. He heard Léa's promise and turned around. "Right. We'll go for a drive," he suggested.

"Yes, yes, just the thing at your age," Madame Peloux poured forth, with emotion. "Edmée will ride in the front with Chéri, he'll drive, and the rest of us will sit in the back. Yield to the young! Yield to the young! Chéri, my love, will you ask for Marie-Laure's car to be brought around?"

Her tiny, round feet teetering on the gravel, she led her visitors to a turn in the walk, then handed them over to Chéri. When she came back in, Léa had taken her hat off and lit a cigarette.

"Aren't they lovely, the two of them!" Madame Peloux said breathlessly. "Don't you agree, Léa?"

"Delightful," Léa breathed out, with a stream of smoke. "But it's that Marie-Laure . . . !"

Chéri was on his way back in. "What's she done, Marie-Laure?" he asked.

"Such beauty!"

"Ah! . . . Ah! . . ." Madame Peloux nodded. "It's true, it's true . . . how pretty she was!"

Chéri and Léa looked at each other and laughed.

"'She was'!" Léa exclaimed. "But she's youth itself! She doesn't have a single wrinkle. And she can wear pale mauve. That awful color! I hate it, and it hates me in return."

The big, relentless eyes and the narrow nose looked away from a glass of brandy.

"Youth itself! Youth itself!" yapped Madame Peloux. "But excuse me! Excuse me! Marie-Laure had Edmée in 1895, no, '94. At that point, she'd run off with a singing master and had dumped Khalil-Bey, who'd given her the famous pink diamond, the one that . . . No! No! Wait! . . . It was a year earlier! . . ."

She was blasting away, loud and off-key. Léa put a hand over her ear. Chéri stated tersely, "An afternoon like this would be ever so beautiful, if it weren't for my mother's voice."

She looked, without anger, at her son. She was used to his impudence. Keeping her dignity intact, she sat far back, feet dangling, in a wing chair too high for her short legs. In her hand, she was warming a glass of eau-de-vie. Léa, swaying in a rocking chair, cast her eyes from time to time on Chéri: Chéri sprawled out on the airy rattan couch, his jacket open, a half-extinguished cigarette hanging from his lip, a lock of hair across his brow; and she stroked him with a whisper, calling him an adorable scoundrel.

The three of them subsisted there, near each other, making no effort to please or to talk; peaceful and, in a way, happy. Long mutual familiarity left them in silence, sank Chéri into torpor, and filled Léa with calm. Because of the increasing heat, Madame Peloux pulled her tight skirt up to her knees, exposing her stout sailor's calves. Chéri angrily tore off his cravat, eliciting a "tsk...tsk..." of reprimand from Léa.

"Oh, leave that boy alone," Madame Peloux objected, as though half waking from a dream. "It's so hot... Do you want a kimono, Léa?"

"No, thank you. I'm quite all right."

These afternoon vulgarities revolted her. Never had her youthful lover surprised her unkempt, or with her bodice unlaced, or wearing slippers during the day. "Completely nude, if you wish," she used to say, "but not just bare-bosomed." She picked up her illustrated journal again but didn't read it. "This Ma Peloux and her son," she mused, "sit them down in front of a well-laid table, or take them out to the country, and in a wink, the mother rips off her corset, and the son his vest. Like tavern-keepers on vacation." She lifted her eyes, vindictively, to the so-called tavern-keeper and saw he was sleeping, his lashes pressed against his pale cheeks, his mouth closed. At its crests, the delectable arc of his upper lip, lit from below, caught two points of silvery light, and Léa had to admit that he looked more like a god than a wine merchant. Without getting up, she gingerly plucked the smoldering cigarette from between Chéri's fingers and tossed it in the ashtray. The sleeping boy's hand relaxed and let his tapered fingers spill like wilted flowers, fingers armed with cruel-looking nails, a hand not at all feminine, but a little more beautiful than one might have wanted, a hand Léa had kissed a hundred times, not in submission, but for pleasure, for the scent...

She looked over the top of her journal, toward Madame Peloux. "Is she sleeping too?" Léa was glad that the mother-and-son siesta might give her—she who was wide awake—an hour of peace and quiet, amid the heat, the shade, and the sunshine.

But Madame Peloux wasn't sleeping. She was sitting, Buddhistic, in her wing chair, staring straight ahead, sucking back her cognac with the intense concentration of an alcoholic nursling.

"Why isn't she sleeping?" Léa wondered. "It's Sunday. She's had a good lunch. She's waiting for the old tramps who turn up for her at-home at five. In view of this, she should be sleeping. If she's not sleeping, she must be up to no good."

They'd known each other for twenty-five years. Inimical intimacy between loose women, women whom one man enriches and then abandons and another man brings to ruin; irascible friendship between rivals, lying in wait for the first wrinkle and the first gray hair; fellowship of worldly, pragmatic women, with a talent for financial risk-taking, but one of them miserly and the other hedonistic ... These connections matter. A different, even stronger bond had drawn them together later in life: Chéri.

Léa remembered Chéri as a child: an astonishing beauty with long curls. When he was very little, he wasn't yet known as Chéri, but simply Fred.

Chéri, by turns neglected and adored, grew up amid bleached-blond chambermaids and lanky, embittered valets. Even though, mysteriously, he'd been born to enormous wealth, you never saw a "Miss" or a "Fräulein" at Chéri's side; he was preserved, by his loud shouts, from "those vampires!"

"Charlotte Peloux, woman of a bygone era!" the aged, dried-up, next-to-expired, and indestructible Baron de Berthellemy used to say, in his free and easy way. "Charlotte Peloux, I salute you. You are the only woman of easy virtue who has dared to raise her boy as the son of a whore! Woman of a bygone era: you don't read, you never travel, you meddle in the affairs of your only neighbor, and you have your child raised by the servants. How pure this is! How like a novel by Edmond About! How like one by Gustave Droz, even! And to think that you haven't the slightest inkling!"

So Chéri tasted all the joys of a debauched childhood. While he was still lisping, he soaked up the sordid gossip of the butler's pantry. He shared the clandestine suppers in the kitchen. He had iris milk baths in his mother's tub, and hasty wipe-downs with the corner of a towel. He suffered from surfeits of sweets, and hunger cramps when they forgot to feed him his dinner. He languished, half-naked, his nose running, at the flower festivals where Charlotte Peloux displayed him sitting on a heap of wet roses. But at the age of twelve, he had a ball in an underground gambling den, where an American dame gave him handfuls of louis d'or for wagering and kept calling him "my little masterpiece." Around the same time, Madame Peloux forced a tutor on her son—a priest whom she dismissed at the end of ten months. "Because," she admitted, "that black robe I saw dragging all over the house, it made me feel like I'd taken in a poor relation, and God knows there's nothing more depressing than a poor relation in your own home."

At fourteen, Chéri got a taste of boarding school. He was not impressed. He rebelled against all forms of restraint and escaped. Not only did Madame Peloux summon the energy to lock him up in school again, but on top of that, faced with her son's tears and insults, she herself ran off, her hands pressed to her ears, crying: "I do not want to see this! I do not want to see this!" A cry so sincere, she did in fact leave Paris, in the company of a man who was young but less than scrupulous, only to come back two years later, alone. This was her last romantic folly.

She returned to find a Chéri who'd grown up too fast: hollow-cheeked and with dark shadows around his eyes; sporting horse-trainer's outfits and talking dirtier than ever. She beat her breast and pulled Chéri out of boarding school. He immediately stopped studying, wanted horses, cars, jewelry, demanded handsome monthly allowances, and when his mother beat her breast and screamed like a peacock, he cut her off with "Ma Peloux, don't worry yourself sick . . . My reverend mother, if there's only me to land you in the poorhouse, you stand a very good chance of dying warm and snug under your American comforter. I have no desire to go to court. Your dough is my dough. Let me manage my own affairs. As for my friends, all they cost me are dinners and champagne. And as for those ladies, surely, Ma Peloux, seeing how you raised me, you wouldn't expect me to offer them more than some artistic trinket, if that!"

He turned a pirouette while she shed tears of relief and proclaimed herself the happiest of mothers. When Chéri began buying automobiles, she trembled once again, but he advised her, "Keep an eye on who's using the fuel, if you please, Ma Peloux!" and sold his horses. He wasn't above combing through the two chauffeurs' logbooks; he made quick, accurate calculations, and the tall, rounded figures he jotted down neatly on the pages were a striking contrast to his clumsy, labored handwriting.

After he turned seventeen, he became more like a fussy little old man of independent means. He was still handsome, but skinny, and short of breath. More than once, Madame Peloux encountered him climbing up the stairs from the cellar, where he'd been counting the bottles in the racks.

"Can you believe it!" Madame Peloux said to Léa, "It's too good to be true!"

"Much too good," Léa answered. "This will end badly. Chéri, show me your tongue."

He stuck it out and added a disrespectful scowl and other crude gestures that didn't shock Léa in the least; she being too close a friend —a sort of indulgent godmother, whom he addressed as an equal.

"Is it true," Léa questioned, "that someone saw you at the bar last night with that old Lili, sitting on her knees?"

"Her knees!" Chéri leered. "She hasn't had any knees for a long time! They've sunk below the surface."

"Is it true," Léa kept on, more sternly, "that she gave you some pepper gin to drink? Do you know it gives you bad breath?"

One day, Chéri, feeling hurt, had answered Léa's query with: "I don't know why you're asking me all that. You must have seen what I was up to, since you were there, in that little back room, with Patron the boxer!"

"That's perfectly accurate," Léa replied, unperturbed. "There's nothing wasted about Patron. He has greater attractions than a cheap little face with bruised-looking eyes."

That week, Chéri caused a big stir at night in Montmartre and Les Halles, with ladies who called him "my child" and "my vice." But he didn't feel aroused anywhere, suffered from migraines, and coughed from his chest. Madame Peloux confided her newfound anxieties ("Ah, for us mothers . . . life, what an ordeal!") to her masseuse, to Madame Ribot her corset-maker, to old Lili, and to dried-up Berthellemy-le-Desséché. She shifted comfortably from happiest of mothers to martyr-mother.

An evening in June, which saw Madame Peloux, Léa, and Chéri gathered under the conservatory roof at Neuilly, changed the destinies of the green young man and the mature woman. By chance, Chéri and his "friends" (Baxter the Younger—a small-time liquor wholesaler; and the Viscount Desmond—an exacting, scornful parasite, barely of age) had gone their separate ways, leading Chéri back to his mother's house, where habit led Léa too.

Twenty years—a past made up of similar dreary evenings; a limited social circle; a certain mistrust; and a sort of indolence that isolates, toward the end of their lives, women who have loved only making love—twenty years kept these two women in each other's presence for one more evening, in anticipation of yet another evening, in mutual suspicion. They were both watching Chéri, who remained silent. And Madame Peloux, who possessed neither the strength nor the authority to look after her son, confined herself to hating Léa a little each time the latter's white nape and rosy cheek leaned closer to Chéri's pale cheek and transparent ear. She would happily have bled that vigorous feminine neck, where "rings of Venus" were beginning to bruise the flesh, in order to tint the slender greenish lily pink, but she never even thought of taking her beloved boy to the country.

"Chéri, why are you drinking brandy?" Léa scolded.

"So as not to be impolite to Madame Peloux, who'd otherwise be drinking alone," Chéri replied.

"What are you doing tomorrow?"

"Don't know. And you?"

"I'm leaving for Normandy."

"With?"

"None of your business."

"With our splendid Spéleïeff?"

"Nothing of the kind. That's been over for two months—you're behind the times. He's in Russia, Spéleïeff."

"My dear Chéri, what's going on in your head?" sighed Madame Peloux. "You're forgetting the charming breakup dinner Léa treated us to last month. Léa, you haven't given me the recipe for those langoustines I enjoyed so much!"

Chéri sat up, eyes sparkling. "Yes, yes, langoustines with a cream sauce! Oh, how I'd love some!"

"You see," chided Madame Peloux. "He who has so little appetite, he'd like to eat some langoustines..."

"Shush!" Chéri ordered. "Léa, are you going into hiding with Patron?"

"No, of course not, my dear child. Patron and I, we're just friends. I'm going alone."

"Woman of fortune!" Chéri shot back.

"I'll take you along, if you like. We'll do nothing but eat, drink, sleep..."

"Where is this backwater of yours?"

He'd stood up and planted himself in front of her.

"You know Honfleur? The Côte de Grâce? Yes...? Sit down, your color's not good. Yes, you do know: on the Côte de Grâce—that wide gateway, the one where your mother and I would always say, when we were passing by..."

She turned in Madame Peloux's direction; Madame Peloux had disappeared.

This sort of discreet disappearance, this evanescence, was so at odds with Charlotte Peloux's accustomed ways, that Léa and Chéri looked at each other, laughing in surprise. Chéri sat down and leaned against Léa.

"I'm tired," he said.

"You're ruining yourself," said Léa.

He straightened up, his vanity pricked.

"Oh no I'm not, I'm still pretty good!"

"Pretty good ... maybe for some ... but not ... not for me, for example."

"Too green?"

"Just the word I was looking for. Will you come to the country, with only good intentions? Real strawberries, clotted cream, tarts, grilled chickens ... Now, that's a healthy diet, and no women!"

He let himself slide down Léa's shoulder and closed his eyes.

"No women ... That's great ... Léa, tell me, are you a pal? Yes? All right then, let's go. Women ... I'm through with them. Women ... I know what they are."

He spoke these low thoughts in a drowsy voice. Léa listened to the rich, soft sound and felt the warm breath on her ear. He'd taken hold of Léa's long necklace and was rolling the heavy pearls between his fingers. She passed her arm under Chéri's head and brought him closer, with no ulterior motive, easy in the familiarity she had with this child, and she rocked him.

"I like this," he sighed. "You're a pal, I like this ..."

She smiled, as though high praise had been bestowed upon her. Chéri seemed to be falling asleep. From close up, she looked at his lashes—gleaming as if wet, pressed against his cheek—and at this wasted cheek that bore the marks of a fruitless struggle. His upper lip, shaved in the morning, had already turned a shade of blue, and the pink lamps imparted a false flush to his lips ...

"No women!" Chéri exclaimed, dreamily. "Then ... kiss me!"

Taken aback, Léa didn't move.

"Kiss me, I'm telling you!"

He gave the order, with knitted brows. And the glare of his eyes, reopened suddenly, disturbed Léa, like a light switched back on abruptly. She shrugged her shoulders and moved slightly to give his forehead a kiss. He wrapped his arms around Léa's neck, bending her toward him.

She shook her head, but only until the instant their mouths touched; then she stayed completely still and held her breath, like someone listening. When he released her, she pushed him away, got up, took a deep breath, and tidied her hair. It hadn't been disturbed. Then, a little pale, she turned back to him with her eyes dimmed. And in a lighthearted tone, she said,

"That's bright!"

He lay back in the depths of the rocking chair and kept quiet, gazing at her with a longing, probing look, so full of defiance and inquiry that she said, after a moment, "What is it?"

"Nothing," said Chéri, "I know what I wanted to know."

She reddened with shame and defended herself smartly. "What do you know? That I like your mouth? My poor child, I've kissed far uglier. What does that prove? You think I'm going to fall down at your feet and cry 'Take me!'? But does this mean you've had only girls? You expect me to lose my head over one kiss!"

She'd calmed down while she was talking, and wanted to show that she'd kept her composure.

"Tell me, my dear," she added for emphasis while she leaned over him, "do you think it would count for anything in my memories, a nice mouth?"

She was smiling at him from above, sure of herself, but she wasn't aware that something stayed on her face—a sort of subtle tremor, and an appealing trace of pain—and that her smile looked like one that follows a fit of tears.

"It really doesn't matter to me," she continued. "Even if I were to kiss you again, even if we—"

She stopped herself, and scowled with contempt.

"No, I definitely don't see us in that light."

"And you didn't see us in that light just a minute ago, either," said Chéri. "Even so, you held on for quite a while. So, you were thinking about doing it, about the other thing? Me, I didn't say a word to you."

They sized each other up as opponents. She was afraid of revealing a desire she hadn't had the time to feed or to conceal, and she held it against this youngster, who'd cooled off in a moment and was now possibly making fun of her.

"You're right," she admitted, lightheartedly. "Let's not think about it. So, as we were saying, I'm offering you a meadow where you can get some country air, and a place to get your meals ... My place, and that's all that needs to be said."

"We'll see," Chéri answered. "I'd bring the Renouhard with the top down?"

"Naturally, you wouldn't leave it with Charlotte."

"I'll pay for the gas, but you'll feed the chauffeur."

Léa burst into laughter.

"I'll feed the chauffeur! Ha, ha! Madame Peloux's boy, enough of you! You don't miss a thing ... I'm not nosy, but I'd like to hear what a love talk between you and a woman would sound like!"

She flopped down in a chair and fanned herself. A sphinx moth and some big mosquitoes with long, trailing legs were circling around the lamps, and the smell of the garden, since night had fallen, had become a country smell. A whiff of acacia came inside, so distinct, so potent, that both of them turned around, as though they expected to see it walking across the room.

"It's the acacia with the pink clusters," said Léa in an undertone.

"Yes," said Chéri. "But tonight it's had so much orange blossom to drink!"

She looked him over, vaguely admiring that he'd thought of this. He was inhaling the scent like a willing victim, and she turned away, all of a sudden fearing he wouldn't beckon her; but he did beckon her, all the same, and she came.

She came to him to kiss him, with a bitter and selfish impulse and thoughts of chastisement. "Wait, hold on ... It's absolutely true: you have a beautiful mouth ... This time, I'm going to drink my fill, because I want to, and I'll let you have your way ... It's a shame, but I don't care, I'm coming ..."

She kissed him so hard that they pulled back drunk, deafened, breathless, trembling as though they'd just fought physically. She took her place again, on her feet, in front of him. He hadn't budged. He nestled still in the depths of the rocker, and she taunted him, softly, "And so?... So?" and braced herself for an insult. But he held his arms out, opened his lovely, trembling hands, laid back his wounded head, and revealed, between his lashes, the matching sparkle of two tears. Meanwhile he murmured words, groans... a feral and amorous ode. She could make out her name and repeated "darling"s, and "come"s, and "never leave you"s. An ode that she listened to while bending over him, full of apprehension, as if she'd unwittingly done him great harm.

When Léa recalled that first summer in Normandy, she would state, in a fair-minded way: "As for bratty nurslings, I've had more amusing ones than Chéri. More likable too, and more intelligent. But, all the same, I've never had another one like him."

"It's laughable," she confided to Berthellemy-le-Desséché, at the end of that summer of 1906. "There are times when I think I'm in bed with a Negro or a Chinaman."

"Have you ever slept with a Chinaman or a Negro?"

"Never."

"So?"

"I don't know. I can't explain. It's just an impression."

An impression that had come to her gradually, along with an astonishment she hadn't always been able to hide. Her first memories of their idyll abounded only in images of delectable treats, choice fruits, and the attentions she lavished like a refined farmwife. Once again, she saw a wasted Chéri—paler in full sunlight—who drifted underneath the Norman hedgerows and dozed on the hot stone banks of the ponds in the parks. Léa would wake him up to cram him with strawberries, cream, frothed milk, and grain-fed chicken. At the dinner table, his eyes staring and vacant, he followed, as though stunned, the flight of mayflies around the basket of roses; checked his wrist for the hour to go to bed; while Léa, disappointed without resentment, pondered the unfulfilled promises of the kiss at Neuilly and simply bided her time.

"If I have to, I'll keep him in this fattening pen up until the end of August. And afterwards, in Paris, ouf! I'll pack him off to his beloved studies..."

Charitably, she'd go to bed early, so that Chéri—snuggled up to her, nuzzling with his forehead and his nose, selfishly sinking into his preferred position—could get to sleep. Sometimes, the lamp switched off, she'd follow a pool of moonlight glowing on the wooden floor. As they melded with the aspens' rustling and the crickets' cry, which never ended, night and day, she listened to the deep, hound-like sighs that lifted Chéri's chest.

"So, what's wrong with me, that I'm not sleeping?" she wondered, vaguely. "It's not this boy's head on my shoulder, I've held heavier ones than this... What lovely weather... For the morning, I've ordered him a big bowl of porridge. Already, you don't feel his ribs sticking out as much. So why am I not sleeping? Ah! Now I remember. I'm going to get Patron the boxer to come and train this boy. We have enough time, with Patron on one side and me on the other, to really impress Madame Peloux..."

She would go to sleep, stretched out flat on her back under the cool sheets, with the dark-haired head of the bratty nursling nestled on her left breast. She would go to sleep, roused at times toward dawn—but so rarely!—by a gesture of insistence from Chéri.

The second month of their seclusion did indeed see Patron arrive with his big valise, his pound-and-a-half dumbbells, his black leggings, his six-ounce gloves, and his high leather boots laced all the way down to his toes; Patron, with his girlish voice and his long lashes; Patron, wrapped in a hide so tanned and beautiful, like his valise, that he didn't appear to be naked when he took off his shirt. And Chéri—by turns belligerent, weak-kneed, or jealous of Patron's effortless power—began the unrewarding yet profitable exercise of slow, repetitive movements.

"One...sss...two...sss...I don't hear you breathing...three... sss...I can see you're not keeping your knee in line...sss..."

The canopy of lindens screened the August sun. A thick red rug, thrown down on the gravel, powdered the bare torsos of trainer and trainee with mauve reflections. Léa, closely attentive, followed the lesson with her gaze. During the fifteen minutes of boxing, Chéri, drunk with his newfound powers, would get carried away. He'd hazard reckless punches and redden with rage. Like a wall, Patron absorbed the swings. From the height of his Olympian glory, he rained down pronouncements on Chéri, oracles more ponderous than his celebrated fists.

"Whoa there! Your left eye is really curious! If I hadn't held back, it would have got a good look at how my right glove is stitched."

"I slipped," Chéri fumed.

"That's nothing to do with balance," Patron went on. "That has to do with fighting spirit. You'll never make a boxer."

"My mother's against it. How sad!"

"Even if your mother wasn't against it, you wouldn't make a boxer, because you're nasty. Nastiness and boxing don't mix. Ain't it so, Madame Léa?"

Léa smiled. She savored the pleasure of being warm, staying still, and witnessing the sparring of the two bare-chested young men. She silently compared them. "How handsome he is, this Patron! He's handsome like a building. The lad is turning out nicely. Knees like his you don't see at every street corner, and I know what I'm talking about. His back, too, it's...no, it *will* be amazing...Where the devil did Ma Peloux cast her net...? And the base of his neck! A real statue. What a brat he is! When he laughs, you'd swear he was a hound getting ready to bite..." She felt glad, and motherly, bathed in easy virtue. "I'd be happy to swap him for somebody else," she said to herself, seeing Chéri shirtless in the afternoon under the lindens, or Chéri shirtless in the morning on top of the ermine bedcover, or Chéri shirtless at night on the lip of the basin of lukewarm water. "Yes, as beautiful as he is, I'd gladly swap him, if it weren't a matter of conscience." She confided her indifference to Patron.

"All the same," Patron objected, "he has the right kind of body. You already see muscles on him like you do on guys from other places, colored guys, even though he couldn't be any whiter. Little muscles that don't show off. You'll never see him with biceps as big as cantaloupes!"

"I hope not, Patron! But I didn't take him on for boxing, not me!"

"Obviously," Patron conceded, lowering his long lashes. "You have to take feelings into account."

He was embarrassed by Léa's unveiled, voluptuous allusions, and by her smile—that intrusive smile, in her eyes—the one she fixed on him when she talked about lovemaking.

"Obviously," Patron carried on, "if he doesn't satisfy you in every way..."

Léa laughed. "In every way, no...but I draw my reward from the purer springs of unselfishness, like you, Patron."

"Oh! Me..."

He dreaded and desired the question that didn't fail to follow.

"No change, Patron? You won't budge?"

"I won't budge, Madame Léa. I've had another letter from Liane, by the noon post. She says she's on her own, that I have no reason to be stubborn, that those friends of hers—those two guys—have taken off."

"So?"

"So, I don't believe it's true...I won't budge because she won't budge. She's ashamed, she says, of a man who has a job like mine, especially a job that requires him to get up early in the morning, to train every day, to give boxing and gymnastics lessons. The minute we get together, it turns into a row. She yells: "People would think I'm not capable of supporting the man I love!" It's a noble sentiment,

I don't deny it, but it's not my way of thinking. Everyone has their little quirks. As you put it so well, Madame Léa: It's a matter of conscience."

They chatted in low tones under the trees: he, modest in his half-undress; she, clothed in white, her cheeks flushed a hearty pink. They revelled in their mutual affection, which sprang from a shared tendency toward simplicity, toward good health, toward a sort of gentility of the demimonde. Yet Léa wouldn't have been the least bit shocked if Patron received luxurious gifts from the beautiful, highly prized Liane. "Give-and-take." And Léa strove, with arguments of old-fashioned fairness, to undermine Patron's "little quirks." Their leisurely chats, which revived the same two gods a little bit every time (love and money), steered away from money and love to come back to Chéri; to his deplorable upbringing; to what Léa called his "basically harmless" good looks; to his character, which Léa said "wasn't one." Chats that satisfied their need for confidences and their distaste for new sayings and new ideas, chats interrupted by the weird apparition of Chéri—they'd assumed he was asleep, or speeding down some dangerous road—Chéri, who would loom up half-naked but armed with an account book, a pen behind his ear.

"Now that's what I call a greeting!" Patron said with wonderment. "He looks just like a cashier."

"What's this?" Chéri shouted from the distance. "Three hundred francs for gasoline? We're drinking it like water! And we've only been out four times in the past two weeks! And seventy-seven francs for oil!"

"The car goes to the market every day," Léa answered back. "And by the way, we hear your chauffeur had three helpings of lamb at lunch. Don't you think that goes a little beyond our agreement...? When you question a bill, you look like your mother."

At a loss for a riposte, he remained unsteady for a moment, shifting back and forth on his delicate feet, rocked by that aerial grace—of a young Mercury—that used to make Madame Peloux swoon and squeal: "That's me at eighteen! Winged feet, winged feet!" While he tried to come up with something cheeky, his whole face trembled, his mouth parted, and his forehead pushed forward in a tense attitude that made the satanic arch of his eyebrows look glaring and strange.

"Give it up," Léa said, with affection. "Yes, you hate me. Come give me a hug. Handsome devil. Fallen angel. Little nitwit."

He came, vanquished by the sound of her voice while offended by the words themselves. Patron, facing the couple, let the truth flow once more from his unblemished lips.

"You have the kind of body it takes to be good-looking. But when I look at you, Monsieur Chéri, it strikes me that, if I was a woman, I'd say to myself: 'I'll come around again in ten years' time.'"

"You hear that, Léa? He says 'in ten years' time,'" Chéri insinuated, while pushing away his mistress's tilted head. "What do you say to that?"

But she didn't deign to listen. Instead, she patted her hands all over the youthful body that owed its renewed vigor to her—on the cheeks, the legs, the bottom—with the saucy delight of a nursemaid.

"What satisfaction do you get from being nasty, monsieur?" Patron then asked Chéri.

Chéri slowly and wholly wrapped the Herculean figure in a savage, inscrutable gaze before answering, "It comforts me. You can't understand."

Truth be told, after three months of intimacy Léa hadn't come to understand a jot about Chéri. If she still spoke to Patron, who came now only on Sundays, or to Berthellemy-le-Desséché, who turned up uninvited but left two hours later, about "letting Chéri get back to his beloved studies," it was in keeping with a kind of tradition, as though to excuse herself for having held on to him for so long. She set herself limits, and exceeded them every time. She was waiting.

"The weather's so lovely... Plus, his Paris escapade last week tired him out... Plus, it will be better if I've really had my fill of him..."

For the first time in her life she was waiting, in vain, for what she'd never gone without: trust, ease, openness, sincerity, the uninhibited expansiveness of a young lover—those hours of total dark when the almost filial gratitude of a teenager pours forth unchecked in tears, confidences, grievances, onto the warm breast of a seasoned, dependable mistress.

"I've had them all," she mused, determined. "I've always known their worth, what they were thinking, what they were after. But this boy, this boy... This boy would be a bit too much to take."

Fit as a fiddle now, proud of his nineteen years, cheerful at table, impatient in bed, he revealed nothing but his presence and remained mysterious like a courtesan. Tender? Yes, if tenderness can manifest itself in an involuntary cry or in the gesture of hugging oneself. But his "nastiness" would return, through his language and through the care he took to conceal himself. How many times, toward dawn, while Léa held her sated lover, soothed, in her arms—his eyes half-closed, his gaze and speech brought back to life as if each morning and each embrace recreated him more beautiful than the day before—how many times—herself overcome at that hour by the urge to possess and the sensual pleasure of confession—had she pressed her forehead against Chéri's and said, "Tell... speak... tell me..."

But no avowal rose from his twisted lips, and hardly any other words besides sulky or drunken diatribes, along with that name of "Nounoune" that he'd given her when he was a little boy, and which he now cast out to her from the depths of his climax, like a cry for help.

"Yes, take it from me, a Chinaman or a Negro," she confided to Anthime de Berthellemy. "I can't explain it to you," she added, listlessly, and at a loss to define the sense, muddied and intense, that she and Chéri didn't speak the same language.

September was drawing to a close when they arrived back in Paris. Chéri returned to Neuilly, to "amaze and impress" Madame Peloux from the very first night. He hoisted chairs in the air, cracked walnuts with his bare fist, leapt up onto the billiards table, and romped around out in the garden like a cowboy, chasing after the terror-stricken guard dogs.

"Phew," sighed Léa when she came home, on her own, to her house in avenue Bugeaud. "Is this ever good—an empty bed!"

But the next evening, while she was nursing her postprandial coffee, trying to prevent herself from finding the night tiresome and the dining room too empty, the sudden apparition of Chéri standing in the doorway—Chéri, who'd arrived on his winged, soundless feet—caused her to emit a nervous shout. Neither friendly nor talkative, he ran toward her.

"What, are you crazy?"

He shrugged his shoulders, wouldn't deign to explain himself. He was running back to her. He didn't ask, "Do you love me? Have you already forgotten me?" He was running back to her.

A moment later, they were resting in the navel of Léa's big iron and brass bed. Chéri—seized by a fit of taciturnity—pretended to be sleepy, sapped of energy, so as to be able to clench his teeth and close his eyes even harder. But she listened to him all the same as she nestled against him; listened with delight to the faint vibration, to the distant and seemingly captive commotion that resonates from a body that denies its anguish, its gratitude, and its love.

"Why didn't your mother tell me about it herself, last night at dinner?"

"She thought it would be more appropriate for me to let you know."

"Really?"

"That's what she says."

"And you?"

"What about me?"

"Do you think it was appropriate too?

Chéri gave Léa a hesitant look.

"Yes."

He appeared to be thinking it over, and he said again, "Yes, it's better this way. Let's get on with it."

So as not to embarrass him, Léa turned her eyes toward the window. A warm rain was shrouding this August morning, dropping straight down onto the three plane trees—already a rusty brown—in the planted courtyard. "You'd think it was fall," Léa remarked, and she sighed.

"What's wrong with you?" Chéri asked.

She looked at him, taken aback.

"Why, nothing's wrong with me, I just don't like this rain."

"Ah! well, I thought..."

"You thought...?"

"I thought you were upset."

She couldn't hold herself back from laughing out loud.

"Upset because you're going to get married? No, really, it's just that...you're...you're so funny..."

She rarely burst into laughter, and her merriment offended Chéri. He shrugged his shoulders, lit a cigarette, and scowled in his usual way, with his chin jutting out too far and his lower lip protruding.

"It's wrong of you to smoke before breakfast," said Léa.

He parried with something impertinent, which she didn't hear, intent as she was, all of a sudden, on listening to the sound of her own voice and to her daily, repetitive advice echoing back to the beginning of the past five years. "It feels like the reflections in two facing mirrors," she mused. Then, with a slight effort, she rose again into the present and a lighter mood.

"It's a good thing I'm handing responsibility over, soon, to somebody else—to enforce the ban on smoking on an empty stomach!" she said to Chéri.

"That one? She has no say in the matter," Chéri declared. "I'm marrying her, right? She can kiss the soles of my heavenly feet, and bless her lucky stars. That's enough."

He thrust his chin even farther out, clenched his teeth on his cigarette holder, and spread his lips wide. In this attitude, in his immaculate silk pajamas, he succeeded only in resembling an Asiatic prince turned pale in the impenetrable shadows of his palace.

Léa, feeling weary, was tightening her pink dressing gown—the pink she referred to as "compulsory"—around herself. She was beset by thoughts that tired her out, and she decided to toss them, one by one, against Chéri's calm façade.

"So, why on earth are you marrying this little girl?"

He leaned both elbows on a table and, without realizing it, imitated Madame Peloux's studied expression.

"You know, darling—"

"Call me 'madame,' or 'Léa.' I am neither your chambermaid nor one of your childish playmates."

Sitting upright in her armchair, she spoke drily, without raising her voice. He wanted to parry. He glared defiantly at her beautiful face—which was a little bruised-looking behind the powder—and at her eyes—which bathed him in a light so blue and so direct. Then he softened and submitted in a manner not habitual for him.

"Nounoune, you were asking me to explain it to you ... Shouldn't we just put it to rest? Besides, there are major interests at stake."

"Whose?"

"Mine," he said, without a smile. "The girl has a fortune of her own."

"From her father?"

He toppled backwards onto the floor, feet in the air.

"Ah! I don't know! The questions you ask! Yes, I think so. The lovely Marie-Laure isn't drawing a million and a half from her personal funds, eh? A million and a half francs, and some high-class jewelry."

"And you?"

"Me, I have more than that," he said, with pride.

"In that case, you don't need any money."

He shook his head. Daylight ran across the smooth surface of his skin, in pulsating bands of blue.

"Need, need ... you know we don't look at money the same way. It's something we don't agree on."

"I'll grant you this much: You've spared me that topic of conversation for five years."

She bent forward, placed a hand on Chéri's knee. "Tell me, little boy, how much have you managed to save from your income, these past five years?"

He made light of it, laughing and rolling at Léa's feet, but she used one of them to push him away.

"Tell me, honestly ... Fifty thousand a year, or sixty? Go on, tell me. Sixty, seventy?"

He sat up on the rug and lolled his head back onto Léa's knees.

"So, are you saying I don't deserve them?"

He stretched himself out in the full daylight, shifted the base of his neck, opened his eyes wide. They looked black, but Léa knew their dark brown and russet hue. With her index finger, as though to point out and select the rarest parts of so much beauty, she touched his eyebrows, his eyelids, the corners of his mouth. Every so often, the physical form of this lover, whom she slightly despised, inspired in her a sort of respect. "To be that beautiful," she thought, "is a sort of nobility."

"Tell me, pretty one . . . The young lady in all of this, how is she with you?"

"She loves me. She admires me. She has nothing to say."

"And you, how do you get along with her?"

"I don't," he answered, straightforwardly.

"A pretty pair of lovebirds," Léa said, picturing them.

He lifted himself up halfway and sat cross-legged. "I see you're very concerned about her," he said harshly. "Does that mean you're not concerned for yourself, in the midst of this big shake-up?"

She looked at Chéri with an astonishment that made her look younger, with her eyebrows raised and her mouth half-open.

"Yes, you, Léa. You, the victim. You, the sympathetic character in the affair, because I'm jilting you."

He'd turned a little pale and looked, while he was treating Léa roughly, like he was wounding himself.

Léa smiled. "But no, my dear, I have no intention of changing anything in my life. For a week, now and then, I'll come across a pair of socks, a tie, a handkerchief, in one of my drawers . . . And when I say 'a week' . . . you know, they're very well organized, my drawers! Ah! And then I'll have the bathroom redone! I have an idea for a glass mosaic . . ."

She stopped talking and put on a look of eager anticipation, sketching a vague plan in the air with her finger. Chéri didn't drop his vindictive gaze.

"You're not satisfied? What is it you would like? For me to go back to Normandy and bury my grief? For me to lose weight? To stop dyeing my hair? For Madame Peloux to come running to the head of my bed?"

Flapping her forearms, she mimicked Madame Peloux's blaring tones: "'The shadow of her former self! The shadow of her former self! The poor woman has aged a hundred years!' Is that what you'd like?"

He'd listened with a forced smile and a quivering of the nostrils that might have been emotional.

"Yes," he shouted.

Léa laid her bare arms—polished smooth, and heavy—on Chéri's shoulders.

"My poor little puppy! But I would have been obliged to die four or five times already if I'd looked at it that way! Losing a young lover... trading one bratty nursling for another..."

She added, more softly and in a lighter tone, "I'm used to it."

"Yes, we know that," he said bitterly. "And I couldn't give a damn! Yes, I really couldn't give a damn that I wasn't your first lover. What I would have preferred, or, more to the point, what would have been... good form... the proper thing... would have been for me to be your last."

With a twist of his shoulders, he caused her heavenly arms to drop.

"Basically, what I'm saying about it—don't you see?—it's for your sake."

"I understand perfectly. You—you're concerned for me; I'm concerned for your fiancée; and it's all...very good, very natural. It's obviously an affair of noble hearts."

She got up, expecting him to answer with some kind of crudeness, but he kept mum, and she felt pained to see, for the first time, a kind of discouragement on Chéri's face.

She leaned forward and put her hands under his arms. "All right, come on, get yourself dressed. I only have to put my dress on, I'm all ready underneath. What better thing to do, on a day like this, than to go to Schwabe's and choose a pearl for you? I certainly have to give you a wedding gift."

He leapt up, his eyes gleaming. "Terrific! How chic! A pinkish pearl for my shirt! I know the very one!"

"Not on your life! A white one, something manly—come on now. I know just the one. Ruining myself again! Think of how much I'll save without you!"

Chéri switched back to his reserved demeanor. "Well, that depends on my successor."

Léa swung round in her bedroom doorway and flashed her sunniest smile, her strong, gourmand's teeth, and the striking blueness of her expertly made-up eyes. "Your successor? Two francs and a packet of tobacco! And a glass of cassis on Sundays, that's all he deserves! And I'll give wedding gifts to your kids!"

They both became very lighthearted during the weeks that followed. Chéri's engagement formalities kept them apart every day for a few hours, sometimes for a night or two. "I have to win their trust," Chéri declared. Léa, whom Madame Peloux was keeping at a safe distance from Neuilly, succumbed to her curiosity and asked Chéri a hundred questions—Chéri, who was full of himself, brimming over with secrets he would start to spill as soon as he came in the door, playing truant again to see Léa.

"My friends!" he cried out one day as he clapped his hat down on Léa's portrait bust. "My friends, the things we've been witnessing at Peloux's Palace since yesterday!"

"First, take your hat away from there. And second, do not mention your pack of filthy friends here, in this house. What's going on now?"

Even while she scolded him, she was laughing in anticipation.

"There are fireworks, Nounoune! Fireworks between those ladies—Marie-Laure and Madame Peloux—they're tearing out each other's hair over my marriage contract!"

"No?"

"Yes! It's a wonderful spectacle. (Move the hors d'oeuvres aside, so I can show you the old dame's arms flapping.) 'Separate accounts! Separate accounts! Why not have it overseen by a public tribunal! It's a personal insult. Personal! *My son*'s financial situation? . . . Now, you listen to me, madame'—"

"She called her 'madame'?"

"As clear as day. 'Take it from me, madame, my son has not had a single sou of debt since he came of age, and the list of investments he has made since 1910 amounts to...' Amounts to this, amounts to that, amounts to my nose, amounts to my ass...In a word, played like a perfect queen mother, like Catherine de Medici, but more diplomatic!"

Léa's blue eyes sparkled with tears of laughter.

"Ah! Chéri! This is funniest you've ever been since I've known you. And the other one, the lovely Marie-Laure?"

"Her, oh! Shocking, Nounoune. That woman must have a couple of dozen corpses lying in her wake. In her jade-green outfit, with that reddish hair, that skin of hers...in a word, an eighteen-year-old, and with that smile. My reverend mother's bullhorn didn't make her bat an eye. She waited until the blast was over to answer: 'It might behoove you, my dear madame, not to go on too much about your son's savings in the years since 1910...'"

"Pow! Right in the eye...your eye! Where were you during all this?"

"Me? In the big armchair."

"You were right there?"

She stopped laughing and put down her canapé.

"You were right there? And what did you do?"

"I made a witty remark...naturally. Madame Peloux was already brandishing one of her precious knickknacks in order to avenge my honor, and I brought her up short, without getting out of my seat. 'My dearest, darling mother...easy now! Follow my example. Follow my charming mother-in-law's example—she's all sweetness...and light.' And with that, I got them to agree to limit the shared property to what we acquire after we get married."

"I don't understand."

"The famous sugar cane plantations that poor little Prince Ceste left to Marie-Laure in his will..."

"Yes...?"

"His forged will. The Ceste family up in arms! A lawsuit in the making! Do you get it?"

He was exultant.

"I get it, but how did you hear this story?"

"Ah! Here's how: Old Lili has just landed head over heels on top of the younger Ceste, who's seventeen and thinks nothing but pious thoughts..."

"Old Lili? How awful!"

"And Ceste the Younger murmured this love story to her in between their kisses..."

"Chéri! I'm sick to my stomach!"

"And old Lili tipped me off at mother's last Sunday. She adores me, old Lili! She has the highest regard for me, because I've never wanted to sleep with her!"

"I should hope not," Léa sighed. "All the same..."

She was thinking the matter over. It seemed to Chéri she was less than enthusiastic.

"Hey, won't you tell me I'm amazing? Won't you?"

He leaned over the table. Sunshine was dancing across the white tablecloth and the porcelain, illuminating his face like a row of footlights.

"Yes..."

"All the same," she thought to herself, "that insufferable Marie-Laure really did treat him like a pimp..."

"Is there any cream cheese, Nounoune?"

"Yes..."

"...and he didn't get any angrier than he would have if she'd thrown him a nosegay," she reflected...

"Nounoune, will you give me the address, the address of the place where you get those creamy heart-shaped cheeses, for the new cook I've hired for October?"

"Where do you think they come from? We make them here. 'Cook,' not 'chef'? Don't expect more than mussel sauce and meat pies."

"...and it's true," she continued to muse. "I've pretty much supported this child for the past five years... All the same, he has three hundred thousand francs of income. Here's the question: Can you be a gold digger when you have three hundred thousand francs of income? The answer doesn't depend on the size of the fortune; it depends on the quality of the mind . . . There are men to whom I could have given half a million, who wouldn't have been gold diggers for all that . . . But Chéri? Even so, I've never given him any hard cash . . . All the same . . ."

"All the same," she burst out loud, "she treated you like a common hustler!"

"Who are you talking about?"

"Marie-Laure!"

His face lit up like a child's. "That's it, isn't it? Isn't it, Nounoune? That's really what she meant?"

"That's what it sounds like to me!"

Chéri lifted his wine glass filled with Château-Chalon the color of eau-de-vie. "Long live Marie-Laure! What a compliment, eh? I hope they can still say the same about me when I'm your age. I couldn't ask for anything more!"

"If that's all it takes to make you happy."

She only half listened to him until the lunch was over. Accustomed as he was to his sensible friend's lengthy silences, he expected no more than her daily maternal injunctions: "Take the crustiest piece of bread," "Don't eat so much of the doughy part," "You've never known how to choose a piece of fruit"—while she, brooding in secret, upbraided herself: "All the same, I do need to know what I really want! What would I have liked? For him to stand up on his own two feet and say: 'Madame, you are insulting me! Madame, I am not what you think!' When you come down to it, I am the one who's responsible. I raised him with a silver spoon, I fed him with every delicacy . . . Who would have dreamt he'd want to play at being the man of the family one day? It certainly hadn't occurred to me! But suppose it had. As Patron says, blood is thicker than water. Even if Patron had given in to Liane's propositions, his blood would have boiled over if anyone within earshot had spoken of dishonorable intentions. Whereas Chéri, he has nothing but the blood of Chéri. He has . . ."

"What were you saying, little one?" she interrupted herself. "I wasn't listening."

"I was saying, never—do you hear me—nothing has ever made me laugh like my scene with Marie-Laure!"

"There you have it," Léa concluded, to herself. "Him—it makes him laugh."

She rose with a weary motion. Chéri passed his arm around her waist, but she slid away from it.

"What day is it again, your wedding?"

"A week from Monday."

He looked so innocent, and so detached, that it shook her.

"It's unbelievable!"

"Why unbelievable, Nounoune?"

"You really don't seem to be thinking about it at all."

"I'm not thinking about it," he said, his voice calm. "Everything's been arranged. Ceremony at two o'clock, so we don't have the headache of putting on a big lunch. Five-o'clock tea at Charlotte Peloux's. And then the sleeping cars, Italy, the lakes..."

"So the lakes are back in fashion?"

"They're back in fashion. Villas, hotels, cars, restaurants...even Monte Carlo!"

"But her! There's her..."

"Of course, there's her. There's not much to her, but she's there."

"And there's no more me."

Chéri wasn't prepared for the clipped phrase, and he showed it. A sickly roll of his eyes, a sudden pallor on his lips, distorted his features. He swallowed some air, guardedly, so that she couldn't hear his breathing, and became himself again.

"Nounoune, there will always be you."

"Monsieur takes my breath away."

"You'll always be there, Nounoune..."—he laughed awkwardly— "whenever I need you to do me a service."

She made no answer. She bent down to retrieve a fallen tortoiseshell hairpin, and as she stuck it back into her hair she hummed. Pleased with her performance, she kept her song going in front of a mirror, proud of having mastered herself so easily; of having extricated herself from the only emotional moment of their separation; proud of having held back the words she mustn't speak: "Say something...beg, insist, wrap your arms around my neck...you've just made me happy."

Madame Peloux must have been talking a lot, for a long while, before Léa came in. The fire on her cheekbones heightened the glare from her large eyes, which expressed nothing but watchfulness: her unabashed, impenetrable curiosity. This Sunday, she was wearing a black cocktail dress with a tight-fitting skirt. It was impossible not to notice that her feet were dainty, and that her belly was firmly cinched. She stopped talking, drank a mouthful from the slender goblet that had been gradually warming in the palm of her hand, and, with languid contentment, tilted her head toward Léa.

"Can you believe how beautiful it is outside? Such weather! Such weather! Would anyone guess it was October?"

"Ah! No...no question about it!" two sycophantic voices answered.

A river of scarlet sage meandered the length of the garden lane between banks of violet asters that were almost a shade of gray. Butterflies—clouded yellows—were flying like it was summertime, but the fragrance of fall chrysanthemums warmed by the sun was wafting in to the open hall. A yellow birch quivered in the breeze, above a bed of Bengal roses that held the last honeybees of the season.

"But what is this weather," declaimed Madame Peloux, suddenly waxing lyrical, "what is this weather, compared to what *they* must be having in Italy?"

"That's a fact...You can say it again!" piped back the servile voices.

Léa, furrowing her brows, turned her head toward the voices.

"If only they didn't open their mouths," she murmured.

At a card table, the Baroness de La Berche and Madame Aldonza were playing a game of piquet. Madame Aldonza—a superannuated ballerina with swaddled legs—suffered from crippling rheumatism. She wore her lacquered ebony wig slightly askew. Facing her, and towering over her by a head and a half, sat the Baroness de La Berche. Her shoulders, as broad and square as a country priest's, framed her large face, a face that old age had made frighteningly masculine. She was nothing but hairs in her ears, shrubbery in her nose and on her upper lip, and bushy fingers . . .

"Baroness, you're not going to forget my ninety points," bleated Madame Aldonza.

"Mark them down, mark them down, my dear friend. As for me, all I want is for everyone to be happy."

She never ceased dispensing her blessings, while hiding a savage cruelty. Léa studied her as though she was seeing her for the first time, with disgust, then shifted her gaze back to Madame Peloux. "At least Charlotte looks like a human being. She . . ."

"What's the matter with you, Léa? Are you feeling out of sorts?" Madame Peloux tenderly inquired.

Léa arched her lovely midriff and answered, "But I am, dear Lolotte . . . It's so pleasant at your place, I'm just taking it easy . . ." while thinking to herself: "Careful . . . there's cruelty here too . . ." And she put on a mask of complacent well-being, of sated reverie, which she emphasized by sighing. "I ate too much . . . I want to lose some weight, that's it! Tomorrow I'm starting a diet."

Madame Peloux waved her arms in the air and simpered, "So, grieving isn't enough for you?"

"Ha, ha, ha!" guffawed Madame Aldonza and the Baroness de La Berche. "Ha, ha, ha!"

Léa stood up, imposing in her fall dress of muted green, beautiful under her hat of satin trimmed with otter, youthful among these relics, whom she surveyed with a tender eye.

"Oh là là, my dears! Give me a dozen of those losses, and let me lose two pounds!"

"You're a knockout, Léa," quipped the baroness through a puff of smoke.

"Madame Léa, you'll pass that hat on to me when you're done with it?" begged the venerable Aldonza. "Madame Charlotte, you remember that blue one of yours? It lasted me two years. Baroness, when you're done with making eyes at Madame Léa, would you deal me some cards?"

"Here you go, my darling. May they bring you luck!"

Léa paused for a moment in the doorway of the hall, then went down into the garden. She picked a Bengal rose, whose petals fell away, listened to the wind in the birch, the streetcars in the avenue, the whistle of a suburban train. The bench she sat down on felt a little warm, and she shut her eyes, letting the sun heat her shoulders. When she reopened her eyes, she turned her head hurriedly toward the house, with the certainty that she was going to see Chéri standing at the entrance to the conservatory, leaning his shoulder against the door...

"What's the matter with me?" she asked herself.

Some sharp bursts of laughter and a faint uproar of greeting in the hall saw her standing up, trembling slightly.

"Am I on the verge of nervous breakdown?'

"Ah, here they are, here they are!" trumpeted Madame Peloux.

And the loud bass of the baroness repeated rhythmically, "The little lovebirds! The little lovebirds!"

Léa shuddered, ran to the doorway, and came to a halt: she saw before her old Lili and her teenage lover, Prince Ceste, who'd just arrived.

Old Lili: possibly seventy, as portly as a eunuch in her corset. One used to say that she "went beyond all bounds," without defining the bounds in question. A ceaseless, childlike gaiety lit up her round, flushed, powdered face, where her big eyes and thin, puckered lips flirted without shame. The venerable Lili followed fashion, outrageously. A striped skirt, in Revolutionary blue and white, encased her lower body; a short blue spencer jacket boldly revealed a bosom whose leathery skin was corrugated like a turkey's; a silver fox stole failed to conceal her bare, flowerpot-shaped neck, a neck as wide as a belly, which had swallowed up her chin.

"It's frightening," Léa thought. She couldn't tear her eyes away from this or that especially dismal detail: the white felt "Breton" sailor's hat, for example, childishly cocked back on a wig of short, pinkish brown hair; or else the pearl necklace, visible one moment, then buried the next in a deep gulley of the sort once known as a "collar of Venus."

"Léa, Léa, my little dear," old Lili exclaimed, hastening toward

Léa. She walked with difficulty on her bulbous, swollen feet bound with leather thongs and gem-studded clips, and she was the first to celebrate the fact. "I waddle like a little duck, it's a style of my own! Guido, my precious, you remember Madame de Lonval? Don't remember too much of her, or I'll scratch your eyes out."

A slender youth with an Italian-looking face, enormous empty eyes, and a weak receding chin quickly kissed Léa's hand and withdrew toward the shadows without saying a word. Lili grabbed him as he went by and pinned him to her grainy bosom, calling on the onlookers to bear witness.

"Do you know what this is, madame, do you know what this is? This, mesdames, is the great love of my life!"

"Control yourself, Lili," admonished Madame de La Berche in her masculine voice.

"But why? But why?" said Charlotte Peloux.

"For the sake of decency," said the baroness.

"Baroness, you are unkind! How sweet they are, the both of them! Ah!" she sighed, "they remind me of my own little ones."

"I was thinking of that," said Lili, laughing with delight. "We're on our honeymoon too, aren't we, Guido! We've come to hear the news about the other young couple! We've come to hear all about it."

Madame Peloux became stern. "Lili, you aren't expecting me to entertain you with bawdy tales, are you?"

"Yes, yes, yes I am," Lili exclaimed, clapping her hands. She tried to take a little hop, but succeeded only in slightly raising her shoulders and hips. "That's how I am, and that's how you have to take me! The sin of curiosity! Nobody can cure me. That little rascal over there knows all about it!"

The tongue-tied youth, under interrogation, didn't open his lips. His black pupils scurried across the whites of his eyes like frightened insects. Léa, rooted to the spot, looked on.

"Madame Charlotte has told us about the ceremony," bleated Madame Aldonza. "Young Madame Peloux was like a dream under her virgin's crown of orange blossom."

"Like a Madonna! Like a Madonna!" Charlotte Peloux overruled at the top of her lungs, roused by a righteous indignation. "Never, ever, have we seen such a sight! My son was walking on clouds! On clouds!...What a couple! What a couple!"

"Under her crown of orange blossom...do you hear that, my sweetheart?" murmured Lili. "So, tell us, Charlotte, what about our mother-in-law, Marie-Laure, how is she?"

Madame Peloux's merciless eyes twinkled.

"Oh! her...! Out of place, absolutely out of place...In a skintight black dress, like an eel wriggling out of the water. Her breasts, her belly...you could see all of her! All of her!"

"The hussy!" snorted the Baroness de La Berche, with martial indignation.

"And that air she has of thumbing her nose at the rest of us, of having some cyanide in her pocket and a pint of chloroform in her purse! Oh yes, out of place—that's the word for it! She made it seem like she had only five minutes to spare. She'd barely put her napkin down before it was "See you, Edmée, see you, Fred," and off she went.

Seated on the edge of an armchair, old Lili was panting, with her tiny, grandmother's mouth, puckered at the corners, hanging half-open.

"And the words of wisdom?" she interjected.

"What words of wisdom?"

"The words of advice—oh, sweetheart, hold my hand!—the words of advice to the young bride? Who gave them?"

Charlotte Peloux, taking umbrage, looked her up and down.

"That might have been the practice in your day, but it's been dropped."

The venerable, strapping dame planted her fists on her hips. "Dropped? Dropped or not, what can you possibly know about it, my poor, dear Charlotte? It's so rare for people to get married in your family!"

"Ha, ha, ha!" the two hangers-on guffawed, heedlessly.

But a single glance from Madame Peloux brought them up short.

"Gently, gently, my little angels! Each of you has your heaven on earth, what more do you want?"

And Madame de La Berche stretched out the firm, pacifying arm of a gendarme between the enflamed faces of these two ladies. But Charlotte Peloux sniffed the scent of battle, like a purebred. "If you're looking for a fight, Lili, you won't have any trouble finding me! Someone your age—I should treat you with respect, but if it weren't for that . . ."

Lili's whole body shook with laughter.

"If it weren't for that, you'd get married yourself, just to prove me wrong? It's not so hard to get married, you know! Me, I'd marry Guido right on the spot, if he were of age!"

"You don't really mean that?" Charlotte asked. Struck by Lili's declaration, she forgot her anger.

"But! . . . I'd be Princess Ceste, my dear! The *piccola principessa! Piccola principessa!* That's what he calls me, my little prince!"

She gathered her skirt and turned around, revealing a golden chain where her ankle ought to have been.

"Except that," she went on mysteriously, "his father . . ."

She was losing her breath, and waved to the silent youngster, who said, speaking low and fast, as though he was reciting from a book: "My father, the Duke de Parese, wants to put me in a convent if I marry Lili—"

"In a convent!" squawked Charlotte Peloux. "In a convent, a man!"

"A man in a convent," Madame de La Berche whinnied, in her basso profundo. "Good God, that's exciting!"

"They're savages!" Aldonza wailed, pressing her misshapen hands together.

Léa got up so abruptly she knocked over a full glass.

"It's just milk glass," observed Madame Peloux with satisfaction. "You'll bring good luck to my newlyweds. Where are you running off to? Is your house on fire?"

Léa managed to give the hint of a little, mischievous laugh. "A fire? Maybe . . . But shush! No questions! It's a secret . . ."

"Really? Another one? It's not possible!"

Charlotte Peloux whimpered with cupidity. "Aha, I thought you were in a funny state."

"Yes! Yes! Tell all!" yapped the trio of oldsters.

Lili's bulging palms, Mama Aldonza's twisted stumps, and Charlotte Peloux's iron fingers had grabbed hold of her hands, her forearms,
her gold mesh purse. She yanked herself away from all these paws and
succeeded in laughing again, with a teasing air. "No, it's too soon, it
would ruin everything! It's my secret!"

And she dashed into the vestibule. But the front door opened
ahead of her, and a wizened elder, a sort of jovial mummy, took her
in his arms. "Léa, my beauty, you'll have to give your little Berthellemy a kiss, or you won't get past!"

She gave a cry of fear and impatience, slapped away the glove-
encased bones that held her, and ran out.

Neither on the avenues of Neuilly nor in the lanes of the Bois—blue
under a rapidly falling dusk—did she allow herself the time to think.
She shivered slightly and raised the window of the car. The sight of
her orderly house, her pink bedroom, her boudoir—so overfurnished
and ornate—comforted her.

"Quick, Rose, light a fire in my room!"

"But the furnace is already set to seventy, like it was wintertime.
It was wrong of madame to take nothing but a fur wrap. The evenings
are unpredictable."

"Put the hot-water bottle in my bed right away, and for dinner I
want a big cup of hot chocolate, nice and thick, with an egg yolk
beaten in, and some toast, and some grapes... Hurry up, my dear,
I'm freezing. I got chilled at that flophouse out in Neuilly."

Once she was lying down, she clenched her teeth and stopped
them from chattering. The warmth of the bed loosened her stiff
muscles, but she didn't really let go of her anxiety yet, and her chauffeur Philibert's account book kept her occupied until the chocolate
arrived. She drank it piping hot and frothy. She picked the Chasselas
grapes one by one, swaying the cluster by its stem. It was a long cluster, amber-green in the lamplight...

Then she turned off her bedside lamp, stretched herself out into
her favorite position—flat on her back—and let herself go.

"What is the matter with me?"

She was gripped again by anxiety and shivering. The image of an empty doorway possessed her: the doorway of the conservatory, flanked by the two sprays of scarlet sage.

"It's morbid. You don't work yourself into a state like that just because of a doorway."

She saw the three old dames again, too: Lili's neck, and the beige blanket Madame Aldonza had been dragging around with her, everywhere, for the past twenty-five years.

"Which one of those three am I most likely to resemble in ten years' time?"

But it wasn't this prospect that distressed her. Even so, her anxiety kept building. She drifted from one image to another, from one memory to the next, trying to distance herself from the empty doorway framed by scarlet sage. She lay restless on her bed, trembling slightly. Suddenly, a profound unease—so intense, at first, that she thought it was physical—lifted her up, twisted her mouth, and tore a sob and a name from her in a husky exhalation:

"Chéri!"

Tears followed, which she couldn't master right away. Once she regained her self-control she sat down, dried her face, turned the lamp back on.

"Ah, well! I see."

She reached into the bedside table, took out a thermometer, and put it under her armpit.

"Normal. So, it's not physical. I see—it's that I'm suffering. Something's going to have to be done about this."

She took a drink of water, got up, washed her enflamed eyes, powdered herself, poked the glowing logs, lay down again. She felt guarded, full of defiance against an unfamiliar enemy: unhappiness. Thirty years of easygoing, congenial living, often amorous, sometimes greedy, had just lifted away. On the eve of her fiftieth birthday, they'd left her youthful and, in a sense, unprotected. She laughed at herself, stopped feeling her pain, and smiled.

"I must have been mad just now. I'm over it."

But a movement of her left arm, involuntarily rounded open as if ready to cradle a sleeping head, brought back all of her pain, and she sat up with a start.

"Well, this is going to be just grand!" she said out loud, harshly.

She looked at the clock and saw it wasn't even eleven yet. Overhead, old Rose's padding tread passed by, reached the staircase to the attic, and faded away. Léa resisted the urge to call to this aging, obliging girl for help.

"Ah, no! Don't give them anything to gossip about downstairs, right?"

She got back up, dressed herself snugly in a quilted silk robe, warmed her feet by the fire. Next, she half opened a window and cocked her ear to listen to something—she couldn't have said what. A warmer, humid breeze had ushered in some clouds, and the nearby Bois, still in leaf, murmured with the gusts. Léa closed the window, picked up a newspaper, and read the date:

"October twenty-sixth. Exactly one month since Chéri got married."

She would never say "since Edmée got married."

Just like Chéri, she hadn't yet given this shadow of a young woman credit for being alive. Hazel eyes, lovely ash-blond hair, a bit frizzy... the rest of Edmée melted away, in Léa's memory, like the outlines of a face glimpsed in a dream.

"No doubt they're making love in Italy at this very hour. And as for that... how little it concerns me..."

This wasn't just swagger. The picture she had formed of the young couple; the commonplace postures it suggested; even the image of Chéri's face—the way he would lie unconscious for a minute with a line of white light between his wasted eyelids... all of this stirred in her neither curiosity nor jealousy. However, a bestial shaking took hold of her again, brought her to her knees in front of a gash in the pearl-gray woodwork: the scar left by one of Chéri's brutalities.

"'The gorgeous hand that left this mark has turned away from me, forever'... Am I ever waxing eloquent! Just wait and see: grief is going to make me poetic!"

She took a few steps back and forth, sat, lay down again, waited for daylight. At eight o'clock Rose discovered her at her desk, writing, a spectacle that upset the old chambermaid.

"Is madame unwell?"

"Yes I am, and no I'm not, Rose. It's age, you know... Doctor Vidal thinks I need a change of air. Will you come with me? They're expecting a rough winter here. Let's go and eat a little southern cooking in the sunshine."

"And where would that be?"

"You ask too many questions. Just bring out the trunks. Give my fur blankets a good beating."

"Madame is taking the car?"

"I think so. Actually, I'm sure. I want all my comforts, Rose. Just imagine: I'm embarking on a pleasure trip, all on my own."

For five days Léa ran around Paris, wrote messages, sent telegrams, received dispatches and correspondence from the south. And she left Paris, leaving Madame Peloux a letter, a short letter, which, nevertheless, she had begun three times:

My dear Charlotte,

You won't hold it against me if I leave without saying goodbye, keeping my little secret to myself. I'm nothing but a big fool! ... Bah! Life is short; at least it ought to be good.

A big affectionate hug from me. You'll pass on my best wishes to the little one when he comes back.

Your incorrigible,

Léa

P.S. Don't go out of your way to come and interrogate my butler or the concierge. Nobody at my place knows anything.

"Do you know what, my darling, precious boy? I don't think you look very well."

"It was the night on the train," Chéri answered curtly.

Madame Peloux didn't risk saying everything she was thinking. She found her son changed.

"He is . . . Yes, there's something ominous about him," she declared to herself; and ended up saying, out loud and with enthusiasm, "It's Italy's fault!"

"If you like," Chéri allowed.

Mother and son had just eaten their breakfast together, and Chéri had deigned to praise, with a few appreciative profanities, his cup of café au lait "concierge-style": a honey-colored, sweet coffee made with whole milk. Pieces of toasted, buttered baguette were broken into it to soak slowly and cover it with a mouthwatering crust. It was then reheated over a bed of low coals.

He felt cold in his white woolen pajamas and hugged his knees. Charlotte Peloux, wanting to please her son, tried on a new burnt-orange dressing gown and a morning cap—tight-fitting around the temples—that gave the bareness of her face a sinister prominence.

While her son was watching her, she said in a mincing tone, "You see, I'm trying out the grandmother look! Soon enough, I'll be powdering my cheeks. Do you like this cap? It's very eighteenth century, isn't it? Who do I look like—Dubarry, or Pompadour?"

"You look like an old galley slave," Chéri hurled at her. "It's not the sort of thing one should show up in without fair warning."

She groaned, then guffawed. "Ha ha! Don't you have a sharp tongue!"

But he wasn't laughing, and he looked out into the garden at the thin layer of snow that had fallen on the lawns during the night. The twitching contractions—barely perceptible—of his jaw muscles were all that betrayed his nervous state. Cowed, Madame Peloux echoed his silence. A muffled trill, the ring of a bell, hung in the air.

"That's Edmée ringing for her breakfast," said Madame Peloux.

Chéri didn't answer.

"So, what's wrong with the furnace? It's cold in here," he said, after a minute.

"It's Italy's fault," Madame Peloux repeated, with lyrical intonation. "You come back here with your eyes and your heart full of sunshine! You've landed at the North Pole! The North Pole! The dahlias didn't last a week! But rest easy, my dearest darling. Your nest is coming along. If the architect hadn't come down with paratyphoid fever it would have been finished by now. I saw it coming. If I told him once, I told him twenty times: 'Monsieur Savaron—'"

Chéri, who'd gone over to the window, turned around abruptly. "What was the date on that letter?"

"What letter?"

"That letter from Léa you showed me just now."

"It wasn't dated, my love, but I received it the day before my last Sunday at home in October."

"Right. And you don't know who he is?"

"Who he is, my treasure?"

"Yes, who is he—the guy she went away with?"

The naked face of Madame Peloux turned malicious. "No! Can you believe it? Nobody knows! Old Lili is in Sicily, and none of the ladies down there have caught wind of the business! A mystery, a deeply disturbing mystery! However, you know me, I've managed to gather a few bits of information here and there..."

Chéri's jet-black pupils shifted.

"What are the rumors?"

"That it's a young man," whispered Madame Peloux. "A young and a rather... a rather disreputable young man—you take my meaning!... A very good-looking one, that's for sure!"

She was lying, choosing the meanest scenario.

Chéri shrugged his shoulders. "Oh là là! A very good-looking one! Poor Léa, I can see him all the way from here: a tough little guy, from Patron's boxing academy, with hairy wrists and damp palms... Look, I'm going back to bed, you've made me sleepy."

Dragging his *babouches*, he made his way back to his bedroom, lingering in the long corridors and on the wide landings of the house he felt he was discovering for the first time. He bumped into a bow-front armoire and exclaimed, "Dammit, if I'd remembered there was an armoire here... Ah, yes, I do remember vaguely... And that guy over there, who could he be?"

He was pondering a photographic enlargement that hung, funereal in its black wooden frame, next to a multicolored faience vase that Chéri also failed to recognize.

Madame Peloux hadn't moved house for twenty-five years. She'd kept, in their place, all the successive errors of her outlandish hoarder's taste. Old Lili—who was avid for paintings, especially by avant-garde painters—would reproach her: "Your house, it's the house of an ant gone berserk." To which Madame Peloux would counter, "Why not leave well enough alone?"

The paint in a sea-green corridor—hospital-green, according to Léa—was it peeling away? Charlotte Peloux had it repainted in green. And to replace the garnet velvet of a chaise longue, she would search zealously for the same garnet velvet...

Chéri came to a halt in the doorway of an open bathroom. A red marble washstand enclosed two monogrammed white sinks, and two electric sconces were crowned with pearl-studded lilies. Chéri lifted his shoulders up to his ears, as if he were caught in a cold draft.

"Good God, it's awful, this hodgepodge!"

He quickly strode away. The window at the end of the hallway he was pacing along was adorned with a border of little red and yellow squares of stained glass.

"And now I have to face this as well," he grumbled.

He turned to his left and shoved open a door—the door to his former bedroom—without knocking. A muffled cry arose from the bed, where Edmée was finishing her breakfast.

Chéri closed the door behind him and regarded his young wife, without approaching the bed.

"Good morning," she said, with a smile. "How surprised you look to see me!"

The snow's reflection bathed her in an even, blue light. She had loosened her frizzy ash-blond hair, which didn't quite cover her low, elegant shoulders. With her white and rosy cheeks, which matched her nightgown, and her pink mouth paled by fatigue, she was a newly painted picture, unfinished, somewhat indistinct.

"Will you say good morning to me, Fred?" she pressed.

He sat next to his wife and took her in his arms. She leaned back gently, taking Chéri with her. He leaned on his elbows to take a close look at this newly minted creature lying underneath him, her bloom unfaded by lassitude. Her lower eyelids, rounded and full, without a crease, seemed to fascinate him, as did the silvery smoothness of her cheeks.

"How old are you?" he asked abruptly.

Edmée opened her eyes, which she had tenderly shut. Chéri saw the hazel color of her irises. Her laugh exposed her diminutive, squarish teeth.

"Oh, come on now... I'll be nineteen on the fifth of January—try and remember!"

He withdrew his arm brusquely, and the young woman slid into the hollow of the bed like an loosened scarf.

"Nineteen, that's a miracle! You know I'm over twenty-five?"

"Yes, of course I know, Fred..."

From the bedside table, he picked up a pale yellow tortoiseshell mirror and gazed at himself.

"Twenty-five years old!"

Twenty-five, with a white marble face that looked invincible. Twenty-five, but at the outer corners of his eyes, and extending below them, two lines—visible only in direct light—subtly accentuated the classical contours of his lids. Two cuts made by a hand so formidable and so deft... He put down the mirror.

"You're younger than me," he said to Edmée. "That shocks me."

"Not me!"

She'd answered in a scathing voice, full of undertones. He paid it no heed.

"Do you know why my eyes are beautiful?" he asked her, in all seriousness.

"No," said Edmée. "Maybe because I love them?"

"You're just waxing poetic," said Chéri, shrugging his shoulders. "It's because my eyes are shaped like a sole."

"Like a..."

"Like a sole."

He sat close to her, to give a demonstration: "Look: Here, in the corner next to my nose, that's the head of the sole. And here, where it curves up, that's the back of the sole, and here, underneath, where it carries on in a straight line, that's the belly of the sole. And the corner that stretches out toward my temple is the tail of the sole."

"Oh?"

"Yes, if I had eyes shaped like a flounder, I mean if they were rounded just as much on the bottom as on top, I'd look stupid. And there you have it. You, with your baccalaureate, did you know that? Did you?"

"No, I admit..."

She went quiet and remained nonplussed, as he'd spoken in a moralizing tone with an excess of emphasis, like an eccentric.

"There are times," she thought, "when he's like a savage. A jungle-dweller. But he knows nothing about plants or animals. And sometimes it seems like he doesn't even know what it means to be human..."

Chéri, seated against her, had one arm around her shoulders, and with his free hand was fondling the little pearls—very lovely, very round, evenly sized—of Edmée's necklace. She breathed in the perfume that Chéri used to excess, and she wilted, overcome, like a rose in a heated room.

"Fred... Come back to bed... we're both worn out."

He appeared not to hear. He fixed the pearls of the necklace with a stubborn and uneasy stare.

"Fred..."

He flinched, stood up, tore his pajamas off in a fury, and threw himself, stark naked, into the bed, searching out the resting place for his head on a youthful shoulder whose slender collarbone still protruded. Edmée submitted with the whole of her body, hollowed her side, and opened her arm. Chéri closed his eyes and stopped moving. She stayed awake, watchful, a bit out of breath under his weight, believing he was asleep. But a second later he tossed over, feigning the groan of an unconscious sleeper, and rolled himself up in the sheet on the other side of the bed.

"As usual," Edmée observed.

All winter long she had to wake up inside this square, four-windowed bedroom. Bad weather was slowing down the completion of a new town house on rue Henri-Martin, as were Chéri's whims; he wanted a black bathroom, a Chinese salon, a basement fitted out with a swimming pool, and a gym. To the objections of the architect, he barked back: "I don't give a damn. I'm paying, I want what I ask for. I don't care what it costs." But at other times he'd obsessively comb through an estimate, swearing that "no one pulls the wool over the eyes of Peloux the Younger." And then he'd ramble on about bulk prices, asbestos cement, and colored stucco with an unexpected facility and a precise recall of sums, which commanded the contractors' respect.

He rarely consulted his young wife, though he did put on a show of authority to impress her. And on occasions when he felt unsure, he took care to mask his uncertainty with terse instructions. She discovered that, while he had an instinctive feel for playing with colors, he disdained beautiful forms and definitive styles.

"You're weighing yourself down with a load of nonsense, my dear... er... Edmée. A decision about the smoking room? Here you go: blue for the walls, a blue that can stand up to anything. A purple rug, in a shade of purple that shrinks away from the blue on the walls. And then, to go along with this, don't be afraid of black, or gold, for the furniture and the knickknacks."

"Yes, you're right, Fred. But it will be a bit relentless, with all these strong colors. There'll be some charm missing, a lighter note, a white vase or a statue—"

"Not so," he interrupted rather abruptly. "The white vase, that'll be me, in the buff. And let's not forget a cushion, a you-know-what, some sort of a thingy in pumpkin red for when I'm lounging around naked in there."

She toyed—secretly seduced and repulsed—with images like these, which transformed their future dwelling into a sort of palace of ambiguity, a temple to the glory of Chéri. But she didn't fight back, just pleaded gently for "a little space" for a tiny, precious set of furniture, upholstered with needlework on a white background, a gift from Marie-Laure.

This compliance—which covered up a willpower so youthful but already so well tested—enabled her to camp out for four months at her mother-in-law's and to withstand, for the whole of the four months, the constant surveillance, the traps laid every day for her peace of mind, for her good humor—still sensitive to coldness—and for her tact; Charlotte Peloux, inflamed by the proximity of such a tender victim, lost a little self-control and was profligate with her darts, firing them off in all directions...

"Keep a cooler head, Madame Peloux," Chéri would interject once in a while. "Who will you have left to feed on next winter, if I don't hold you back now?"

Edmée lifted eyes, in which fear and gratitude trembled together, toward her husband and tried not to think too hard or look too much at Madame Peloux. One evening, as if distracted, Charlotte lobbed the name "Léa"—instead of "Edmée"—three times over the chrysanthemums in the centerpiece.

Chéri lowered his satanic brows. "Madame Peloux, I believe your memory is failing. Do you think you might need to spend some time in an isolation ward?"

Charlotte Peloux kept mum for a week, but Edmée never risked asking her husband: "Is it because of me that you're upset? Is it really me you're defending? Is it not the other woman, the one before me?"

Her childhood and adolescence had taught her patience, hope, silence, and a prisoner's easy employment of dodges and wiles. The fair Marie-Laure had never scolded her daughter; she had restricted herself to doling out punishment. Never a harsh word, never a tender one. Solitude, then boarding school, then solitude once more during a few holidays when she was frequently relegated to a prettily decorated bedroom; finally, the threat of marriage, any marriage, once her too-fair mother discerned in her the dawn of another kind of beauty, a shy beauty, as if suppressed and all the more touching... Compared to this mother of unfeeling ivory and gold, Charlotte Peloux's overt nastiness was a bed of roses...

"Are you afraid of my reverend mother?" Chéri asked her one evening.

Edmée smiled and put on a pout of indifference.

"Afraid? No. When a door slams, I might jump, but I'm not afraid. What I am afraid of is the snake sliding under it..."

"Quite the snake, that Marie-Laure, eh?"

"Quite."

He waited for a confidence that wasn't forthcoming and wrapped an arm around the narrow shoulders of his wife, in a comradely gesture. "We're a bit like orphans, aren't we?"

"Yes, we're orphans! Such sweet ones!"

She pressed herself against him. They were alone in the conservatory. Madame Peloux, as Chéri called her, was upstairs concocting her poisons for the following day. The night, cold still on the other side of the windows, mirrored the furniture and the lamps, like the surface of a pond. Edmée felt warm and protected, confident, in the arms of this stranger. Suddenly, shocked, she raised her head and cried out: he was leaning back under the chandelier with a magnificent and desperate look on his face, his eyes closed over two tears, withheld and sparkling between his lashes.

"Chéri, Chéri, what's wrong with you?"

In spite of herself, she'd called him by this overly indulgent pet name, which she never liked to use. He answered the summons distractedly and turned his gaze back onto her.

"Chéri! My God, I'm frightened... What's the matter with you?"

He moved her a short distance away and held her by the arms, facing him.

"Ah! Ah! This little girl... this little girl... So, then, what *are* you afraid of?"

He offered up his velvety eyes, made more lovely by his tears: peaceful, wide-open, indecipherable. Edmée was going to beg him to be quiet, when he said, "What fools we are! ... It's that idea that we're orphans... It's idiotic. And so true..."

He resumed his air of maudlin self-importance, and she breathed a sigh of relief, confident that he wouldn't go on talking. As he began carefully to snuff out the candelabras, he turned toward Edmée and said, with a conceit that was either very innocent or very cunning, "Tell me, then, why shouldn't I have a heart, too?"

"What are you up to there?"

Even though he'd accosted her almost silently, the sound of Chéri's voice affected Edmée so much that she bent forward as if pushed. Standing in front of an open bureau, she had her hands resting on top of some scattered papers.

"I'm doing some tidying up..." she said. She lifted one hand, which halted in midair as though numb. Then she seemed to wake up, and stopped lying.

"All right, Fred...You told me, for our upcoming move, that you had a horror of having to deal on your own with what you want to take: the stuff in this room, these pieces of furniture...I intended, in good faith, to tidy up, sort things out...and the next thing I knew, the poison, the temptation came over me—the evil thoughts...I beg your pardon. I've meddled with things that don't belong to me."

She trembled bravely and waited. He stood in a menacing attitude, with his head bent and his hands clenched, but didn't appear to be seeing his wife. His gaze was so clouded that, from that moment on, she would always recall having had a conversation with a man with pale eyes...

"Ah, yes!" he said, at last. "You were searching...You were searching for love letters."

She didn't deny it.

"You were searching for my love letters!"

He gave one of his awkward, forced laughs. Edmée reddened, feeling hurt.

"You must think I'm stupid, it's obvious. You're not the kind of man who'd fail to put them away somewhere safe, or burn them. And besides, they're none of my business. I'm only getting what I deserve. You won't hold it against me too badly, will you, Fred?"

She was forcing herself to plead a bit, and she was deliberately making herself look pretty, with her lips spread wide and the upper half of her face obscured by the shadow of her puffed-out hair. But Chéri didn't alter his stance, and she noticed for the first time that his beautiful, smooth complexion had taken on the transparency of a white winter rose, and the ovals of his cheeks were sunken.

"Love letters..." he repeated. "What a joke."

He took a step forward, grabbed the papers and leafed through them. Postcards, restaurant bills, letters from suppliers, telegrams from one-night stands, three- or four-line pneumatic tube scrolls from his sponger friends, a few narrow sheets slashed with Madame Peloux's piercing script...

Chéri turned back toward his wife. "I have no love letters."

"Oh!" she protested. "Then why do you want—"

"I don't have any," he interrupted. "You wouldn't understand. I hadn't even thought of it this way myself: I can't have any love letters, because—"

He stopped himself.

"Ah! Wait, wait. There was one time, I remember, I hadn't wanted to go to the spa at La Bourboule, and so... Wait, wait..."

He was opening drawers and feverishly hurling papers on the rug.

"This is too much! What have I done with it? I could have sworn it was in the top drawer on the left... No..."

He slammed the empty drawers shut and fixed Edmée with a heavy stare. "You didn't find anything? Might you have taken a letter that began, 'But no, I'm not bored. It's always better to spend one week a month apart'? And after that it carried on, I don't remember just how anymore, about a honeysuckle climbing up the window..."

He stopped talking—only because his memory was failing him—and he made a slight gesture of impatience. Edmée, slender and stiff, facing him, kept strong. "No, no, I haven't *taken* anything," she stressed, with annoyance. "Since when am I capable of *taking*? A letter so precious to you, that you just left it lying around? A letter like that—do I need to ask if it came from Léa!"

He gave a slight start, but not in the way Edmée was expecting. A half-smile flitted across his beautiful, impenetrable face; with his head tilted to the side, his watchful eyes, and the delectable arch of his slackened mouth, perhaps he was hearkening to the echo of a name...All of Edmée's youthful strength—amorous and uncontrolled—burst into shouts, tears, and the twisting, or stretching and scratching, movements of her hands.

"Get out of here! I hate you! You've never loved me! You couldn't care less if I didn't even exist! You hurt me, you despise me, you're crude, you're...you're...You think about no one but that old woman! You have the tastes of a sick man, a degenerate...a...a...You don't love me! Why, why on earth, why did you marry me?...You're... You're..."

She was shaking her head like a tethered animal. When she bent her neck, gasping for air, you could see the milk-white, diminutive, even-sized pearls of her necklace glowing. Chéri gazed in astonishment at the unruly movements of this charming, sinuous throat, the entreaty of her two knotted hands, and above all, the tears, the tears... He'd never seen so many tears...Who had ever cried in front of him, or for him? No one...Madame Peloux? "But," he reflected, "Madame Peloux's tears don't count...Léa's...? No." In the depths of his inmost memories, he scanned two eyes of genuine blue that had never shone with anything but pleasure, mischief, and a slightly mocking tenderness...So many tears coming from this young woman thrashing around in front of him! What can you do about so many tears? He didn't know. All the same, he held out his arms, and when Edmée backed away, fearing, perhaps, some act of violence, he placed his lovely, soft hand, steeped in perfume, on her head, and stroked that disheveled head while trying to imitate a voice and some words whose power now became apparent to him.

"There...there...What's the matter?...What's this about... There..."

Edmée succumbed. She dropped down onto a settee, huddled up and sobbing, in a passion, in a frenzy of what seemed to be convulsive laughter and spasms of joy. Her graceful, arched body heaved with grief, jealous love, anger, and unconscious servility, and at the same time—like a warrior in the heat of battle, like a swimmer breasting a wave—she felt immersed in a new element, natural and bitter.

She cried for a long while, and she recovered slowly, her periods of calm punctuated by fits of choking and shuddering. Chéri had taken a seat near her and continued stroking her hair. He'd moved past the fever pitch of his own emotion and was losing interest. He cast his eyes over Edmée, who lay sprawled across the dry surface of the couch. He wasn't happy to see this outstretched body, with its dress hauled up and its scarf unwound, adding to the disorder of the room.

However quietly he'd sighed with boredom, she heard him and sat up.

"Yes," she said, "I'm too much for you ... Ah! It would be better if—"

He cut her off, dreading a flood of words. "That's not it, but I don't know what you want."

"What do you mean, 'what I want'... How does what I ..."

She lifted her face, inflamed by her tears.

"Listen to me closely."

He took her hands. She tried to break free.

"No, no! I know that voice of yours! You're going to make another one of your outrageous arguments. When you put on that voice and that face, I know you're going to prove to me that your eyes are shaped like some kind of a fish and your mouth looks like an upside-down number 3! No, no, I won't listen!"

She was railing childishly, and Chéri loosened up, sensing that they were both very young. He shook her warm hands and kept them in his.

"But you have to listen to me! For God's sake, I'd like to know what it is you hold against me! Do I go out at night without you? No! Do I leave you alone a lot during the day? Do I keep up a secret correspondence?"

"I don't know... I don't think so ..."

He was swiveling her this way and that, like a puppet.

"Do I sleep in a separate bedroom? Don't I make love to you well?"

She hesitated, then smiled with a wary incisiveness.

"You call that love, Fred..."

"There are other words, but none that you'd appreciate."

"What you call love...couldn't it be, really...a sort of...alibi?" She added abruptly, "I'm speaking in general terms, Fred, you understand...I'm saying it *could* be, at certain times..."

He let go of Edmée's hands. "That," he said coldly, "that is a big blunder."

"Why?" she asked, in a muted voice.

He gave a hiss, with his chin in the air, as he stepped back a few steps. Then he came back at his wife and looked her up and down, as if she were a stranger. A scary beast doesn't need to pounce to instill fear. Edmée could see that his nostrils were flaring and the tip of his nose was white.

"Bah!" he breathed, while looking at his wife. He shrugged his shoulders and turned to go. From the far end of the room, he came back again.

"Bah!" he repeated. "It speaks."

"What?"

"It speaks, and what does it say? Oh my! It lets itself go..."

She rose in a fury. "Fred," she cried, "you will never again speak to me in that tone of voice! Who do you take me for?"

"For a blunderer, obviously. Didn't I just have the honor of telling you so?"

He placed a stiff index finger on her shoulder. She felt that it would leave a heavy bruise.

"You who've earned your degree, isn't there a saying somewhere...a saying that goes: 'Don't touch the knife,' or 'the dagger,' or whatever?"

"The ax," she said, mechanically.

"That's it. And so, my deary, don't touch the ax. Which means: don't disparage a man...for the favors he bestows...if I may be so bold. You've disparaged me for the gifts I've given you...You've disparaged my favors."

"You...you talk like a...cocotte!" she stammered.

She flushed, lost her strength and her composure. She hated him for not reddening, for maintaining a superiority whose whole secret resided in the attitude of his head, the straightness of his legs, the looseness of his shoulders and arms . . .

The stiff index finger pressed into Edmée's shoulder once again.

"Pardon me, pardon me. I could really floor you by claiming that it's you, on the contrary, who thinks like a whore. When it comes to sizing something up, one can't fool a Peloux. I have some knowledge of 'cocottes,' as you call them. I know a little bit about them. A 'cocotte' is a lady who arranges, by and large, to receive more than she gives. Do you understand me?"

What she understood, most of all, was that he was no longer using the singular, intimate form of address.

"Nineteen years old, unblemished skin, hair smelling of vanilla; and in bed, eyes closed and arms dangling. All of that is very fetching, but is it really that rare? Do you think it's really rare?"

She flinched at every word, and every sting readied her for the duel between female and male.

"It's possible that it might be rare," she said in a steady voice, "but how would you know?"

He didn't answer, and she made haste to gain an advantage.

"As for me," she said, "in Italy, I saw men handsomer than you. They were nothing unusual. At nineteen, I'm just as good as the next girl, and one pretty boy is worth just as much as another. Come on now, everything can work out . . . In this day and age, marriage is a meaningless bond. Instead of making each other bitter with ridiculous quarrels—"

He stopped her with an almost merciful shake of his head. "Ah, poor kid! . . . it's not so simple . . ."

"Why? Divorces can go quickly, if you're willing to pay the price."

Her tone was sharp. like a runaway schoolgirl's, and painful to hear. Her hair, swept back above her forehead, and the soft folds and outline of her cheeks made her worried, intelligent eyes look darker—the clearly defined eyes of an unhappy woman, in an uncertain face.

"That wouldn't solve anything," said Chéri.

"Because?"

"Because..."

He lowered his forehead, his eyebrows flaring like pointed wings. He closed his eyes and opened them again, as though he'd just swallowed a bitter mouthful.

"Because you love me..."

She was attentive only to his using, once more, the intimate form of "you"; and most of all to the tone of his voice, which was full but a little muffled, the tone of their happiest hours. She acquiesced in the very depths of her being. "It's true, I do love him! At this point, there's no cure."

The dinner bell sounded out in the garden, a too-small bell from before Madame Peloux's time, a sad, clear bell from a provincial orphanage. Edmée shivered.

"Oh! I don't like that bell..."

"No?" said Chéri, distracted.

"In our home, we'll announce the meals instead of ringing a bell. In our home, we won't keep up these boarding house practices; you'll see, in our home..."

She talked without turning around as she walked down the hospital-green corridor. She didn't see, behind her, the fierce attention that Chéri paid to her last words, nor his silent smirk.

He walked, light on his feet, enlivened by an understated spring, a season sensed only in the humid, fitful breeze and in the heady scent—from squares and gardens—of the earth. From time to time, along the way, a mirror reminded him that he was wearing a flattering fedora lowered over his right eye; a light and roomy overcoat; long kid-leather gloves; and a terracotta-colored cravat. Behind him, women paid mute homage, and the most candid among them accorded him that fleeting look of astonishment, which they could neither feign nor conceal. But Chéri never looked at women in the street. He'd departed from the town house on avenue Henri-Martin after leaving some instructions—contradictory, but delivered with an air of authority—for the decorators.

At the end of the avenue, he breathed deeply, savoring the smell of vegetation—borne from the Bois on the heavy, moist wing of the west wind—and then quickened his steps toward the Porte Dauphine. In a few minutes he reached the lower end of avenue Bugeaud and came to a halt. For the first time in six months his feet were treading the familiar path. He unbuttoned his overcoat.

"I've walked too fast," he thought to himself. He started again, then stopped again, and this time he aimed his gaze at a particular spot: fifty yards away—hatless, his chamois in hand—Ernest, Léa's concierge, was "doing" the brass ornaments on the gate in front of Léa's town house. Chéri started to hum as he walked, but on hearing the sound of his own voice he remembered that he never hummed, and he stopped.

"How goes it, Ernest? Busy as always?"

The concierge cautiously opened up.

"Monsieur Peloux! I'm delighted to see monsieur. Monsieur hasn't changed."

"Neither have you, Ernest. Is madame doing well?"

He was talking with his head turned sideways; his attention was focused on the closed blinds upstairs.

"I believe so, monsieur. We've only had a few postcards."

"From where? From Biarritz, I expect?"

"I don't think so, monsieur."

"Where is madame?"

"I'd be hard pressed to tell monsieur. We're forwarding her mail—there's been next to nothing—to madame's lawyer."

Chéri pulled out his wallet, giving Ernest an affectionate look.

"Oh, Monsieur Peloux, money coming between us? You can't really mean it. A thousand francs can't get information out of a man who knows nothing. Would monsieur like the address of madame's lawyer?"

"No, thanks anyway. When is she coming back?"

Ernest spread his arms. "Now there's another question that's beyond me. Maybe tomorrow, maybe in a month ... I'm keeping things up, you see. With madame you have to stay on guard. If you said to me: 'There she is now, coming around the corner of the avenue,' I wouldn't be the least bit surprised."

Chéri swung around and looked toward the corner of the avenue.

"Is there nothing else I can do for monsieur? Was monsieur passing by, out on a stroll? It's a lovely day..."

"No, thanks, Ernest. Till the next time, Ernest."

"Always at Monsieur Peloux's service."

Chéri walked up as far as place Victor-Hugo, twirling his cane. Twice he tripped and almost fell, the way people do when they think someone's staring at them, hard, from behind. Having reached the stairs of the metro station, he leaned his elbows on the railing and looked down at the black and pink shadows of the underground passage. He felt crushed by fatigue. When he straightened up again, he saw the gas lamps lighting up in the square, and that night was turning everything blue.

"No, it's impossible. I must be ill."

He'd reached the very depths of a gloomy reverie and roused himself with difficulty. The requisite words came to him at last: "Come on, come on, good God... Peloux the Younger, are you going off the rails, old pal? Don't you have an inkling that it's time to go home?"

This final word revived a specter that an hour had sufficed to banish: a square room—Chéri's big childhood bedroom; a worried young woman standing by the window; and Charlotte Peloux, mollified by a martini cocktail...

"Ah, no!" he said out loud. "No... That—that's finished."

He raised his cane, and a taxi halted.

"To the restaurant... uh... to the Blue Dragon restaurant."

To the sound of violins, he passed through the grill room, bathed in an atrocious glare of electric light that he found bracing. He shook the hand of a maître d', who recognized him. In front of him a tall, lean young man got up, and Chéri gave a tender sigh.

"Ah! Desmond! I'd been wanting to see you so badly! And look, here you are!"

The table they sat at was decorated with pink carnations. A diminutive hand and a tall plume waved to Chéri from a neighboring table.

"It's la Loupiote, the Little Tyke," Viscount Desmond warned.

Chéri didn't recall la Loupiote, but he smiled at the tall plume and, with the tip of a cheap folding fan, touched the little hand without getting out of his seat. Next, putting on his most imperious, sober air, he gave the once-over to a couple he didn't know, because the woman had stopped paying attention to her food ever since Chéri had taken his seat not far from her.

"He has the head of a cuckold, eh, that guy?"

He leaned toward his friend's ear to murmur these words, and the joy in Desmond's eyes glittered like overflowing tears.

"What do you drink, now that you're married?" asked Desmond. "Chamomile tea?"

"Pommery," Chéri answered.

"And before the Pommery?"

"Pommery before and after!"

He widened his nostrils while he inhaled, in his memory, the rose-scented sparkle of a vintage 1889 champagne, which Léa had reserved for him alone...

He ordered a meal fit for a tradesman on a binge: cold fish in a port wine sauce, roasted songbirds, a piping hot soufflé whose interior hid a sour red sorbet...

"Hey ho," la Loupiote shouted out, waving a pink carnation toward Chéri.

"Hey ho," answered Chéri, raising his glass.

An English timepiece, fastened to the wall, chimed eight o'clock.

"Oh, damn!" Chéri grumbled. "Desmond, do me a favor and make a call."

Desmond's pale eyes hoped for revelations.

"Call Wagram 17-08, ask for my mother, and tell her we're dining together."

"And what if it's the younger Madame Peloux who answers the phone?"

"The same thing. I'm very free, you see. I've got her trained."

He drank and ate a lot, preoccupied with looking solemn and blasé. But the least burst of laughter, a glass breaking, a drunken waltz, all enhanced his enjoyment. The hard blue sheen of the wainscoting revived his memories of the Riviera, of the noontimes when the too-blue sea would turn dark around a patch of molten sun. He abandoned the customary indifference of the good-looking man and began to scan the brunette facing him with professional looks that left her all aquiver.

"And Léa?" Desmond abruptly asked.

Chéri didn't flinch; he'd been thinking about Léa.

"Léa's in the south."

"Is it over with her?"

Chéri stuck his thumb into an armhole of his vest.

"Oh, of course it is! We parted very nicely, on very good terms. It couldn't have lasted the rest of our lives. What a charming, intelligent woman... Anyway, you knew her! Very broad-minded... Truly remarkable. Dear friend, I admit, if there hadn't been the issue of age... But there was the issue of age, and isn't there—"

"Clearly," Desmond interrupted.

This youth with washed-out eyes, who knew all the ins and outs of his tough and exacting trade as a parasite, had just given in to curiosity and was faulting himself for doing so, as though he'd committed a careless act. But Chéri, wary and tipsy at once, couldn't stop talking about Léa. He said reasonable things that brimmed with conjugal common sense. He lauded marriage, but also did justice to Léa's virtues. He sang the praises of his young wife's submissive sweetness, to give himself the opportunity to criticize Léa's willful character. "Ah, the vixen, I guarantee you she had her designs, that one!" He took his confidences a step further. Concerning Léa, he turned severe, even insolent. And while he spoke, shielded by the inane words that came into his tormented lover's head, he savored the subtle pleasure of talking about her freely. A little further yet, and he would have dragged her through the mud, while extolling his heartfelt memory of her; her sweet name, so easy to say, which he hadn't let himself utter for the past six months; the whole merciful image of Léa leaning over him, her brow lined with a few big, deep, irreparable furrows; beautiful, lost to him, but—ach!—so present . . .

Around eleven, they got up to leave, their spirits dimmed by the almost empty restaurant. But at the next table, la Loupiote was busy with her correspondence. She was calling out for the little blue forms to send by pneumatic tube. She lifted her harmless blond sheep's head toward the two friends as they passed by.

"Hey there, you don't even say good night?"

"Good night," Chéri said, compliantly.

La Loupiote called on her girlfriend to bear witness to Chéri's beauty: "Can you believe it? And to think he has so much dough! Some guys have it all."

But Chéri offered her only his open cigarette case, and she turned acerbic.

"They have it all, except the knack of knowing what to do with it . . . Go home to your mother, honeybun . . . !

"Actually," Chéri said to Desmond, when they'd reached the street. "Actually, I wanted to ask you, Desmond . . . Let's wait till we get away from this bottleneck where we're being crushed to death . . ."

Strollers were lingering in the soft, humid evening, but past rue Caumartin, the boulevard hadn't filled up yet with the crowds coming out of the theaters. Chéri took his friend's arm. "Here's the thing, Desmond . . . I'd like you to go back to the telephone."

Desmond came to a halt. "Again?"

"You'll call Wagram . . ."

"17-08 . . ."

"You're adorable. You'll say I'm at your place, feeling unwell—where are you staying?"

"At the Hotel Morris."

"Perfect—and that I'll be home tomorrow morning, that you're making me some mint tea . . . Go, my friend. Here, you can give this to the telephone boy, or else keep it for yourself . . . Come back quick. I'll be waiting for you on the terrace at Weber's."

The lanky, obliging, arrogant young man went away crumpling

the banknotes in his pocket and holding himself back from making a comment. When he rejoined Chéri, the latter was hunched over a full glass of orange soda, in which he seemed to be reading his fortune.

"Desmond!...Who answered you?"

"A woman," the messenger replied tersely.

"Which woman?"

"I don't know."

"What did she say?"

"That it was fine."

"In what sort of tone?"

"The one I just used."

"Ah! Good; thanks."

"It was Edmée," thought Chéri. They were walking toward the place de la Concorde, and Chéri had taken hold of Desmond's arm again. He was reluctant to admit he felt worn out.

"Where do you want to go?" asked Desmond.

"Ah, dear friend," Chéri sighed with gratitude, "to the Morris, and right away. I'm beat."

Desmond lost his composure. "What, really? We're going to the Morris? What is it you want to do? No joking, eh? You want..."

"To sleep," Chéri answered. And he closed his eyes like he was ready to drop, then reopened them. "To sleep—to sleep, is that clear?"

He was gripping his friend's arm with too much force.

"Let's go," said Desmond.

In ten minutes, they were at the Morris. The sky-blue and ivory tints of a bedroom and the faux-Empire style of a little salon smiled at Chéri like old friends. He bathed, borrowed a silk nightshirt—too tight for him—from Desmond, got into bed, and, wedged between two fat, soft pillows, sank into a state of dreamless happiness, a dark and heavy sleep that defended him on all fronts...

Days of shame slid by. He counted them: "Sixteen...seventeen... When three weeks are up, I'm going home to Neuilly." He wasn't going home. He was lucidly assessing a situation he no longer had the strength to remedy. At night, or in the morning, he sometimes indulged in thinking his cowardly behavior would end in a few hours. "No more strength? Oh, beg your pardon . . . no strength yet. But it will return. What do I bet that I'll be in the dining room on boulevard d'Inkermann at the stroke of noon? Or at one . . . or two . . . or . . . ?" At the stroke of noon, he'd be found taking a bath, or driving his car with Desmond at his side.

Mealtimes offered him a chance, which recurred as punctually as a fever, to feel some conjugal optimism. While sitting across from Desmond at their bachelor's table, he'd see Edmée appear, and he'd reflect in silence on the inconceivable deference of his youthful wife. "She's too kind, that girl! Has anyone ever seen such a darling wife? Not a word, not a complaint! I'm going to clap one of those bracelets on her when I get home . . . Ah! It's her upbringing . . . There's no one better than Marie-Laure when it comes to raising a girl." But one day in the grillroom of the Morris, the apparition of a green dress with a chinchilla collar, which looked like a dress of Edmée's, painted all the marks of abject terror onto Chéri's face.

Desmond was finding life very agreeable and putting on a little weight. He reserved his arrogance for the times when Chéri, on being urged to visit a "prodigious Englishwoman, blackened with vices," or "an Indian prince in his opium palace," would flatly refuse, or else consent only with unconcealed disdain. Desmond no longer understood anything about Chéri, but Chéri paid the bills and paid them better than he had in the best years of their adolescence. One night they encountered the blond Loupiote again at the place of her friend, the one whose dull-sounding name they could never remember. "What's-her-name . . . you know who . . . la Loupiote's pal . . ."

La Copine smoked opium and she shared it with others. As soon as you entered her modest mezzanine apartment, you could smell leaking gas and the residue of the drug. She won you over with a tearful cordiality and constant inducements to be sad, which were far from being harmless. At her place, Desmond was known as "a big incorrigible boy," and Chéri as "a beauty who has it all, which only makes him unhappier." But Chéri didn't smoke; he regarded the box of opium with the repugnance of a cat who's about to be fed a purgative, and he spent almost the whole night sitting on the floor mat with his back against the upholstered wall, between Desmond, who was asleep, and la Copine, who never stopped smoking. Almost the whole night, Chéri, watchful and reserved, inhaled the fragrance that satisfies hunger and thirst, and he seemed perfectly happy, except that he frequently looked, with a painful, probing intensity, at la Copine's withered neck—an inflamed and grainy neck—where a string of fake pearls was gleaming.

At a certain point, Chéri stretched out his hand and, with his fingertips, caressed the hennaed hair on the nape of la Copine's neck; he gauged the weight of the big, hollow, insubstantial pearls; then he withdrew his hand with the nervous shiver of someone who's caught his fingernails on a piece of frayed silk. A short while after that, he got up and left.

"Have you not," Desmond asked Chéri, "had enough of these dives where we eat, or we drink, and you don't avail yourself of the women, and of this hotel where they're always slamming the doors? And of the nightclubs, and of running around in your roadster from Paris to Rouen, Paris to Compiègne, Paris to Ville-d'Avray...Why not the Riviera! The high season down there isn't December or January, it's March, it's April, it's—"

"No," said Chéri.

"Then?"

"Then nothing."

He softened, without conviction, and put on what Léa used to call his "connoisseur face."

"My dear friend...you don't appreciate the beauty of Paris at this time of year...This...this hesitancy, this springtime that can't uncloud its brows, this soft sunlight...whereas the humdrum of the Riviera...No, don't you see, I like it here."

Desmond almost lost his valet-like patience. "Yes, and besides, maybe with Peloux the Younger's divorce..."

Chéri's sensitive nostrils turned white.

"If you're in cahoots with a lawyer, tell him it's off, right away. There's no 'Peloux the Younger's divorce.'"

"My dear boy!" Desmond objected, trying to look hurt. "You have a curious way of reacting to a childhood friend, one who at every turn..."

Chéri wasn't listening. He was puckering his chin and screwing up his mouth like a miser, pointing them at Desmond. For the first time, he was hearing an outsider meddle with his personal business.

He was pondering. Peloux the Younger's divorce. He'd mused on it for many an hour, day and night, and these words evoked freedom, a sort of second childhood, maybe something even better... But Desmond's voice, intentionally nasal, had just summoned up the necessary image: Edmée departing from the Neuilly house, determined, under her little driving hat and her long veil, heading to an unknown house where an unknown man lived. "Obviously, that would settle everything," Chéri the bohemian agreed. But at the same time another Chéri, strangely timid, was rearing back. "No, that's not how things are done!" The image grew sharper, took on color and movement. Chéri heard the low, melodious sound of the gate and saw—on the other side, on a bare hand—a gray pearl, a white diamond...

"Farewell..." the small hand was saying.

Chéri pushed back his chair and stood up.

"It's mine, all of it! The woman, the house, the rings, they're mine!"

He hadn't spoken out loud, but his face betrayed such savage violence that Desmond thought the last hour of his prosperity had come. Chéri commiserated ungenerously. "Poor little pussycat, have you taken a fright? Ah, these old aristocrats. Come on, I'll buy you some underpants like my linen shirts, and some shirts like your underpants. Desmond, is it the seventeenth?"

"Yes, why?"

"March seventeenth. In other words, spring. Desmond, the fashionable crowd, I mean the truly elegant ones, women or men, can't wait any longer to buy their wardrobes for the coming season, can't they?"

"Not easily…"

"The seventeenth, Desmond!…Come on then, everything's good. We're going to buy a big bracelet for my wife, an enormous cigarette holder for Madame Peloux, and a nice little tiepin for you!"

Two or three more times, in similar fashion, he had the stunning premonition that Léa was on her way back, that she'd just gotten home, that the opened blinds on the second floor were exposing the flowery pink of the half-drapes, the tracery of the big lace curtains, and the gold of the mirrors…April 15 passed by, and Léa didn't return. Annoying events marred the course of Chéri's mournful existence. There was the visit from Madame Peloux, who thought she was going to expire when she saw Chéri as skinny as a greyhound, his mouth sealed shut, and his eyes wandering. There was the letter from Edmée, entirely consistent in tone, startling, in which she explained she would go on living at Neuilly "until instructed otherwise" and undertook to pass on to Chéri the "warmest compliments of Madame de La Berche"…He thought he was being mocked, didn't know how to respond, and ended up tossing away this incomprehensible letter; but he didn't go to Neuilly. While April—green and cold, blooming with paulownias, tulips, hyacinths in bunches, clusters of laburnum—was imbuing Paris with fragrance, Chéri was holed up alone in a forbidding realm of shadows. Desmond—abused, harassed, discontented, but well paid—was tasked at times to protect Chéri from loose young women and indiscreet young men, and at other times to round up some of each to form a gang that ate, drank, and whooped it up from Montmartre to the restaurants of the Bois and the cabarets on the Left Bank.

One night, la Copine, who was smoking alone and lamenting, on that particular evening, a major infidelity on the part of her girlfriend, la Loupiote, saw that young man—the one with the devilish, tapering eyebrows—come into her place. He asked for "some really cold water" for his lovely, dried-out mouth, which was parched by a secret burning desire. He didn't manifest the least concern for la Copine's sorrows, which she recounted while pushing the lacquered platter and the pipe toward Chéri. He would accept nothing but his share of the floor mat, in silence and half-darkness, and stayed there until daylight, minimal in his movements, like someone who's afraid to budge and reopen a wound. At sunrise, he asked la Copine, "Why weren't you wearing your string of pearls today, you know, your big necklace?" and then courteously departed.

He developed the unconscious habit of walking by himself at night. His quick, long stride led him to a clear but inaccessible goal. After midnight he'd cut himself loose from Desmond, who'd find him, toward dawn, asleep on his hotel bed, flat on his stomach with his head between his folded arms, in the attitude of an afflicted child.

"Ah! Good, he's here," Desmond would say, relieved. "With a crackpot like that, you never know..."

One night when Chéri was out on one these walks, with his eyes wide open in the dark, he went up avenue Bugeaud, because all day long he'd managed to resist the fetishistic impulse that brought him back there every forty-eight hours. Like the fanatics who can't go to sleep without having touched a doorknob three times, he would run his fingers over the gate, place his index finger on the doorbell, call out softly in a mocking tone, "Ha ha ha!" and then go on his way.

But one night—this very night—standing in front of the gate, he felt his heart pound in his throat: the electric globe in the courtyard was glowing like a mauve moon over the front steps; the open door of the service entry lit up the paving stones; and on the second floor the louvered shutters filtering the interior light gave the impression of a golden comb. Chéri leaned back against the nearest tree and bowed his head.

"It isn't real," he said. "I'll open my eyes again and everything will be dark."

He straightened up to the sound of the voice of Ernest, the concierge, who was shouting in the corridor. "Around nine tomorrow morning, Marcel will help me bring up the big black trunk, madame!"

Chéri hurriedly spun around and ran all the way to the avenue du Bois, where he sat down. The illuminated globe he'd looked at—a muted purple ringed with gold—was dancing in front of him against the dark background of the leafless shrubbery. He pressed his hand against his heart and breathed deeply. The night was redolent of half-opened lilacs. He tore off his hat, unbuttoned his coat, slumped against the back of the bench, stretched out his legs, and let his opened hands dangle loosely. A crushing, velvet weight had just come down on top of him.

"Ah!" he said to himself, under his breath. "Is this happiness?... I didn't know..."

He had time to feel pity and scorn for himself, for everything he hadn't made the most of in the course of his wretched life as a rich and heartless young man. Then he stopped thinking for a moment, or maybe an hour. After this, he was capable of believing that he no longer desired anything in the world, even to go to Léa's.

When the cold made him shiver and he heard the blackbirds signalling the dawn, he got up, unsteady and unburdened, and headed back toward the Hotel Morris, avoiding the avenue Bugeaud. He stretched his limbs, filled his lungs, and exuded a universal goodwill.

"Now," he sighed, as if exorcised. "Now... ah! Now I'm going to be ever so kind to my little wife ..."

Up at eight, shaved, shoes on, and bursting with energy, Chéri gave Desmond, who was sleeping, a shake. The latter was pallid, frightening to look at, bloated with slumber like a drowning victim.

"Desmond! Hop to it, Desmond!... Enough! You're too ugly to look at when you sleep!"

The sleeper sat up and let his eyes—the color of cloudy water—settle on his friend. He pretended to be groggy so that he could carry on making a close inspection of Chéri: Chéri clothed in blue, pathetic, superb, pale under a velvet layer of skillfully applied powder. There were times when Desmond, in his affected ugliness, still suffered from Chéri's beauty. Desmond gave a long, intentional yawn. "What is it now?" he wondered, still yawning. "This imbecile is more beautiful than he was yesterday. It's these lashes, most of all, these lashes of his ..." He looked at Chéri's eyelashes, lustrous and full, and at the shadows they cast on his dark pupils and the bluish whites of his eyes. Desmond also noticed, this morning, that when Chéri's arched, contemptuous mouth opened, it was moist, refreshed, a little breathless—as though he'd just come to a hasty climax.

Desmond then banished his jealousy to the nether reaches of his emotional concerns and interrogated Chéri in a tone of weary condescension. "Might one be permitted to know if you're going out at this hour, or if you're coming back?"

"I'm going out," said Chéri. "Don't worry about me. I'm going to run some errands. I'm going to the florist's. To the jeweler's, to see my mother, to see my wife, to see ..."

"Don't forget the papal nuncio," said Desmond.

"I know the right way to do things," Chéri shot back. "I'll bring him some gold shirt buttons and a bunch of orchids."

Chéri rarely responded to pleasantries, and he always received them coldly. The exceptional tone of this jaded riposte enlightened Desmond as to his friend's unusual state of mind. He observed Chéri's image in the mirror—noted the paleness of his flaring nostrils, the unsteadiness of his wandering gaze—and he hazarded the most discreet of inquiries: "Will you be coming back for lunch?... Hey, Chéri, I'm talking to you. Are we having lunch together?"

Chéri shook his head, "No." He was whistling softly while he squared his reflection in the oblong mirror. It was just the right height for him, like the one between the two windows in Léa's bedroom. Any time now, surrounding that other mirror, a heavy gold frame would be the setting—against a pink, sunlit background—for his naked image, or his image loosely draped in silks: the opulent picture of a beautiful, beloved, pampered young man who plays with his mistress's necklaces and rings ... "Could it be there, already, in Léa's mirror: the young man's image ...?" So virulent was this thought that, in his joyous mood, in a daze, he believed he'd actually spoken it out loud.

"What were you saying?" he asked Desmond.

"I wasn't saying nothing," answered his meek, affected friend. "They're talking out in the courtyard."

Chéri walked out of Desmond's room, banged the door shut, and went back to his suite. The rue de Rivoli, come to life, filled the interior with a gentle, continuous din, and Chéri could glimpse, through the open window, the springtime leaves, firm and transparent, like blades of jade in the sunshine. He closed the window and sat down on a small, superfluous chair next to the wall, in a sad-looking space between the bed and the bathroom door.

"How can this be ... ?" he began, in an undertone. Then he went quiet. He didn't understand why, for a period of six and half months, he'd hardly ever thought about Léa's lover.

"I'm nothing but a big fool," Léa's letter, piously preserved by Charlotte Peloux, had said.

"A big fool?" Chéri shook his head. "It's strange, I don't see her like that. What kind of a man could she love? A Patron type? More likely than a Desmond type, naturally... A little slicked-back Argentinian? Just as unlikely... But all the same ..."

He smiled naively. "Other than me, who could really be attractive to her?"

A cloud obscured the March sun and the room went dark. Chéri pressed his head back against the wall. "My Nounoune ... My Nounoune ... have you betrayed me? Have you horribly betrayed me? ... You've done that to me?"

He lashed his hurt with words and images that he put together painfully, in astonishment, but without anger. He tried to summon up the morning games they used to play at Léa's; certain afternoons of prolonged, perfectly silent pleasure at Léa's; the delicious wintertime slumber, in the warm bed, in the cool boudoir at Léa's ... But he never saw anyone—in Léa's arms, in the cherry-colored daylight that danced like flame behind Lea's curtains in the afternoon—other than one single lover: Chéri. He got up, as if brought back to life by an instinctive burst of faith.

"It's so simple! If I don't see anybody else with her, it's because there isn't anybody else!"

He grabbed hold of the telephone, almost put the call through, then gently replaced the receiver on the hook.

"No fooling around."

He went out, very upright, throwing back his shoulders. His car, with its top down, brought him to the jeweler's, where he fell for an elegant little bandeau—brilliant blue sapphires in an invisible blue steel setting, "just right for Edmée's hair"—which he took. He bought some flowers, which were a little silly and ceremonious. Since it was barely eleven o'clock, he killed another half hour here and there: at a savings and loan where he withdrew some cash, next to a kiosk where he leafed through some English magazines; at an oriental tobacco emporium; at his perfumer's. Finally, he got back into his car and sat down between his bouquet and his parcels tied with ribbons.

"To the house."

The chauffeur turned around in his bucket seat. "Monsieur? ... Monsieur said ... ?"

"I said: to the house, boulevard d'Inkermann. Do you need a map of Paris?"

The car sped off toward the Champs-Élysées. The driver was over-zealous. His back, loaded with speculations, seemed to be leaning forward, anxiously, over the abyss that separated the deflated youth of the month before—the youth of "As you wish," and "A shot, Antonin?"—from "Monsieur Peloux the Younger," hard on the staff, and strict with the gasoline.

"Monsieur Peloux the Younger," leaning against the morocco seat cushion with his hat on his knees, drank drafts of wind and focused all his willpower on not thinking. Between avenue Malakoff and the Porte Dauphine, he sheepishly shut his eyes in order not to see avenue Bugeaud go by, and congratulated himself: "I'm brave enough for this!"

At boulevard d'Inkermann, the driver blew his horn at the gate, which sang a long, low, harmonious note from its hinges. The concierge, cap on head, rushed out, and the guard dogs barked at the familiar scent of the arriving party. Very much at ease, inhaling the fragrant green of the clipped front lawn, Chéri entered the house. He climbed the stairs, with a master's stride, toward the young woman he'd deserted three months before, deserted in the way a European sailor leaves behind, on the other side of the world, a savage little bride.

Léa flung far away from herself—onto the open desk top—the photographs she'd pulled out of the last of the trunks. "How ugly people are, my God! And they have the audacity to give me these. And do they think I'm going to set them in effigy on my mantelpiece, in a nickel-plated frame, maybe, or in a little folding album? Into the waste basket, yes, and in four pieces!"

She went and retrieved the photos. Before she tore them up, she gave them the hardest stare her blue eyes were capable of giving. Against a black postcard background, a sturdy, tightly corseted dame had covered her hair and the lower parts of her cheeks with a tulle veil, which was lifted by the breeze. "To my dear Léa, in memory of some delectable hours at Guéthary —Anita." Centered on a piece of cardboard, as rough as mortar made with straw, another photo showed a large and mournful family group: a sort of penal colony governed by a short-legged, made-up matriarch. She was lifting a beribboned tambourine up in the air and resting one foot on the extended knee of a sort of youthful butcher, robust and shifty-eyed.

"Their kind doesn't deserve to live," Léa decided, while ripping apart the coarse cardboard.

An unmounted print, which she unrolled, brought back the vision of that elderly couple of provincial spinsters—eccentric, voluble, combative—sitting every morning on a south-facing wayside bench, and every evening between a glass of cassis and the square of silk on which they were embroidering a black cat, a toad, a spider. "To our lovely sprite!" the inscription read, "her little companions from Trayas—Miquette and Riquette."

Léa destroyed these travel souvenirs and brushed her hand across her forehead. "How dreadful. And after those two, the same as it was before those two, there'll be others, others just like them. There's no getting around it. That's the way it goes. It could be that, wherever there's a Léa, some sort of a Charlotte Peloux, or a de La Berche, or an Aldonza, rises up out of the earth: old horrors who once were young beauties, people who—ah! Impossible people, impossible, impossible..."

Fresh in her memory, she heard the voices that had hailed her on the front steps of the hotel; that had shouted out to her, from afar, "Hou-hou!" across the golden sands; and she lowered her forehead in a bull-like gesture of aggression.

After six months, she'd come back a bit thinner and less toned, less composed. A grumpy little twitch would sometimes jerk her chin down onto her collar, and makeshift hennaings had ignited excessively red highlights in her hair. But the amber shade of her complexion— buffeted by the sun and the sea—glowed like a healthy farmwife's and could have made do without rouge. She still had to carefully drape, if not altogether hide, her faded neck, ringed with deep folds that her tan had failed to penetrate.

Seated in her chair, she dawdled over trivial arrangements and kept trying to rediscover in her surroundings—as she might have searched for a missing piece of furniture—her former rhythm, her readiness to circulate through her salubrious domain.

"Ah! That trip," she sighed. "How could I have... How tiresome it was!"

She wrinkled her brows and put on her new grumpy pout when she discovered that someone had cracked the glass of a little painting by Chaplin: the half-length portrait of a young girl, pink and silvery, which Léa found ravishing.

"And a tear, as wide as two hands, in the lace curtain... And that's all I've seen so far...What was I thinking when I went away for so long? And for whose sake?... As if I couldn't have done my grieving here, in peace and quiet."

She got up to ring for the maid, gathering the chiffon of her dressing gown, while bluntly upbraiding herself. "Go on, you old shopgirl..."

The chambermaid came in, laden with lingerie and silk stockings.

"Eleven o'clock, Rose. And my face not yet done! I'm running late..."

"Madame has nothing pressing to attend to. Madame no longer has those old Mégret sisters coming around to drag madame out on excursions, and turning up first thing in the morning to gather all the roses from around the house. There's no more Monsieur Roland to drive madame to distraction by tossing little pebbles into her bedroom..."

"Rose, there are things we have to attend to in the house. I don't know if people are right when they say "three moves are as bad as a fire," but I am sure that being away for six months is every bit as bad as a flood. Have you seen the lace curtain?"

"That's nothing... madame hasn't seen the linen closet: mouse droppings everywhere, and the floorboards eaten away. And isn't it awfully strange that when I leave twenty-eight tea towels for Éméran-cie I get only twenty-two back?"

"No, really?"

"It's as I say, madame."

They looked at each other in a state of mutual indignation, each of them attached to this comfortable house where sounds were softened by carpets and silk hangings; attached to its fully stocked cupboards and its enamel-painted cellar rooms. Léa slapped her knee with her firm hand.

"Things are going to change, my dear! If Ernest and Émérancie don't want their week's notice, they'll come up with the six tea towels. And that big idiot Marcel—you've written to him to come back?"

"He's here, madame."

Having dressed herself quickly, Léa opened the windows and leaned forward on her elbows to contemplate, with complacency, her avenue of budding trees. No more fawning old maids, and no more Monsieur Roland, that stocky, athletic young man from the spa at Cambo-les-Bains.

"Ah! The numbskull...!" she sighed.

But she forgave that passing fancy his simplemindedness and went on holding against him only his failure to satisfy. In her memory—that of a clearheaded woman whose body readily forgets—Monsieur Roland was nothing more than a big and slightly ridiculous oaf who'd shown himself to be ever so clumsy ... At this point, Léa would have denied that on a certain rainy night, when the scented showers were drenching the rose geraniums, a blinding flood of tears had briefly hidden Monsieur Roland behind the image of Chéri ...

The brief encounter left Léa with neither regrets nor embarrassment. The "numbskull" and his old ninny of a mother would have found—after the fact, just as before, in Léa's rented villa at Cambo—the generous spread of afternoon snacks, the rocking chairs on the wooden balcony, the inviting comfort that Léa knew how to share and of which she was proud. But the numbskull, wounded, had taken off, leaving Léa in the care of a stiff and handsome graying officer, whose stated aim was to wed "Madame de Lonval."

"Our ages, our fortunes, our shared taste for independence and worldliness, do all of these not destine us to be with each other?" the colonel, who'd kept himself slim, would say to Léa.

She laughed and took pleasure in the company of this rather slender man, who ate well and drank without getting tipsy. He misunderstood her good humor, read in her beautiful blue eyes, in the confiding and lingering smile of his hostess, a consent she was slow to give ... One of his reactions, in particular, marked the end of their incipient friendship. Léa was sorry to lose it, while, in her conscience, she frankly blamed herself.

"It was my mistake! You don't treat a Colonel Ypoustègue from an old Basque family the way you treat a Monsieur Roland. My mistake ... to have jilted him ... that's what it's called, what I did: I jilted him ... He would have shown a lot of class, a lot of spirit, if he'd come back the next day, in his shooting brake, to smoke a cigar *chez moi* and flirt with my old maids ..."

She failed to comprehend that a mature man can accept being dismissed but can't abide certain glances that measure him up physically, that openly compare him with someone else, someone unknown, someone unseen ...

Léa, being kissed unexpectedly, hadn't held back that terrible, protracted gaze: the gaze of the woman who knows the places where age lays waste to a man. From his hands—dried-up and manicured, crisscrossed with tendons and veins—her eyes climbed to his drooping chin; then to his forehead, lined with deep wrinkles; and then returned, cruelly, to his mouth, pinched between creases like quotation marks... And all the refinement of the "Baroness de Lonval" blew up in an "Oh là là!" so insulting, so explicit and vulgar, that the handsome Colonel Ypoustègue crossed the threshold for the last time.

"My last idylls," Léa mused, leaning on the windowsill. But the fine, Parisian weather; the view of the clean, resounding courtyard; the topiary balls of the laurels in their green planter boxes; the warm wafts of scented air escaping from the bedroom and caressing her neck; all of these gradually replenished her mischievousness and good humor. Women were passing by in silhouette on their way over to the Bois. "There go the skirts, changing again," Léa observed, "and the hats are getting taller." She envisaged visits to the dressmaker's, to Lewis the milliner. A sudden desire to look beautiful had her standing upright.

"Beautiful? For whom? Why, for myself. And, on top of that, to aggravate Ma Peloux."

Léa wasn't ignorant of the fact that Chéri had flown the coop, but that was all she knew. Even while she censured Madame Peloux for her investigative methods, Léa put up with a young milliner (on whom she showered favors) who smoothly dispensed her gratitude through streams of gossip either poured into Léa's ear during a fitting, or scrawled—"with a thousand thanks for the delectable chocolates"— across a big sheet of business letterhead. A postcard from old Lili had reached Léa at Cambo, a postcard in which the doddering elder— foregoing periods and commas and in tremulous script—had reeled off an incomprehensible tale of love, of flight, of a young wife housebound in Neuilly...

"The weather's the same," Léa recalled, "as it was on that morning when I read old Lili's postcard, in my bath, at Cambo..."

Once again, she saw the yellow bathroom: the sun was dancing on the surface of the water and across the ceiling. She heard the echoes from the narrow, noisy villa hurl back a big burst of laughter, rather savage and not very spontaneous—it was her own—and then the shouts that had followed: "Rose!...Rose!..."

With her shoulders and breasts clear of the water, and resembling more than ever—dripping and robust, with her superb arm stretched out—a piece of fountain statuary, she was fluttering the damp piece of card from her fingertips.

"Rose, Rose! Chéri...Monsieur Peloux has flown the coop! He's left his wife!"

"Madame, it doesn't surprise me," said Rose. "Their divorce will be happier than their marriage—it was a living hell for the both of them..."

For the rest of that day Léa was beset with an awkward giddiness. "Oh my little curse! Oh the little brat! Now you see...!"

And she shook her head, while laughing under her breath like a mother whose son has shared another woman's bed for the first time...

A varnished phaeton flitted past the gate, glinted, and disappeared, nearly silent on its rubber-treaded wheels and the delicate hoofs of its trotters.

"There goes Spéleïeff," Léa noted. "Good sort. And there's Merguillier on his pinto: eleven o'clock. Dried-up Berthellemy will be the next one to come along, and he'll go to the Bois to thaw out his bones on the Sentier de la Vertu...It's odd that people can go on doing the same thing for their entire lives. If Chéri were here, you could imagine I'd never left Paris. My poor, dear Chéri, he's had it, for now. Whooping it up, womanizing, eating at any hour, drinking too heavily...It's a pity. Who knows whether he might have made something of himself, if he'd only had the face of a little sausage-maker—nice and pink—and flat feet?"

She left the window, rubbing at the numbness in her elbows, and shrugged her shoulders. "You can save Chéri once, but not twice."

She buffed her nails, blew "Ha!" onto a tarnished ring, studied the reflection of the botched hennaing of her hair and its whitening roots, wrote a few lines in a notebook. She was moving very quickly and with less poise than usual in an effort to combat an insidious attack of anxiety, one she knew well and which she called—in denial even of the memory of her grief—her "moral indigestion." She felt the desire, in short order and in rapid bursts, for a well-sprung victoria carriage drawn by an easygoing horse; then for an extremely fast automobile; then for a set of Directoire furnishings for her salon. She even contemplated changing the style of her hair, which she'd worn up for twenty years with the nape of her neck exposed. "A little low roll, like that actress, Lavallière?...That would give me the chance to try out those loose-belted dresses that are in fashion this season. Altogether, if I go on a diet, and I get my henna redone properly, I could still pretend to be ten—no, let's say five— years less than..."

With an effort, she came fully back to her senses, and to all of her clear-sighted pride.

"Wouldn't a woman like me have the courage to know when to quit? Come on, come on. We've had more than our share, my lovely." She examined the reflection in the mirror: the imposing Léa, drawn to her full height, hands on her hips, smiling back at her.

"This kind of a woman doesn't end up in the arms of an old man. This kind of a woman, who's had the luck never to have soiled her hands or her mouth on a withered carcass!...Yes, here she is: the 'ghoul' who wants only fresh flesh..."

She called to mind the casual affairs and lovers of her younger years, during which she was immune from any contact with older men. And she considered herself to be pure and proud, having been dedicated, for another thirty years, to radiant Adonises or sensitive adolescents.

"And that fresh flesh owes a lot to me! How many of them owe their good health to me, their beauty, the little heartbreaks that make them stronger, the milk and egg punches for their runny noses, and the habit of making love with attention and variety?... And would

I really go now and provide myself with some old gentleman, just so my bed won't be empty? Someone as old as ..."

She thought about it for a moment and made up her mind with majestic complacency.

"As old as forty?"

She wiped her long, shapely hands, one against the other, and wheeled around in disgust. "Ugh! Goodbye to all that, it's cleaner this way. Let's go buy some playing cards, some fine wine, some score sheets for bridge, some knitting needles, all the baubles it takes to fill a big hole, everything you need to conceal that monster: the old woman ..."

In place of knitting needles, she had mounds of dresses, and robes like auroral clouds. The Chinese pedicurist came once a week, the manicurist twice, and the masseuse every day. You'd see Léa at the theater and—before the theater—in restaurants she'd never frequented during her time with Chéri.

She accepted invitations—from young women and their boyfriends; from Kühn, her former tailor, now retired—to join them in their private boxes or at their dinner tables. But the young women showed her a deference she didn't require, and Kühn addressed her as "my dear friend," to which she replied, at the very first banquet, "Kühn, you're not cut out to be a client."

As though she were seeking refuge, she went to find Patron, who was now a referee and the manager of a boxing gym. But Patron was married to a young bar owner; she was diminutive and as viciously keen-scented as a guard dog. To go and meet the sensitive athlete, Léa had to expose to view—all the way to the place d'Italie—her dark, sapphire-blue dress trimmed with gold, her bird-of-paradise hat feathers, her conspicuous jewels, and her hair with its new tint of mahogany. She breathed in the smell of sweat, vinegar, and turpentine that the young "contenders" in training with Patron exhaled, and she left, sure she would never revisit the low cavernous hall with its hissing of greenish gas.

These attempts to reconnect to the restless life of an idle crowd cost her a weariness she couldn't comprehend.

"So, what is the matter with me?"

She stroked her ankles, a little swollen at night; examined her strong teeth and vigorous gums; tested her lungs by punching her capacious ribcage with her fist, the way you give a sharp rap to a barrel; and did the same to her sensual belly. Something unnameable inside her was pitching over, deprived of a missing prop, and it was dragging the whole of her down along with it. The Baroness de La Berche—encountered sitting at a zinc-covered bar, washing down two dozen snails with inferior white wine—finally informed Léa of the return of the prodigal son and the dawn of a new honeymoon on boulevard d'Inkermann. Léa listened to this moral tale with indifference. But the following day she grew pale with painful emotion when she recognized a blue limousine in front of her gate and saw Charlotte Peloux walking across the courtyard.

"At last! At last! You're back! Léa, my dearest, my best friend! More beautiful than ever! Thinner than last year! Be careful, Léa dear, we shouldn't get too skinny at our age! Just this much, but not more! And even . . . But what a joy to see you again!"

Never had that piercing voice seemed so palatable to Léa. She let Madame Peloux go on talking. Léa was grateful for this caustic flood, which gave her time to collect herself. She'd seated Charlotte Peloux in a low armchair, in the soft light of the little salon with its painted-silk walls, just as in times past. Reflexively, just as in times past, Léa sat down in the chair with the stiff back, which forced her to throw back her shoulders and thrust out her chin. Between them, the table—covered with a rough, embroidered antique cloth—held, just as in times past, the big cut-glass carafe half-filled with aged eau-de-vie, the ringing chalices as thin as mica, the ice water, and the shortbread cookies.

"Dearest friend! We're going to be able to spend time together leisurely, leisurely," Charlotte wept. "You know my motto: Leave your friends alone when you're down in the dumps; only let them know when you're feeling good. During the whole time Chéri was playing truant, I deliberately lay low, you understand? Now that everything's going well, now that my children are happy, I'm saying to you loud and clear: I'm here for you, completely, and we're picking up where we left off—"

She stopped herself and lit a cigarette. Like an actress, she was well versed in this sort of suspension.

"Without Chéri, naturally."

"Naturally," Léa conceded, with a smile.

She watched and listened to her old enemy in a state of stunned satisfaction. These huge, inhuman eyes, this chattering mouth, this short, plump, agitated body: all of this, sitting across from her, had turned up only to put her determination to the test, to shame her, as in the past, always as in the past. But, just as in the past, Léa knew how to react, how to scorn, to smile, to hold her head high. Already, that weight of sadness that had loaded her down yesterday, and in the days before, seemed to be lifting. An ordinary, familiar light bathed the salon and played in the curtains.

"So, here we are," Léa mused lightheartedly. "Two women, a little bit older than last year; their usual malice and idle chitchat, their mild suspicions, the meals they share; reading the financial papers in the morning, exchanging spicy gossip in the afternoon: all of this has to start over again, because it's life, because it's my life. The Aldonzas and the de La Berches, the Lilis and a few rootless old men, the whole lot of them crowded around a gaming table, where a brandy glass and a deck of cards may be sitting next to a pair of little booties, which someone's started to knit for a child who will soon be born ... Let's start over again, because this is the way of the world. Let's go at it with spirit, because I'm falling back into it effortlessly, back into the same old rut ..."

And she readied herself—with her eyes clear, and her lips loosely parted—to listen to Charlotte Peloux, who was talking excitedly about her daughter-in-law.

"You know, don't you, dear Léa, that my lifelong ambition has been peace and tranquility? Well, now I have them. When Chéri ran off, he was sowing a few wild oats—that's all, nothing more. Far be it from me to blame you for that, my dear. But admit it: From the time he was nineteen until he was twenty-five, he hardly had the chance to lead the life of a bachelor. Well, now, for three months he has led the life of a bachelor. What's all the fuss about?"

"It's all for the best," said Léa, without losing her composure. "It's a guarantee that he's giving to his young wife."

"Just, *just* the word I was I searching for!" Madame Peloux squealed, all aglow. "A guarantee! Since that day, it's been a dream come true! And you know, when a Peloux comes home after a big blowout, he never leaves again!"

"So it's a family tradition?" asked Léa.

But Charlotte wasn't listening.

"And what's more, he was welcomed back in his home. His little wife ... ah! There's a fine specimen for you, Léa ... You know, I've seen lots of them—these little wives—and I'm telling you, I've never seen one who could get the upper hand over Edmée."

"Her mother is so special."

"Just try to imagine, try to imagine, my dearest: Chéri had just left her on my hands for nearly three months. And, by the way, she was lucky I was there!"

"Exactly what I was thinking," said Léa.

"Well, my dear, not a groan, not a scene, not a single awkward step, nothing, nothing! Patience itself, sweetness itself, the face of a saint, of a saint!"

"It's frightening," said Léa.

"And can you believe it? When our little rogue showed up one morning, all smiles, like he'd just taken a turn around the Bois, do you think she let herself say a single word? Nothing! Not a thing! So he—and, deep down, he must have felt a bit embarrassed—"

"Oh! Why?" asked Léa.

"Come on, you can imagine ... He was charmed by the welcome, and they made it up in the bedroom—wham! Just like that—wasting no time. Oh! Believe me, while that was happening, there was no woman in the world happier than me!"

"Except for Edmée, perhaps," Léa suggested.

But Madame Peloux was quick to react. She fluttered her wing tips impressively. "What on earth are you going on about? Me—I was thinking only about them being together again in their own home."

She changed her tone and screwed up her eyes and her lips. "Besides, I can't really picture that child in the throes of passion, howling in ecstasy. Twenty years old, with her collarbones sticking out. Bah!... At that age, you blubber. Anyway, between you and me, I'm sure her mother is frigid."

"Your cult of the family is carrying you away," said Léa.

Charlotte Peloux nakedly exposed the depths of her big eyes, where you couldn't read a thing.

"No, not that, not that! It's heredity! Heredity! That's what I believe in. The same with my son: he's whimsical...What, you don't know that he's as whimsical as they come?"

"It must have slipped my mind," Léa apologized.

"Well, I believe in my son's future. He'll love his home like I love mine, he'll manage his fortune, he'll love his children the way I've loved him..."

"Please don't predict so many sad things!" Léa pleaded. "What's it like, the inside of their house?"

"Creepy, creepy," cheeped Madame Peloux. "Purple carpets! Purple! A black and gold bathroom. A salon with no furniture, full of Chinese vases as big as I am! And so, what happens? They never leave Neuilly. Anyway, with all due modesty, the girl adores me."

"Didn't she have some sort of nervous disorder?" asked Léa, with concern.

Charlotte Peloux's eyes glinted. "Her? No risk of that. We're dealing with a powerful adversary."

"Who's 'we'?"

"Sorry, dearest, force of habit...We're up against...what I'll call a brain, a real brain. She has a way of giving orders without raising her voice, of putting up with Chéri's provocations, of swallowing insults like they were milk and honey... I really do wonder, I wonder if there isn't a danger in this for my boy in the future. I'm afraid, my dear Léa, I'm afraid she might go too far in subduing his nature, which is so unusual, so—"

"What? He's being submissive?" Léa interrupted. "Have some more of my brandy, Charlotte, it's some of Spéleïeff's, seventy-four years old, you could serve it to a baby..."

"'Submissive' isn't the right word, but he's ... inter ... impertur ..."

"Imperturbable?"

"That's it. For example, when he knew I was coming to see you ..."

"What, he knows?"

Léa's cheeks flushed uncontrollably; she cursed the intensity of her emotion and the bright daylight in the little salon. Madame Peloux, with her velvety gaze, feasted on Léa's distress.

"But of course he knows! No need to be ashamed of that, my dearest! Are you a child?"

"First of all, how did you know I'd come back?"

"Oh, come on, Léa, don't ask questions like that. People have seen you everywhere ..."

"Yes, but Chéri ... So, you're the one who told him I'd come back?"

"No, my dearest, he's the one who told me."

"Ah, he's the one ... That's strange."

She could hear her heart beating through her voice, and didn't risk letting her sentences run on.

"He even added: 'Madame Peloux, I'd be glad if you went and got some news about Nounoune.' He still feels so much fondness for you, that child!"

"How nice!"

Madame Peloux, rosy-faced, seemed to be surrendering to the influence of the aged eau-de-vie. She was speaking dreamily, swaying her head. But her hazel eyes stayed fixed, steely. She was lying in wait for Léa, who sat upright, on guard against herself, not knowing what sort of blow to expect ...

"It is very nice, but it's only natural. A man doesn't forget a woman like you, dear Léa. And ... Do you want to know my true feelings? You'd only have to give him a sign, for him to ..."

Léa placed a hand on Charlotte Peloux's arm. "I don't want to know your true feelings," she said sweetly.

Madame Peloux let the corners of her mouth sink. "Oh, I understand. I think you're right," she sighed, in a dreary voice. "Once you've rearranged your life, as you have ... I haven't even asked you about yourself!"

"But I thought you had ..."

"Fulfilled?"

"Fulfilled."

"Big romance? Lovely trip? ... Is *he* nice? Where's his photo?"

Léa, relieved, smiled thinly and shook her head. "No, no, you won't get anything out of me! Just try! ... So, you don't have any more detectives, Charlotte?"

"I don't rely on any detective," Charlotte shot back. "It's not because Monsieur So-and-So or Madame So-and-So has told me ... that you've met with a new disappointment ... that you've had any serious troubles, even financial ... No, no! You know I don't pay any attention to rumors!"

"No one knows that better than I do. My dear Lolotte, leave your worries behind. Relieve our friends of theirs. And tell them I hope they've raked in half as much as I did on petroleum shares between December and February."

The alcoholic cloud that had been softening Madame Peloux's features now dissolved; her face looked clear, taut, alert. "You invested in petroleum! I should have guessed. And you didn't tell me!"

"You didn't ask ... You were only thinking about your own family, it's entirely natural."

"Luckily, I also thought about Pellet Fuel," trilled the muted trumpet.

"Ah, and you didn't tell me either."

"Disturb a romantic idyll? Never! Léa my dear, I'll be on my way now, but I'll be back."

"You'll be back here on Thursdays, because from now on, my dear Lolotte, your Sundays at Neuilly ... they're over for me. Would you like it if we had some little Thursday get-togethers here? Only good friends—Ma Aldonza, our Reverend Father the Baroness...We'd have your poker, at least, and my knitting..."

"You knit?"

"Not yet, but that's bound to come, eh?"

"It makes me jump for joy! Just look and see if I'm not jumping! And, you know, I'm not going to mention it to anyone back at the house: the boy should be capable of coming here for a glass of port on his own on Thursday! One more kiss, my dearest...God, do you ever smell good! Have you noticed, when your skin starts to sag, perfume soaks in better? It's really quite pleasant."

"Go, go..." Léa, trembling, kept her eyes fastened on Madame Peloux, who was crossing the courtyard. "Go back to your nasty designs! Nothing's stopping you. You twisted your foot? Yes, you did, but you won't fall down. Your chauffeur, who's cautious, won't go into a skid and ram your car into a tree. You'll get back to Neuilly and you'll choose your moment—today, tomorrow, next week—to say the things you never ought to say. You'll try and stir up the people around you who may actually be at peace. The very least damage you might do is to make them shake a little, like I did, temporarily..."

Her legs were shaking like a horse's at the end of an uphill climb, but she wasn't feeling any pain. The care with which she'd handled herself, and her quick retorts, made her rejoice. A winning vitality suffused her complexion and her gaze. Because she had some excess energy to expend, she was kneading her handkerchief into a ball. She couldn't shift her thoughts away from Charlotte Peloux.

"We've met again," she said to herself, "the way two dogs meet up over the slipper they're in the habit of tearing to pieces. How bizarre! This woman is my enemy, and it's from her I get my comfort. How bound together we are..."

She went on reflecting at length, now dreading, now accepting her fate. For a short spell, once her nerves had settled, she fell asleep. Seated, her cheek resting on the arm of the chair, in her dreams she delved into her encroaching old age; pictured the sameness of her days, one after another; saw herself sitting across from Charlotte Peloux, and preserved for a long time—by an intense rivalry that swallowed up the hours—from the degrading indifference that leads older women first to neglect their corsets, then the dyeing of their hair, and finally their delicate lingerie. She tasted, in advance, the pernicious pleasures of the aged, which are nothing more than a war waged in secret: homicidal urges; keen hopes, continually renewed, for catastrophes that spare only a single being, a single corner of the world; and she awoke—amazed—in the light of a pink dusk that resembled dawn.

"Ah, Chéri..." she sighed.

But this was no longer the hoarse and famished cry of the past year; nor the tears; nor that revolt of the whole body, which feels pain and resists when a sickness of the mind threatens to overwhelm it... Léa stood and rubbed her cheek where the embroidery of the cushion had left its pattern.

"My poor Chéri... Isn't it strange to think that by your losing your worn-out old mistress, and my losing my scandalous young lover, we've lost the purest and most honorable possession we had on earth..."

Two days passed after Charlotte Peloux's visit. Two gray days that passed slowly for Léa, that she bore patiently, in a spirit of apprenticeship. "Since it will be necessary to live this way," she told herself, "let's get started." But she went at it clumsily, with a kind of excessive deliberation, which was bound to check the impetus of her novitiate. By eleven in the morning on the second day, she wanted to venture out on foot as far as the lakes in the Bois.

"I'll buy a dog," she declared. "It will keep me company and guarantee that I go for walks." Rose had to search, in the recesses of the summer closets, for a pair of yellow ankle boots with stiff soles and a somewhat rugged outfit that smelled like mountainsides and forests. Léa headed off with the determined gait that certain shoes and certain rough-textured garments impart to those who wear them.

"Ten years ago, I would have been bold enough to bring a cane," she reflected. While she was still close to her house, she heard a light, rapid footstep to her rear, one that she thought she recognized. A numbing fear, which she didn't have time to banish, left her almost senseless, and it was against her own will that she allowed herself to be met up with, and then overtaken, by a young stranger in a hurry, who didn't give her a single look.

She breathed in, relieved.

"I'm so stupid!"

She bought a dark red carnation for her jacket and started out again. But in front of her, at thirty paces, planted upright in the diaphanous mist that enveloped the lawns of the avenue, stood a man in silhouette, waiting.

"Now, this time, I recognize the cut of his coat and the way he twirls his cane... Ah! No thanks! I don't want to be wearing a postman's boots and a thick jacket that makes me look fat when he sees me again for the first time. If I do have to run into him, I'd prefer him to see me in a different outfit—he never could stand chestnut brown, anyway... No... no, I'm going home, I'm..."

Just then, the waiting man hailed an empty taxi, got into it, and passed by in front of Léa; he was young, fair-haired, and wore a little clipped moustache. But Léa didn't smile; nor did she breathe a sigh of relief; she turned on her heels and went back to her house.

"It's one of those lazy days, Rose... Give me my peach-blossom tea gown, the new one, and the big embroidered sleeveless cape. I'm suffocating in all these woolens."

"There's no point in dwelling on it," Léa mused. "Twice in succession, it wasn't Chéri; the third time, it would have been. I know all about these little ambushes. There's no way to prevent them, and today I have no fight in me, I'm limp."

She returned, for the rest of the day, to her patient attempts at solitude. Cigarettes and newspapers distracted her after lunch, and she welcomed, with a momentary joy, a phone call from the Baroness de La Berche, and another from Spéleïeff, her former lover, the handsome horse-dealer, who'd seen her passing by the day before and had offered to sell her a pair of horses.

And after that, a long, scary hour of total silence.

"Come on, come on . . ."

She was pacing, with her hands on her hips, trailing behind her the magnificent long cape embroidered with gold and roses that left her arms exposed.

"Come on, come on . . . let's try and take stock. This isn't the time—now that this kid isn't pulling on my heartstrings any longer, it's no time to let to myself be dispirited. I've been living on my own for six months. Down south, I handled it very well. I began by keeping on the move. And those acquaintances I made, on the Riviera and in the Pyrenees, were good for me. Whenever any of them went away, they left me with such a feeling of freshness . . . Starch poultices on a burn: they don't heal, but they do soothe, as long as you keep changing them all the time. The story of my six months of shifting around is the same as that hideous Sarah Cohen's, who married a monster: 'Every time I look at him,' she says, 'I feel pretty.'

"But even before those six months, I knew what it was like to live alone. For example, how did I manage after I left Spéleïeff? Ah, yes, I hung around with Patron in bars and bistros, and right after that, I had Chéri. But before Spéleïeff, that kid Lequellec was snatched away from me by his family, who married him off . . . poor kid, with his beautiful eyes full of tears . . . After him, I stayed single for four months, I recall. How I cried the first month! Ah, no, it was for Bacciocchi that I cried so much. But once I finished crying, you couldn't hold me back, I was so glad to be alone. Yes! But at the time of Bacciocchi I was twenty-eight, and then after Lequellec I was thirty, and in-between them, I had . . . no matter. After Spéleïeff, I was sick and tired of squandering so much money. Whereas now, after Chéri, I'm . . . I'm fifty, and I was foolhardy enough to hold on to him for six years."

She wrinkled her forehead and made herself look ugly by putting on a dismal pout.

"It serves me right, you don't hold on to a lover for six years, not at my age! Six years! He spoiled what was left of me. From those six years, I could have come away with two or three trouble-free little satisfactions, instead of one big regret ... A six-year affair is like following your husband to the colonies: when you get back, nobody recognizes you and you no longer know how to dress."

To conserve her energy, she rang for Rose, and together they rearranged the lace cabinet. Night came, which caused the outdoor lamps to bloom and called Rose back to her housekeeping.

"Tomorrow," Léa said to herself, "I will ask for the car and go for a spin—up to Normandy—to visit Spéleïeff's stud farm. I'll bring Ma La Berche along, if she wants to come—it will remind her of her horse teams of the past. And, my goodness, if Spéleïeff's youngest son makes eyes at me, I'm not saying that I ..."

She took the trouble to smile in a mysterious, alluring way, so as to deceive the phantoms that might be wandering around the dressing table and the imposing bed, which was glimmering in the shadows. But she felt completely devoid of passion, and full of contempt for other people's sensual pleasures.

Her dinner of fine fish fillets, with pastries for dessert, revived her spirits. Instead of a Bordeaux, she drank a dry champagne, and hummed as she left the table. The chime of eleven took her by surprise while she was measuring, with a cane, the width of the wall panels between the windows of her bedroom; she was planning to replace all of the big mirrors with antique canvases painted with flowers and balustrades. She yawned, scratched her head, and called for her nightclothes. While Rose was removing her mistress's long silk stockings, Léa reviewed her vanquished day, its petals stripped and scattered in the past; it satisfied her, like a finished piece of schoolwork. Kept sheltered, for the night, from the perils of idleness, she was counting on the hours of sleep as well as those of wakefulness; since, with the coming of night, an uneasy person regains the right to yawn out loud, to sigh, to curse the milkman's wagon, the street sweepers, and the awakening sparrows.

While she was getting ready for bed she pondered plans for some benign projects, projects she wouldn't carry out.

"Aline Mesmacker has taken over a bar-restaurant and she's turned it into a goldmine ... Obviously, it's a job as well as an investment ...

But I don't see myself sitting at a cash desk, and if you hire a manager, it's not worth it anymore. Dora and Fat Fifi are running a nightclub together, Ma La Berche told me. It's very much in fashion. And they put on detachable collars and smoking jackets to attract a special sort of clientele. Fat Fifi has three kids to raise, so that's an excuse . . . And then there's Kühn, who's bored, and who'd gladly get hold of my capital to found a new fashion house . . ."

Stark naked, and tinted brick-red by the reflections from her Pompeian bathroom, she sprayed herself with her sandalwood perfume and unfolded, with unconscious pleasure, a long silk nightdress.

"All of this, it's just empty talk. I'm perfectly aware of the fact that I don't like to work. To bed with you, madame! You'll never have another establishment, and the clients are all gone."

She wrapped herself in a white Moroccan tunic—its colorful lining infused it with an elusive, rosy light—before returning to her dressing table. She lifted both her arms to comb and put up her henna-stiffened hair, and they framed her weary face. They were so beautiful still, her arms—from the full and muscular underarms all the way to the rounded wrists—that she considered them for a moment.

"Lovely handles, for such an old vase!"

With a careless gesture, she stuck a pale yellow comb at the nape of her neck and chose, without much expectation, a detective novel from a shelf in a shadowy cabinet. She had no taste for fancy covers and had never gotten over the habit of banishing her books to the backs of cupboards, along with empty cardboard boxes and medicine bottles.

As she was bending over to smooth out the fine, cool cambric of her big turned-down bed, the heavy bell rang in the courtyard. Its deep, full, unexpected sound violated the midnight hour.

"What on earth . . . ?" she asked out loud.

She listened with her mouth half-parted, holding her breath. A second ring sounded, even louder than the first. In an instinctive reaction of modesty and self-defense, Léa ran to powder her face. She was on her way to summon Rose when she heard the front door slam, the sound of footsteps in the vestibule and on the stairs, and two voices intermingled—the chambermaid's and another voice. She had no time to make up her mind, a heavy hand opened her bedroom door: Chéri was there in front of her—with his overcoat unbuttoned over his dinner jacket and his hat on his head—pale and nasty-looking.

He leaned back against the door and didn't budge. He wasn't looking at Léa in particular, but at the whole of the room, in a shifty sort of a way like a man under attack.

Léa, even though she'd trembled this morning because of a shadowy profile she thought she'd made out in the fog, didn't feel any more distress now than the displeasure of a woman caught off guard while arranging her hair. She wrapped herself in her dressing gown, fastened her comb, and felt around with her foot for a slipper that had dropped. She flushed, but once the blood had left her cheeks she'd already regained a semblance of calm. She raised her head and looked taller than the young man who was leaning, all in black, against the white door.

"Now that's one way of making an entrance," she said, quite loudly. "You could take off your hat and say hello."

"Hello," said Chéri, in a haughty tone.

The sound of his own voice seemed to surprise him. He looked around more benignly, and a kind of smile moved from his eyes down to his mouth. He said again, gently this time: "Hello . . ."

He removed his hat and took two or three steps forward.

"May I sit down?"

"If you like," said Léa.

He sat down on a cushioned footstool and saw that she stayed standing.

"Were you getting dressed? Weren't you on your way out?"

She shook her head, sat down at a distance, picked up a nail buffer, and didn't speak. He lit a cigarette, then asked for permission to smoke it after it was lit.

"If you like," Léa repeated, with indifference.

He stopped talking and lowered his eyes. The fingers that held his cigarette were trembling slightly; he became aware of it, and rested this hand on the edge of a table. Léa was buffing her nails with slow movements, casting a brief glance at Chéri's face from time to time, especially at his lowered lids and the dark fringe of his lashes.

"It was still Ernest who opened the door for me," Chéri said at last.

"Why wouldn't it be Ernest? Was I obliged to change my staff because you got married?"

"No ... of course not, I was just saying ..."

Silence fell again. Léa broke it.

"Might I know if you intend to remain on that footstool for long? I'm not even going to ask why you've taken the liberty of coming into my home at midnight."

"You can ask me why," he said eagerly.

She shook her head. "I'm not interested."

He jumped up, toppling the footstool behind him, and walked toward Léa. She felt him leaning over her as if he were going to strike her, but she didn't flinch. She thought: "Why should I be afraid of anything in this world?"

"Ah! You don't know what I've come here for? Don't you want to know what I've come here for?"

He tore off his coat, tossed it through the air onto the chaise longue, and crossed his arms while shouting close to Léa's face in a choked and triumphant tone: "I'm back!"

She was using a delicate pair of nail clippers, which she closed calmly before wiping her fingers. Chéri fell into his chair, as if he'd used up all his strength.

"Fine," said Léa. "You're back. That's very nice. Who have you asked about this?"

"Me," said Chéri.

Now it was her turn to stand up, the better to dominate him. Her heartbeat had subsided, allowing her to breathe more easily, and she wanted to play her hand perfectly.

"Why didn't you ask me for my opinion? I'm an old pal and I know your boorish ways. How could it not have occurred to you that, by coming in here, you might upset ... somebody?"

With his head lowered he made a horizontal survey of the bedroom:

its closed doors; the bed in its metallic armor with its rampart of luxurious pillows. He saw nothing unusual, nothing new, and shrugged his shoulders. Léa was expecting better than this, and she didn't let up.

"Do you understand what I mean?"

"Indeed," he answered. "Hasn't 'monsieur' come back yet? Does 'monsieur' spend the night somewhere else?"

"It's none of your business, child," she said, calmly.

He bit his lip and nervously flicked his cigarette ash into a jewelry dish.

"Not in there, I'm forever telling you that!" cried Léa. "How many times do I have to—"

She cut herself short, while reproaching herself for having reverted, in spite of herself, to the tone of a domestic quarrel. But he seemed not to have heard, and was staring at a ring—an emerald Léa had purchased during her time away.

"What . . . what is this?" he stammered.

"This? This is an emerald."

"I'm not blind! I mean, who gave it to you?"

"Someone you don't know."

"Delightful!" said Chéri, bitter.

His tone restored to Léa all of her authority, and she allowed herself the pleasure of leading him—who'd lost the upper hand—a little further astray.

"Isn't it just delightful? People compliment me on it everywhere. And the setting—did you notice?—those gems like stardust, that . . ."

"Enough," Chéri shouted in a rage, slamming his fist onto the fragile tabletop.

Some roses dropped their petals from the shock, and a porcelain dish slid, without breaking, onto the thick carpet. Léa reached for the telephone. Chéri blocked her hand with his arm, roughly. "What do you want with that telephone?"

"To call the police station," said Léa.

He took hold of both her arms and pretended to be playful, while pushing her away from the receiver.

"Come on, come on, it's okay, don't be stupid! I can't say anything without you making a scene right away."

She sat down and turned her back on him. He stayed standing, empty-handed, his mouth half-open and puffy like a sulky child's. A lock of dark hair draped itself over his brow. Surreptitiously, in a mirror, Léa kept her eyes on him; but he sat down, and his face disappeared from the glass. Now it was Léa's turn to feel, self-consciously, that he was seeing her back looking broad inside her billowing tunic. She returned to her dressing table, smoothed her hair, replanted her comb, and opened, as though absentmindedly, a vial of perfume. Chéri turned his head toward the scent.

"Nounoune!" he called out.

She didn't answer.

"Nounoune!"

"Say you're sorry," she ordered, without turning around.

"As if!" he sneered back.

"I'm not forcing you. But you have to leave. And straightaway."

"I'm sorry!" he said smartly, with a snarl.

"Better than that!"

"I'm sorry," he repeated, in a whisper.

"That's more like it!"

She came back to him and passed her hand lightly over his lowered head.

"All right then, let's hear it."

He flinched, and shook off the caress.

"What do you want me to tell you? It's not complicated. I'm back here, and that's that."

"Tell me about it. Come on, tell me."

He was rocking back and forth on his seat, clenching his hands between his knees. He raised his head toward Léa without looking at her. She could see Chéri's pale nostrils throbbing and hear the sound of rapid breathing trying to get itself under control. She needed only to say, one more time, "Come on, tell me . . ." and to nudge him with her finger, as though to make him fall backwards. He cried out: "Nounoune, darling! Nounoune, darling!" and threw himself at her with all his might, hugging her long legs, which buckled. Sitting, she let him slide to the floor and wallow over her, with tears, with confused words, and with groping hands. He was grabbing on to her lace and her string of pearls, searching under her robe for the shape of her shoulder, and through her hair for her ears.

"Nounoune, darling! I've rejoined you, my Nounoune! Oh, my Nounoune, it's your shoulder, and your same perfume, and your necklace, my Nounoune. Ah! It's amazing... And that hint of something burnt in your hair, ah!... It's amazing..."

Leaning back, he breathed out these foolish words as if they were his last gasp. On his knees, he held Léa tightly in his arms, offered up to her his fringed forehead; his quivering mouth, wet with weeping; and his eyes, joyfully filled with radiant tears. She gazed at him so intently, so completely forgetful of everything other than him, that it didn't occur to her to give him a kiss. She wrapped her arms around Chéri's neck and embraced him gently, to the rhythm of the words she was murmuring: "My child... my naughty boy... Here you are... Here you are, you're back... What did you go and do again? You're so bad... my beauty..."

He was moaning, softly, with his mouth closed, barely talking anymore: he was listening to Léa and pressing his cheek to her breast. He pleaded, "More!" when she paused in her tender litany, and Léa, who was afraid she might cry too, scolded him in the same tone: "Horrible creature... Heartless little devil... Dirty rotter..."

He looked up at her with gratitude. "That's it, bawl me out! Ah! Nounoune..."

She moved him away, to see him better.

"So, you were still in love with me?"

He lowered his eyes with a childish flutter. "Yes, Nounoune."

A short burst of stifled laughter—which she couldn't hold back—warned Léa that she was close to abandoning herself to the most terrible joy of her life. An embrace, the tumble, the open bed; two bodies that fuse together like two live segments of a single, severed beast... "No, no," she said to herself, "not yet, oh! Not yet..."

"I'm thirsty," sighed Chéri. "Nounoune, I'm thirsty..."

She got up quickly, felt the carafe—which had gone warm—left the room, and returned at once. Chéri, curled up on the floor, had set his head on the cushioned footstool.

"Rose will bring you some lemonade," said Léa. "Don't stay there. Come over to the chaise longue. Does this lamp bother you?"

She was trembling with the pleasure of serving and arranging. She settled deep into the chaise, and Chéri lay stretched out on the floor, half leaning against her.

"Now, you're going to tell me a little—"

Rose's entrance interrupted her. Chéri, without raising himself up, turned his head lazily toward Rose. "Evening, Rose."

"Good evening to you, monsieur," said Rose, discreetly.

"Rose, for tomorrow morning, at nine, I'd like—"

"Some brioches and some chocolate." Rose finished the sentence for him.

Chéri closed his eyes again, with a sigh of well-being. "You're a clairvoyant! . . . Rose, where will I get dressed tomorrow morning?"

"In the boudoir," Rose answered, obligingly. "Only, no doubt, I'll have to get the sofa bed removed and your toiletry chest put back in place, like before?"

She glanced at her mistress for approval. Léa, reclining proudly, was supporting the torso of her "bratty nursling" while he drank.

"If you like," said Léa. "We'll see. Go back up, Rose."

Rose left. During the moment of silence that followed, they heard nothing but the confused murmur of the breeze and the call of a bird deceived by the moonlight.

"Chéri, are you sleeping?"

He heaved his big, hunting-dog sigh.

"Oh no, Nounoune, I feel too good to sleep."

"Tell me, dear . . . You didn't cause any harm over there?"

"At my place? No, Nounoune. Not at all, I swear."

"A scene?"

He looked at her from below without raising his trusting head.

"But no, Nounoune. I left because I left. The girl is very nice. Nothing happened."

"Ah!"

"Well, I wouldn't swear that she didn't have an inkling. Tonight she had what I call her 'orphan's look.' You know—such gloomy eyes under such beautiful hair... You do know she has beautiful hair?"

"Yes..."

She was emitting only monosyllables, under her breath, as if she were listening to a dreamer talking in his sleep.

"I even think," Chéri continued, "that she must have seen me go out through the garden."

"Ah?"

"Yes. She was on the balcony in her beaded white dress. Such an icy white. Ah! I don't like that dress... Because of that dress I've been wanting to clear out ever since dinnertime."

"Really?"

"But yes, Nounoune. I don't know if she saw me. The moon hadn't come yet. It came up while I was waiting."

"Where were you waiting?"

Chéri stretched his hand out vaguely toward the avenue.

"Out there. You know, I was waiting. I wanted to see. I waited a long time."

"But, what for?"

He left her abruptly and sat down farther away. He resumed his expression of savage mistrust. "Look, I wanted to make sure there was no one else here."

"Ah, yes... You were thinking about..."

She couldn't hold back a laugh full of scorn. A lover, in her home? A lover, while Chéri was still alive? The idea was grotesque. "What a dunce he is!" she thought, keen with anticipation.

"You laugh?"

He stood in front of her and pushed her head back, with his hand against her brow.

"You laugh? You're mocking me? You have... you have a lover? You have somebody?"

As he talked, he leaned forward and pressed the base of her neck against the back of the chaise longue. On her eyelids she could feel the breath of an abusive mouth, but made no effort to free herself from the hand that was roughing up her forehead and her hair.

"Just dare to say it, that you have a lover!"

She batted her eyelids, blinded by the proximity of his fiery gaze bearing down on her, and she said, finally, in a muted voice, "No. I don't have a lover. I love you..."

He let her go and started pulling off his dinner jacket, his vest; his tie hissed through the air and wrapped itself around the neck of the sculpted bust of Léa that sat on the mantlepiece. But he stayed close and kept her seated, his knees against hers, on the chaise longue. When she saw him half-naked, she asked him, almost sadly, "So, you do want to?...Yes...?"

He didn't answer, absorbed in the idea of his approaching pleasure and the desire he had to take her back. She yielded and served her young lover in the way a good mistress does...with attention and seriousness. Yet, with a sort of terror, she could feel the instant of her own defeat coming closer; she endured Chéri like a torture; she held him off with her powerless hands and held on to him between her powerful knees. At last, she grabbed him by the arm, cried feebly, and sank into that abyss from which love resurfaces pale, taciturn, and full of nostalgia for death.

They didn't detach, and no speech disturbed the long silence during which they came back to life. Chéri's torso had slid down Léa's side, and his drooping head, with his eyes closed, rested on the sheet as if someone had stabbed him while he was lying on top of his mistress. A little turned toward the other side, she bore almost the whole weight of this body, which showed no concern for her. She was panting slightly; her left arm, crushed, was hurting; and Chéri could feel the back of his neck going numb; but each of them waited, respectful and motionless, until the waning lightning bolts of pleasure had moved off into the distance.

"He's sleeping," thought Léa. Her free hand was still holding on to Chéri's wrist; she squeezed it gently. His knee—she knew its unusual shape—was bruising hers. She could make out the regular, hushed beating of his heart, level with her own. Lingering, sharp—a blend of succulent flowers and exotic wood—Chéri's favorite perfume drifted around them. "He is here," Léa thought. And a blind sense of security enveloped her whole being. "He is here, for good!" she shouted inwardly. Her caution, born of experience; the cheerful common sense, which had guided her life; the doubts and humiliations of her advancing years; along with her acts of renunciation: all of these shrank and vanished before the presumptuous violence of love. "He's here! He's given up his home, his pretty, simpleminded little wife, he's come back, he's come back to me! Who can take him away from me? Now, now I'm going to sort out our lives . . . He never knows what he wants, but I do. A trip away will be needed, for sure. We won't be going into hiding, but we will be looking for peace and quiet . . . Plus, I need some time to look at him. I can't have looked at him—really looked at him—when I didn't know that I loved him. I need a place where there'll be enough space for his whims, and for my choices . . . I'll do the thinking for both of us—he can do the sleeping."

While she gingerly detached her left arm, which was tingling painfully, and her shoulder, gone stiff with immobility, she looked at Chéri's averted face and saw that he wasn't sleeping. The whites of his eyes were glistening, and the little black wings of his lashes were batting irregularly.

"What—you aren't asleep?"

She felt him start against her, and he rolled his body over in one movement.

"But you aren't asleep either, Nounoune."

He stretched his hand out toward the night table and found the lamp; a blanket of pink light covered the big bed, sharpening the pattern of the lace, darkening the hollows between the plump pockets of the down-filled comforter. Chéri, stretched out wide, reviewed his resting place, his voluptuous playground. Léa, on her elbows next to him, caressed the long eyebrows she loved and pushed back his hair. Lying down like this, with his hair swept away from his forehead, he looked as though he'd been knocked down by a furious wind.

The enameled clock sounded from the mantel. Chéri abruptly sat up.

"What time is it?"

"I don't know. What difference could it make to us?"

"Oh, I was just wondering..."

He gave a short laugh and didn't lie down again right away. Outside, the first milk wagon jangled its glass chimes, and he made an imperceptible gesture toward the avenue. A cold blade of breaking daylight slid in between the strawberry-colored curtains. Chéri turned his gaze back toward Léa and studied her; studied her with the same power and fixity that makes the watchfulness of a puzzled child, or of an incredulous dog, so formidable. An inscrutable thought rose up from the depths of his eyes. Their shape, their hint of very dark carnation, their alternately harsh and languid glare, had served him only to conceal, not to disclose. His naked torso, broad across the shoulders, narrow at the waist, emerged from the bedsheets—stirred up as though by an ocean swell—and his whole being exuded the melancholy of a perfect work of art.

"Ah, you!" Léa sighed in ecstasy.

He didn't smile, accustomed as he was to receiving such homages as a matter of course.

"Tell me, Nounoune..."

"Yes, my beauty?"

He hesitated, fluttered his eyelids, and shivered.

"I'm tired... And, besides, tomorrow, how are you going to be able..."

With a tender push, Léa laid his naked torso and heavy head back onto the pillow. "Don't worry. Lie down. Isn't your Nounoune right here? Don't think about anything. Sleep. I bet you're cold... Here, take this, it's warm."

She wrapped him in the silk and wool of a little feminine garment that lay rolled up on the bed, and turned off the light. In the darkness, she gave him her shoulder to rest on, hollowed out her shapely flank, and listened to him breathing in unison with her. No desire was disturbing her, but she wasn't in the mood to sleep. "He can do the sleeping, I'll do the thinking," she repeated to herself. "Our trip—I'll organize it very smartly, very discreetly; my goal is to cause the least possible fuss and bother ... It's still the south that will suit us best in the spring. If I were concerned only for myself, I'd prefer to stay here, in peace and quiet. But there's Ma Peloux to think about, and young Madame Peloux ..." The image of a young woman in her nightgown, standing anxiously next to a window, didn't occupy Léa's thoughts for any longer than it took her to shrug her shoulders with cold impartiality. "There's nothing I can do about that. What makes some people happy ..."

Silky-haired and dark, Chéri's head stirred on her breast; her sleeping lover moaned as he dreamt. Fiercely, with her arm, Léa protected him from his nightmare. She kept him cradled so that he'd stay there for a good long while—sightless, without memories, with no visions of the future—looking like the "bratty nursling" she'd been unable to bear.

Awake for some time now, he kept still. Cheek on bent arm, he tried to guess what time it was. A speckless sky must be pouring unseasonable heat down onto the avenue; no cloud shadows passed across the flaming pink of the curtains. Maybe ten o'clock? Hunger racked him; he'd had very little for dinner the night before. Last year, he would have leapt up, interrupted Léa's slumber, and cried out voraciously for his creamy chocolate and chilled butter ... He didn't budge. He feared that by stirring he'd break up a vestige of delight, an optical pleasure he could savor in the fiery pink of the curtains, and in the steel and brass volutes of the bed, glinting within the tinted atmosphere of the room. The elation he'd felt yesterday seemed to have gone into hiding—reduced to next to nothing—in a reflection, in the rainbow dancing on the side of a pitcher filled with water.

Rose's cautious footsteps brushed along the carpet on the landing. A discreet broom swept the courtyard. Chéri caught a distant clinking of porcelain in the pantry. "How it drags on, this morning ..." he thought to himself. "I'm going to get up!" But he kept completely still because Léa, behind him, yawned and stretched out her legs. A gentle hand came to rest on the small of Chéri's back, but he closed his eyes, and his whole body began to tell a lie—without knowing why—by feigning the slackness of sleep. He felt Léa get out of bed and saw her pass in dark silhouette in front of the curtains, which she half opened. She turned toward him, looked at him, and nodded with a smile that wasn't victorious, just determined, one that accepted all of the risks. She wasn't in any hurry to leave the room, and Chéri, letting a sliver of daylight part his lashes, secretly observed her. He saw that she was opening a railway timetable and tracing columns of numbers with her finger. Then she seemed to be calculating, with her head lifted up to the sky and her brows furrowed. With no make-up on yet, a meager braid of hair on her nape, her double chin and her ravaged neck, she was exposing herself recklessly to his unseen gaze.

She stepped away from the window, took her checkbook out of a drawer, wrote several checks, and tore them out. Then she laid a pair of white pajamas at the foot of the bed and left without a sound.

Alone now, Chéri, inhaling deeply, realized he'd been holding his breath ever since Léa had gotten out of bed. He got up, put on the pajamas, and opened a window. "It's stifling," he whispered. He couldn't shake the vague, uneasy feeling that he'd done something quite bad.

"Because I pretended to be asleep? But I've seen Léa a hundred times in her dressing gown. Only this time, I pretended to be sleeping."

The dazzling daylight restored to the room its rose-petal hue, and the delicate shades of the blond and silvery Chaplin portrait laughed from the wall. Chéri bowed his head and closed his eyes, so that his memory could restore the bedroom of the night before, mysterious and richly colored like the inside of a melon; the magical dome of lamplight; and, most of all, the exaltation, whose exquisite delights had left him reeling...

"You're up! Your chocolate is on its way."

He noticed, with gratitude, that in a few minutes Léa had brushed her hair, put on some light makeup, and perfumed herself with her usual scent. The sound of her kind, cordial voice suffused the room, along with the aroma of toasted bread and cocoa. Chéri sat down next to the two steaming cups, took the thickly buttered bread from Léa's hands. He was at a loss for words, but Léa didn't guess this, as she was used to him being quiet and withdrawn during his meals. She ate heartily, with the haste and the distracted high spirits of a woman who eats breakfast, with her bags already packed, before catching a train.

"Your second tartine, Chéri...?"

"No, thanks, Nounoune."

"Not hungry?"

"Not hungry."

She poked a finger at him as she laughed. "You'll be forced to take two rhubarb laxatives, I can see it coming!"

He wrinkled his nose in alarm. "Listen, Nounoune, you're far too concerned with—"

"Tut, tut! It's my concern. Stick out your tongue. You don't want to stick out your tongue? Then wipe away your chocolate moustache, and let's have a little talk, but a good one. It's best to deal quickly with tiresome subjects."

She drew one of Chéri's hands across the table and enclosed it in hers.

"You've come back. It was our destiny. Do you trust me? I'll take care of you."

She halted without intending to and closed her eyes, as though she were overwhelmed by the weight of her crown of victory; Chéri saw his mistress's impulsive blood light up her face.

"Ah!" she continued, more quietly. "When I think of everything I didn't give you, of everything I didn't say to you...When I think of how I saw you as a passing fancy, like the rest of them—only just a little more precious than the rest of them... How stupid I was not to realize you were my love, my one true love, the love of my life..."

She reopened her eyes, which looked even bluer, a blue steeped in the shadows of her eyelids, and she breathed haltingly.

"Oh," Chéri pleaded inwardly, "don't let her pose a question, don't let her ask me for an answer now, I can't say a single word..."

She shook him by the hand.

"All right, all right, let's be serious. So, as I was saying: We're leaving, we've already left. What will you do about the situation *over there*? You should have Charlotte handle your financial obligations, that's the wisest course, and be generous, please! How will you let them know *over there*? In a letter, I imagine. Not easy, but you can pull it off, if you're brief and to the point. We'll see about it together. There's also the question of your belongings—I have nothing of yours here anymore . . . Trivial things like these are more vexing than big decisions, but don't worry too much about them . . . Would you please stop picking at the skin next to your toe? With bad habits like these, you'll end up with an ingrown nail!"

He let his foot drop mechanically. His own silence was crushing him, and it was all he could do to focus his attention on listening to Léa. He studied his mistress's animated, joyful, imperious face and asked himself, vaguely, "Why does she seem so happy?"

His torpor became so obvious that Léa, who was now ruminating over the opportunity she had to purchase old Berthellemy's yacht, cut herself short. "Do you think this one would even offer me an opinion? Ah, you! You're still no better than a twelve-year-old!"

Chéri, roused from his stupor, gave his forehead a wipe and cast a melancholy gaze on Léa. "With you, Nounoune, I might be twelve years old for half a century!"

She blinked several times, as if he'd breathed onto her eyelids, and she let silence fall between them.

"What do you mean by that?" she asked, at last.

"Nothing but what I'm saying, Nounoune. Nothing but the truth. Can you deny it, honest person that you are?"

She decided to laugh, with an air of easy unconcern that was already hiding a major fear.

"But your childishness is half of your charm, little nincompoop! Later on it will be the secret of your perpetual youth. And you complain about it! . . . And you have the nerve to come complaining about it to me!"

"Yes, Nounoune. Who else should I complain to?"

He took hold again of the hand she'd withdrawn.

"My darling Nounoune, my wonderful Nounoune, I'm not just complaining, I'm accusing you."

She felt her hand being gripped firmly. And his big, dark eyes, with their lustrous lashes, instead of avoiding hers, fixed on them mournfully. She didn't want to start trembling yet.

"It's nothing, nothing... It will take only a few really harsh words, words he'll answer with some horrible insult, and then he'll sulk, and I'll forgive him... It's nothing more than that..." But she didn't come up with the stern reprimand that would have altered his expression.

"Come on, come on, my dear... You know there are certain jokes I don't put up with for long."

Even as she spoke, she heard her own voice sounding weak and false. "How awkward that was... Like something in a bad play." The mid-morning sunlight glanced off the table that separated them and made Léa's polished fingernails shine. But the bright shaft also lit up her large, shapely hands. It carved—into the loose, soft skin on the backs of her hands and around her wrists—complex traceries, concentric folds, minuscule parallelograms, like the webs etched into clay soil by severe drought after the rainy season. Léa rubbed her hands distractedly, while turning her head to draw Chéri's attention toward the street; but he persisted in his doglike, gloomy contemplation. Abruptly, he took hold of her two nervous hands—which pretended to fiddle with a fold of fabric at her waist—kissed them, kissed them again, and then laid his cheek on them as he murmured, "My Nounoune... oh, my poor Nounoune..."

"Leave me alone!" she cried, with inexplicable rage, tearing her hands away from his.

She took a moment to regain control of herself, and felt horrified at her weakness, since she'd come close to breaking out in sobs. As soon as she could, she spoke, and smiled: "So, you feel sorry for me now? Why were you accusing me a minute ago?"

"I was wrong," he said humbly. "You—you've been, for me..."

He made a gesture that expressed his inability to find words worthy of her.

"'You've *been*!'" she stressed, in a biting accent. "Now, there's something fit for a eulogy, my dear boy!"

"But don't you see..." he said, reproachfully.

He shook his head, and she could tell clearly that she wouldn't upset him. She tensed all her muscles and reined in her thoughts with the help of two or three phrases—always the same, repeated deep inside herself: "He's right here, right in front of me...Come on now, he's still here...He isn't out of reach...But is he still here, in front of me, really...?"

Her thoughts escaped from this rhythmic constraint, and a deep interior lamentation replaced the incantatory phrases. "Oh, if I could only go back, if I could only go back to the moment when I said, 'Your second tartine, Chéri?' That moment is still so close to us, it's not lost forever, it's not yet in the past. Let's start our life over again at that moment; the little that's happened since then won't count; I'm wiping it away, I'm wiping it away...I'm going to talk to him just as if we've gone back to a few minutes ago...Yes, let me see: about the trip, his belongings..."

She did, in fact, speak, and said, "I see...I see that I can't consider to be a man, a being who's capable, because he has no spine, of throwing two women's lives into disarray. Do you think I don't understand? When it comes to trips, you like them short, eh? Yesterday, Neuilly; today, here; but tomorrow...So, where, tomorrow? Here? No, no, my dear, it's not worth lying. That convict's look wouldn't even fool a woman more stupid than me, if there is one over there..."

Her impulsive gesture, pointing in the direction of Neuilly, knocked over a cake stand, which Chéri set back up. As she went on talking, she augmented her suffering, changed it into stinging, aggressive, jealous grief, the voluble grief of a young woman. The makeup on her cheeks turned the color of red wine; a lock of her hair, twisted with a curling iron, crawled down the back of her neck like a skinny little snake.

"Even that one, over there, even your wife, you won't always find her at home when it pleases you to go back. A woman, my dear, you don't really know how she allows herself to be won, but you understand even less how she sets herself free!...You'll get Charlotte to hold on to her, your woman, eh? Now there's an idea! Ah! I'll have a good laugh, the day when—"

Chéri stood up, bloodless, somber. "Nounoune!"

"'Nounoune' what? 'Nounoune' what? You think you're going to frighten me? Ah! You want to go off on your own? Go! You're sure to travel far, with a daughter of Marie-Laure's. She has no flesh on her arms, and a flat behind, but that won't stop her from—"

"I forbid you, Nounoune—!"

He grabbed her by her arms, but she got up, wrenched herself away, and burst into hoarse laughter. "But of course! 'I forbid you to say one word against my wife!' That's it, isn't it?"

He walked around the table and came right up to her, trembling with indignation. "No! I forbid you—do you understand me?—I forbid you to ruin my Nounoune!"

She shrank back farther into the room, stammering, "What do you mean...what do you mean..."

He came after her, as if he were ready to chastise her.

"Yes! Is this the way Nounoune ought to talk? What sort of manners are these? Dirty little insults—Madame Peloux's style, now? And they're coming from you, from you, Nounoune!"

He threw his head back proudly. "I know how Nounoune ought to talk! I know how she ought to think! I've had time to learn. I haven't forgotten the day when you said to me, a little before I was going to marry that girl: 'At least don't be mean...Try not to make her suffer...To me it looks a little like they're handing a doe over to a wolfhound.' That's how to talk! That was you! And the day before my wedding, when I escaped to come and see you, I remember, you said to me..."

He lost his voice. All of his features lit up with the fire of a memory.

"Darling, carry on..."

He placed his hands on Léa's shoulders. "And, again, last night," he continued, "wasn't one of your first concerns to ask me if I hadn't caused too much harm *over there*? My Nounoune, when we started out, I knew you were someone classy and kind, I loved you as a person with class. If we have to end it, are you going to turn out to be just like other women?"

She vaguely sensed the ruse behind his homage, and sat down, hiding her face between her hands.

"How hard you are, how hard-hearted," she stammered. "Why did you come back ... I was so calm, so solitary, so used to—"

She could hear herself lying and stopped short.

"Not me!" Chéri shot back. "I came back because ... because ..."

He spread his arms, let them fall, opened them again.

"Because I couldn't go on without you anymore. There's no need to look for any other reason."

They remained silent for a moment.

Slumped in her chair, she contemplated this impatient young man—as white as a seagull—whose light feet and open arms seemed poised for flight ...

Chéri's dark eyes wandered above her head.

"Ah! You can boast," he said, all of a sudden, "you can boast of having made me, for the past three months especially, lead a life ... a life ..."

"Me?"

"Who else, other than you? If a door opened—it was Nounoune; the telephone—it was Nounoune; a letter in the garden mailbox—it could be Nounoune ... Even in the wine I was drinking, I kept on trying to find you, and I could never find the Pommery you serve here ... And then, at night ... oh my!"

He was walking, very quickly and noiselessly, back and forth across the carpet.

"I can say I know what it means to suffer for a woman, yes, I can! I know what to expect, now, of the ones who'll come after you ... they'll be worthless! Ah, did you ever poison me ... !"

She straightened up slowly and followed, with a swaying of her upper body, Chéri's to-ing and fro-ing. Her cheekbones were dry and shiny, a feverish red that made the blue of her eyes almost unbearable. He was striding, his head bent forward, and he didn't stop talking.

"Can you imagine—Neuilly without you, the first days after I went back! And besides, everything was without you ... I nearly lost my mind. One night, the girl was sick, I don't remember what it was anymore, aches and pains, neuralgia ... I felt bad for her, but I left the room, because nothing in the world would have stopped me from saying 'Wait, don't cry, I'm going to go and get Nounoune, who'll make you better.' And anyway, you would have come, wouldn't you, Nounoune? ... Oh my, the life I led! ... At the Hotel Morris I took on Desmond, paid him well, and talked to him about it, sometimes, at night ... 'My old friend, skin like hers, it's beyond belief ... And, you see your sapphire ring? Well, old friend, put it away, because the blue of her eyes—her own blue—it doesn't turn gray in strong light.' And I'd tell him how you could be mean when you wanted to, and how no one could have the last word with you ... I no more than anyone else ... I'd say to him, as if he didn't know you: 'That woman, old friend, when she's wearing the right hat—your marine blue one with the wings, Nounoune, from last summer—and dressing the way she does—put any other woman next to her, and there's absolutely no comparison!' And then there's her amazing way of talking, of walking, her smile, her classy ways. I'd say to him, to Desmond: 'Ah! She really is something, a woman like Léa!'"

He snapped his fingers with proprietary pride and came to a stop, out of breath from talking and walking.

"I never said any of that to Desmond," he thought to himself. "But, even so, what I just said isn't a lie. Desmond could tell what I was thinking, all the same." He wanted to go on talking, and looked at Léa. She was still listening to him. Sitting very upright now, she was letting him see her face in the full light of day: it was noble and distraught, caked with dried, burning tears. An invisible weight pulled her chin and her cheeks downward, saddened the trembling corners of her mouth. In this wreckage of beauty, Chéri could still recognize, intact, the pretty, dominating nose, the pupils of floral blue ...

"Isn't it so, Nounoune, that after months of living that life, I get here, and—"

He stopped, frightened by what he'd almost just said.

"You get here, and you find an old woman," Léa said, her voice faint, but calm.

"Nounoune! Listen, Nounoune!"

He threw himself down at her knees, revealing through his features the cowardice of a child who can no longer come up with the words to conceal a mistake.

"And you find an old woman," Léa said again. "So what are you afraid of, my dear?"

She wrapped Chéri's shoulders in her arms and felt the stiffness, the protectiveness of this body, which was suffering because she'd been wounded.

"Come, now, my Chéri...What are you afraid of? Of having made me sad? Don't cry, my beauty...It's the other way around, I'm so grateful to you..."

He gave a groan of protest and struggled weakly. She leaned her cheek against his dark, tangled hair.

"Did you say all of that, did you think all of that, about me? Tell me, then, was I so beautiful in your eyes? So very fine? At the age when so many women have stopped living, for you I was the most beautiful, the very best of women, and you loved me? How grateful I am to you, my darling...The kindest woman, you said?...Poor little one..."

He stopped resisting, and she held him up in her arms.

"If I'd been the kindest. I'd have made you a man, instead of thinking only of your bodily pleasure, and mine. The classiest? No, no, I wasn't that, my darling, because I held on to you. And now it's too late..."

He seemed to be sleeping in Léa's arms, but his stubbornly clenched eyelids didn't stop wincing, and he kept clinging, with a steady grip, to her dressing gown, which was slowly tearing apart.

"It's too late, it's too late...All the same..."

She leaned over him.

"My darling, listen to me. Wake up, my beauty. Listen to me with your eyes open. You shouldn't be afraid of seeing me. You know I'm still the same woman you loved, the classiest woman of all..."

He opened his eyes, and his first, tearstained look was already full of a selfish and imploring hope. Léa turned her head away. "His eyes... Ah! Let's get this over with quickly..." She rested her cheek on Chéri's brow.

"It was me, dear, it really was me, the woman who said to you: 'Don't cause any needless harm, spare the little doe...' I'd forgotten my advice. Fortunately, you remembered it. You've waited a long, long time to wean yourself from me, my bratty nursling, I've held you to my breast for too long, and now it's your turn to carry a heavy load: a young wife, maybe a child... I'm responsible for everything you lack... Yes, yes, my beauty, here you are, thanks to me, at twenty-five, so heedless, so spoiled, and so gloomy, all at once... It really worries me. You're going to suffer, you're going to cause suffering. You, who've loved me..."

The hand that was slowly tearing her dressing gown tightened its grip, and Léa felt the claws of the bratty nursling on her breast.

"You, who've loved me," she picked up, after a pause, "will you be able to... I don't know how to make myself understood..."

He pulled away from her to listen; and she came close to crying out to him: "Put your hand back on my bosom, and your nails back where they've scratched! I lose my strength as soon as your flesh leaves mine." Now she, in turn, pressed herself against him, who'd gone down on his knees in front of her. She continued: "You, who've loved me, you, who'll miss me..."

She smiled at him, and looked him in the eyes.

"What vanity, eh!... You, who'll miss me... when you feel on the verge of frightening that little doe—who belongs to you, who needs your protection— I want you to hold yourself back, to figure out, at those moments, all the things I haven't taught you... I've never spoken to you about the future. Forgive me, Chéri: I've loved you as if each of us was bound to die within the hour. Because I was born twenty-four years before you, I was doomed, and I was dragging you along with me..."

He was listening with a concentration that made him look harsh. She passed her hand across his uneasy brow to wipe away the crease.

"Can you see us, Chéri, going to have lunch together at Armenonville?... Can you see us inviting Madame and Monsieur Lili to join us?..."

She laughed sadly, and shivered.

"Ah! I'm just as worn out as that old dame... Quick, quick, my dear, go and recover your youthfulness, the crones have only taken the edges off it, it's not finished for you, it's still there, in that girl who's waiting for you. You've gotten a taste of it from her, of youthfulness! It's not satisfying, but you'll go back for more... You didn't just start comparing last night, did you?... And what business do I have, giving you advice and flaunting my magnanimity? What do I know about the two of you? She loves you: it's her turn to tremble, she'll suffer like a lover, not like a misguided mother. You'll talk to her as her master, not as a capricious gigolo... Go, go, quick!"

She spoke in a tone of rash entreaty. He was listening standing up, feet firmly planted, bare-chested, his hair in wild disorder; he was so tempting, she clasped her hands together... they were going to grab hold of him. He might have guessed her intention, but he didn't back away. An utterly foolish hope, of the kind that occurs to people as they're falling from a tower, glimmered between them and evanesced.

"Go," she said, softly. "I do love you. It's too late. Get away from here. But make it quick. Get dressed."

She got up and brought him his shoes, laid out his wrinkled shirt, his socks. He was turning in circles, rubbing his fingers awkwardly as though they'd gone numb, and she herself had to fetch his suspenders, his necktie; but she avoided coming near him and didn't help him put anything on. While he dressed, she cast frequent glances at the courtyard, as though she were expecting a car.

Once he was dressed he looked even paler; a halo of fatigue enlarged his eyes.

"You aren't feeling ill?" she asked. And she added timidly, her eyes lowered, "You could... you could rest..." But right away she pulled herself together and looked at him like he was in great danger. "No, no, you'll be better off at your place... Get home quick, it isn't noon yet, a good, hot bath will set you right, and then some fresh air...

Here, take your gloves...Ah, yes, your hat's on the floor!...Put on your overcoat, you might catch cold. Farewell, my Chéri, farewell... That's right...You'll tell Charlotte..." She closed the door behind him, and silence ended her vain and desperate chatter. She heard Chéri trip on the stairs, and she ran to the window. He was walked down the front steps and stopped in the middle of the courtyard.

"He's coming back up! He's coming back up!" she cried, raising her arms.

In the full-length mirror a breathless crone mimicked her motions, and Léa wondered what she could possibly have in common with that madwoman.

Chéri went on his way again toward the street, opened the gate, and left. Out on the sidewalk, he buttoned up his overcoat to hide his day-old linens. Léa let the curtain drop. But she still had time to see that Chéri was lifting his head up to the spring sky and the chestnut trees loaded with blossoms; and that, as he walked, he was filling his lungs with air like an escapee.

THE END OF CHÉRI

CHÉRI shut the wrought iron gate of the front garden behind him and sniffed the night air. "Ah! It's nice out." He changed his mind at once. "No, it's not." The boughs of the tightly spaced chestnut trees weighed heavily on the captive heat below. Above the nearest gas lamp, a dome of charred greenery pulsed. From now until dawn, avenue Henri-Martin, choked with vegetation, would await the faint stirrings of freshness emanating from the Bois de Boulogne.

His head bare, Chéri gazed at his brightly lit town house, emptied now of dinner guests. He heard the noise of clashing crystal, then Edmée's voice: clear, hardened in reprimand. He saw his wife approach the bay window in the hall on the second floor and lean forward. In the greenish glare of the gaslight, her beaded dress lost its snowy whiteness, then flared yellow as she brushed against the silk lamé curtain.

"Is that you down there on the sidewalk, Fred?"

"Who else would it be?"

"So you didn't drive Filipesco home?"

"No, he'd already taken off."

"I would have liked . . . Anyway, it doesn't matter. Are you coming back in?"

"Not yet. Too hot. I'm going for a walk."

"But . . . Well, whatever you like."

She paused for a moment. Then she must have laughed—he saw all the frosted beads on her dress shimmer.

"From up here, all I can see of you is your white shirtfront and your white face floating in the dark... You look like a poster for a dance hall. It's devastating."

"How fond you are of my mother's turns of phrase," he said, pensively. "You can let everybody else go to bed, I have my key."

She gave him a wave, and, one by one, the lights went out. A particular muted blue glow told Chéri that Edmée was passing through her boudoir on her way to the bedroom, which overlooked the garden at the back of the house.

"No doubt about it," he mused. "These days, the boudoir has turned into the study."

The clock tower at Janson-de-Sailly sounded the hour, and Chéri, his head cocked, caught the ringing of the bells in flight, like drops of rain.

"Midnight. She's in such a rush to go to bed... Ah, right, she has to be at her hospital at nine tomorrow morning."

He took a few nervous steps, shrugged, and settled down.

"I might as well have married a ballerina. Nine o'clock, barre class: it's a sacred duty. The most important of all."

He walked as far as the entrance to the Bois. A sky hazy with dust dimmed the twinkling of the stars. A steady tread kept time with Chéri's; he stopped and waited; he didn't like anyone walking behind him.

"Good evening, Monsieur Peloux." The night watchman tipped his cap.

Chéri answered by lifting a finger to his temple—a condescending gesture he'd picked up from his fellow staff sergeants during the war—and carried on past the watchman, who was checking the locks on the iron gates of the private gardens.

Inside the entrance of the Bois, a pair of lovers, sitting on a bench, were rumpling each other's clothes and exchanging muffled words. For a moment, Chéri listened to the hushed sound—like a prow slicing through placid water—that issued from their tightly clasped bodies and invisible mouths.

"The man's a soldier," he observed. "I just heard the buckle of his army belt."

All his senses were on the alert now, purged of thought. On certain calm nights during the war, this feral refinement of perception had brought Chéri problematic pleasures, well-founded fears. Blackened with earth and human filth, his soldier's fingers had learned to identify, by touch alone, the effigies on medals and coins, how to recognize the stems and leaves of plants whose names he didn't know… "Hey, Peloux, guess what I've got ahold of here?" Chéri could picture the redheaded kid who used to slide to him, in the dark, a dead mole, a little snake, a tree frog, a piece of overripe fruit, or some bit of muck, and then cry out: "Ah! He's on to it every time!" He smiled impassively at the memory of this dead redheaded pal. He often recalled the image of Pierquin—laid out on his back, gone to sleep for good with a wary look on his face—and he often talked about him. Again, this evening after dinner, Edmée had deftly elicited the brief anecdote—strung together with a studied awkwardness—which Chéri knew by heart. It ended with: "Then Pierquin said to me, 'Old chum, I dreamt I saw a cat, and then I dreamt the river back home was full of disgusting filth…There's no surviving that…' This was the very moment he got picked off, by nothing but a piece of shrapnel. I wanted to drag him back…They found us—him on top of me—a hundred yards from the spot…I'm telling you all this because he was a decent guy…I got this partly because of him."

Right after coming to this modest conclusion, Chéri dropped his eyes to the green and red ribbon of his medal of bravery and tapped the ash from his cigarette, as if to stay calm and collected. To his mind, it was nobody else's business that a chance explosion had hurled one of them across the other's shoulders, Chéri alive, Pierquin dead. Because the truth—more ambiguous than a lie—was that a living Chéri, full of rage and hatred, lay half-smothered under the enormous weight of a Pierquin gone suddenly stiff…Chéri held a grudge against Pierquin. What's more, Chéri scorned the truth, ever since a day when it had exited his mouth, like a spasm, to degrade and to harm…

But this evening, here at his place, the American majors Atkins and Marsh-Meyer and the American lieutenant Wood seemed not to be listening to him. Their athletic choirboys' faces, their clear gazes—fixed, vacant—were only waiting, with almost painful anxiety, for it to be time to head to the dance hall. As for Filipesco... "Keep an eye on him," Chéri told himself, succinctly.

A humid fragrance encircled the lake in the Bois, emanating more from the clipped banks than from the silt-filled water. While Chéri was resting his back against a tree, a woman's shadow swept boldly across him. "Evening, kid..." He started at the last word, delivered by a deep, raspy voice, a voice redolent of thirst, of the desiccated night, of the dusty road... He gave no reply, and the hard-to-make-out woman took a step toward him on her soft-soled shoes. But he got a whiff of black wool, dirty linen, and dampened hair, and he strode quickly back to his house.

The muted blue light was still keeping watch there: Edmée hadn't yet left the boudoir-study. No doubt she was filling out and signing orders for medicines and dressings, reading the day's case notes and some memos from a secretary... She was leaning over some papers... with her frizzy hair and its reddish highlights, her pretty schoolmistress's forehead. Chéri pulled the small flat key, at the end of a fine gold chain, out of his pocket.

"Here we go. She's going to make love to me by the book, again..."

As was his wont, he entered his wife's boudoir without knocking. But Edmée didn't give a start, and didn't interrupt her telephone conversation. Chéri listened in.

"No, not tomorrow... But you don't need me for that. The general knows you well enough. And at the chamber of commerce, we have... What do you mean, do I 'have' Lémery? No, not at all! He's charming, but... Hello?... Hello?"

She laughed, showing her small teeth. "Oh, come on! You're exaggerating... Lémery flirts with any woman who isn't one-eyed or lame... What? Yes, he's back, he's standing right here. No, no, I'll be discreet... Bye... see you tomorrow."

Edmée's white charmeuse negligée, the same shade of white as her string of pearls, slipped off her shoulder. Her chestnut hair, as frizzy as an African's and stiffened a little by the dryness of the air, moved with her head.

"Who was that?" Chéri asked.

As she hung up the receiver, she asked, "Fred, you'll let me have the Rolls tomorrow morning? It would be better for bringing the general here for lunch."

"General who?"

"General Haar."

"Is he a Boche?"

Edmée frowned.

"Fred, believe me, jokes like that are a little childish for someone your age. General Haar is visiting my hospital tomorrow. When he gets back to America, he'll be able to say my hospital is every bit as good as the same kind of establishments over there. Colonel Beybert will be showing him around. They'll have lunch with us afterwards, both of them."

Chéri slung his dinner jacket over a chair.

"I couldn't care less. I'm eating lunch in town."

"You mean . . . ? What do you mean . . . ?"

A wave of intense emotion passed across Edmée's face, but she smiled, carefully picked up his jacket, and changed her tone. "You asked who I was talking to? To your mother."

Chéri sank deep into an armchair and said nothing. His loveliest, most inflexible mask hid his expression. A censorious calm settled on his brows, on his lowered eyelids—which, as he neared thirty, were turning a yellowish brown—and on his mouth, which he was careful to keep unclenched, shut softly, as if he were asleep.

"You know," Edmée went on, "she wants Lémery, at the chamber of commerce, to do something about her three shiploads of leather . . . Three shiploads of leather sitting in the port of Valparaíso . . . You know, it might not be a bad idea . . . The thing is, Lémery won't grant the import license—at least, that's what he says . . . Do you have any idea how much of a commission the Soumabis have offered your mother, at a minimum?"

With his hand, Chéri swept away the ships, the hides, and the commission.

"Enough," he said tersely.

Edmée demurred and tenderly went to her husband.

"You are having lunch here tomorrow, right? I might invite Gibbs, the reporter from *Excelsior*, who'll take photos of the hospital and your mother."

Chéri shook his head and stayed collected. "No," he said. "General Hagenbeck—"

"Haar."

"...and a colonel—and my mother in her uniform. Her tunic— what do you call it? Her jerkin?—with its little leather buttons... her elastic corset...her epaulettes...her mandarin collar, with her chin hanging out...and her cane. No, you know...I won't pretend to be more valiant than I really am. I'd prefer to go out."

He laughed, mirthlessly, under his breath. Edmée placed a hand already quaking with annoyance on his arm, but kept her manner light.

"You can't be serious?"

"But I am. I'm going to have lunch at Brekekekex...or somewhere else."

"With whom?"

"With whomever I like."

He sat, kicked off his low-cut shoes. Edmée leaned back against a black lacquered chair and tried to think of something to say that would bring Chéri back to his senses. The white satin of her negligée rose and fell to the rhythm of her rapid breathing, and she crossed her hands behind her back like a martyr. Chéri regarded her with feigned deference.

"She really is a fine-looking woman. Even with her hair down, in a nightdress, in a bathrobe, she's a fine-looking woman."

She lowered her gaze, lifted it to meet Chéri's, and smiled. "You're teasing me," she said dolefully.

"No," Chéri replied. "I won't be having lunch here. That's all there is to it."

"But why?"

He stood up, walked as far as the open doorway of their dimly lit bedroom—perfumed by the nocturnal garden—then turned back toward her.

"Because. If you force me to explain myself, I'll get loud, and I'll get mean. You'll cry, and 'in your distress' you'll let your nightdress slip down, and . . . and unfortunately it won't affect me at all."

Another intense wave of emotion passed across the young woman's features. But her patience wasn't exhausted yet. She laughed, then shrugged her curvaceous shoulder, bare under her loosened hair.

"You can say that as much as you like, that it won't affect you at all."

He was pacing around, now wearing only his white silk shorts. With every step he took, he carefully checked the flexibility of the back of his knee and his instep. He was rubbing the pair of matching scars below his right breast, to revive their fading shade of yellowish brown. Less bulky than he'd been at twenty, but more muscular and more finely sculpted, he gladly paraded in front of his wife. But he did so as a rival rather than as a lover. He knew himself to be more beautiful than her, and he looked down with the detachment of a connoisseur at her flat hips, her girlish bust, and her graceful, vanishing outlines, which Edmée was so skilled at dressing in formfitting robes and slinky tunics. "So, you've gotten skinnier?" he'd sometimes ask, for the pleasure of wounding her a little and seeing her surprisingly strong body rear up in annoyance.

His wife's comeback upset him. He liked her to look chic and stay silent, if not unresponsive, in his arms. He stopped, lowered his brows, looked her up and down.

"Nice manners," he said. "Is it your chief of staff who's training you? This means war, madame!"

She shrugged her bare shoulder.

"What a child you are, my poor, dear Fred! Thank goodness we're all alone. To chide me for a little joke . . . which was actually a compliment . . . To try to teach me manners—you . . . you! After seven years of marriage!"

"How do you come up with seven years?"

He sat down, as though prepared for a long discussion—naked, with his legs apart in a V, stretched out in athletic display.

"But of course ... 1913 ... 1913 ..."

"Wait a minute! We're not counting by the same calendar. By my reckoning—"

Edmée bent her knee and stood on one leg, revealing her fatigue, and Chéri cut her off: "Where's this getting us? Come on, let's go to bed. You have to teach your ballet class at nine a.m., don't you?"

"Oh, Fred!"

She twisted up and tossed away a rose that had been steeping in a black vase, and Chéri stoked the choleric fire, dampened with tears, that shone in Edmée's eyes.

"That's what I call your leftover troop of injured soldiers, when I'm not thinking..."

Without looking at him, she murmured, her lips trembling, "A brute ... a brute ... a vile creature."

He didn't back down. And he laughed.

"What do you want me to say? For you, it's all settled, you're performing a sacred task. But for me? ... It wouldn't make any difference if you spent every day in the upper gallery at the opera. I'd be just as ... just as left out. And the ones I call your 'leftover troop,' well, they're injured, aren't they? Injured men who happen to be a bit luckier than the rest. I have nothing in common with them, either. With them, too, I'm ... left out."

She wheeled back toward him in an impulse that sent her hair flying.

"Darling! Don't be hurt! You're not left out. You're above it all!"

He stood up, drawn to a pitcher of ice water, on whose surface the mist was slowly condensing into sky-blue tears. Edmée hurried to ask, "With or without lemon, Fred?"

"Without. Thanks."

He drank; she took the empty glass from his hand and went off toward the bathroom.

"By the way," he said, "that leak in the cement of the swimming pool ... We should ..."

"It's all arranged. The man who does the glass tile mosaics is a cousin of Chuche's, one of my wounded soldiers. He won't need to be called twice, you can be sure of that."

"Good."

He was on his way out, but turned around. "So, tell me, that business with the ranch shares—we talked about them yesterday—should we sell, or not? What if I try and have a word with Papa Deutsch tomorrow morning?"

Edmée burst into schoolgirl laughter. "Do you think I waited around for you? Your mother had an inspiration this morning, while we were bringing the baroness home from the hospital."

"You mean Ma La Berche?"

"Yes, the baroness. Your mother 'had a word' with her, as you put it so nicely. The baroness is one of the original shareholders, she's in constant touch with the chairman of the board—"

"Except when she's busy knocking back a big bottle of white."

"Can you not constantly interrupt me! . . . By two o'clock, everything had been sold, my dear! Everything! The little burst on the Exchange—it lasted only a few minutes after lunch—put two hundred and sixteen thousand francs* into our pockets, Fred! That covers the medications and the dressings! I wanted to wait and let you in on the news tomorrow, by handing you one of those big fat wallets . . . Give me a kiss?"

He was standing, pale and undressed, behind the drawn-back folds of the doorway curtain, watching his wife's face attentively.

"Fine . . ." he said at last. "And where do I fit in to all of this?"

Edmée gave a mischievous shake of the head.

"Your power of attorney is still in force, my love. 'The right to sell, to buy, to sign a lease in my name . . .' et cetera. By the way, I'm going to send a token of appreciation to the baroness."

"A stubby pipe," said Chéri thoughtfully.

"Don't laugh! That brave creature is so valuable to us!"

"Who's 'us'?"

*Equivalent to about U.S. $10,000 in today's money.

"Your mother and me. The baroness knows how to talk to those men in their own language. She tells them stories that are a little racy and full of zest...They adore her!"

A bizarre laugh twitched across Chéri's face. He let the door curtain drop behind him. Its fall erased his presence, the way sleep wipes away a nascent fantasy. Like a form floating in midair, he advanced noiselessly—because he'd insisted that the house be carpeted from top to bottom—down a corridor that was bathed in a blue half-light; noiselessly. He preferred silence and stealth, and never knocked before entering the room that his wife, since the war ended, had called her "study." She showed no impatience with this. She could sense Chéri's presence, and didn't flinch.

He took a bath, didn't linger as the water cooled, scented himself absentmindedly, and returned to the little salon.

He could hear a body rustling the bedsheets in the adjoining room and a paper knife strike against some porcelain on the night table. He sat down and rested his chin on his hand. The menu for the following day, written out daily by the butler, was sitting on a little stand beside him. He read: "'Lobster thermidor, lamb cutlets Fulbert-Dumonteil, chaudfroid of duck, Charlotte salad, Curaçao soufflé, cheese straws Chester...' Nothing wrong with all this. 'Six place settings.' Now, here, I do need to make a change."

He corrected the number and set his chin back on his hand.

"Fred, do you know what time it is?"

He didn't respond to the muted voice, but came into the room and sat down by the big bed. One of her shoulders was bare, the other draped in a fold of white linen. Edmée was smiling, in spite of her fatigue. She knew she looked prettier lying down than she did standing up. But Chéri remained seated, with his chin on his hand.

"*The Thinker*," Edmée said, to make him laugh, or to get him to move.

"How right you are," Chéri shot back sententiously.

He wrapped his legs in the folds of his Chinese bathrobe and crossed his arms in exasperation.

"What the hell am I doing here?"

Either she didn't understand, or didn't want to.

"That's what I'm asking myself, Fred. It's two o'clock in the morning, and I have to get up at eight. Another one of those 'light' days tomorrow . . . It isn't fair of you to loaf around the way you do. Come on, there's a breeze picking up. We'll go to sleep in some fresh air, like we're lying out in the garden . . ."

He gave in, and hesitated for only a second before he tossed away his silk robe, while Edmée turned off the single lamp. She slid over to face him in the darkness, but he adroitly rolled her the other way, put one arm firmly around her waist, murmured, "This way. As though we're in a bobsled," and dropped off to sleep.

The next morning, he hid in the linen room and watched through the little window as they left. The duck-egg-blue Rolls and a long American sedan were idling in the avenue, almost inaudibly, under the dense, low-hanging chestnuts. An illusion of freshness emanated from the hosed-down sidewalk and the leafy shadows. But Chéri knew that a June morning—June, the month of scorching heat in Paris—was drying out the lake of blue forget-me-nots and its banks of pink carnations in the garden behind the town house.

He'd felt a pang of anxiety when he spied two khaki uniforms, some gold stars, and a military cap trimmed with garnet velvet approaching the gate.

"In uniform, naturally, the schnook!"

This is how Chéri referred to the chief of staff at Edmée's hospital. Unknowingly, Chéri hated this reddish-blond man who traded technical terms in flattering tones with Edmée. Chéri muttered some indistinct, heartfelt insults, aimed particularly at the medical corps and people who wore military uniform in peacetime. He sniggered because the American officer was growing paunchy ("For somebody from a nation of athletes, what a gut he has!"), then fell silent when Edmée appeared—vivacious in a white dress and white shoes—and held out her white-gloved hand. She spoke loudly, quickly, cheerfully. Chéri didn't miss one of the words that flew from her ruby mouth, which revealed such tiny teeth when she laughed. She went up to the cars, came back, asked a servant to go and fetch an order-book she'd left behind, then chatted while she waited. She addressed the American colonel in English and lowered her voice, in reflexive deference, to reply to Dr. Arnaud.

Behind the tulle curtain, Chéri kept still. Whenever he suppressed a lively emotion, his habits of defiance and prevarication froze his features. Even when he was alone, he kept a close eye on himself. His gaze traveled from Edmée to the doctor, from the American colonel back to Edmée. Chéri saw her lift her eyes a number of times toward the second floor, as if she'd been warned of his presence.

In a convertible touring car driven by a young chauffeur, who was flawless and aloof, Charlotte Peloux pulled up. Tightly wrapped in gabardine, she held her head high under a little peaked cap, and you could see the fringe of red hair, cropped short, on her neck. She didn't step out, deigned to be greeted, and accepted Edmée's kiss. She must have asked after Chéri, because she raised her head toward the second floor and exposed her magnificent eyes, as large as a mollusk's, where an inhuman dream drifted inscrutably.

"She has her little cap on," Chéri murmured to himself.

He shuddered in a peculiar way, scolded himself, and smiled when the three automobiles drove away. He waited patiently for his own roadster to draw up to the curb at eleven o'clock, then let it sit there for a while. Twice, he stretched his hand out toward the telephone, and twice let it drop again. His vague desire to summon Filipesco subsided quickly; then he thought he wanted to pick up Maudru Junior and his girlfriend.

"Or even better, Jean de Touzac... But at this time of day, he's still dead-drunk and sawing logs. Ah, but for sure, not one of them... not one of them holds a candle to Desmond... Poor old sport..."

He thought of Desmond as a casualty of war. But, for Desmond, he felt the pity he refused to feel for the dead. Desmond—alive and lost to Chéri—inspired in him an almost tender melancholy and the envious respect due to a man with an "occupation." Desmond ran a dance hall and sold antiques to Americans. Though he'd been ailing and listless during a war that saw him bear everything but arms (bundles of papers, mess kits, soiled chamber pots from hospitals), Desmond tore into peacetime with the fury of a warrior. In short order he reaped gains that astonished Chéri. Desmond's dance hall was squeezed into a private residence on the avenue de l'Alma. Inside its thick stone walls, below its ceilings decorated with swallows and hawthorns, between its stained-glass windows picturing reeds and flamingoes, it was a haven for frenetic, voiceless couples. They danced at Desmond's day and night, the way you dance when a war has ended: the men, young and old—freed from the burden of thinking and of being afraid—innocent, with nothing on their minds; the women, intent on a satisfaction greater than any climax: a man's company, a man's touch, his smell, his invigorating warmth, the certainty, felt from head to foot, of being prey to a man who was alive in every part, and of submitting, in his embrace, to a rhythm as intimate as that of sleep.

"Desmond would have gone to bed at three, or three thirty," Chéri calculated. "He's had enough sleep."

But he let his hand, stretched out toward the telephone, drop again. He went downstairs at a rapid pace, treading the plush, springy carpet that covered every floorboard in his house; as he passed by the dining room, he glanced indulgently at five white plates arranged in a circle around a black crystal basin decorated with pink, free-floating nymphs—the same pink as the tablecloth—and didn't stop until he reached the mirror that backed the heavy door of the ground-floor parlor. He was drawn to, and dreaded, this mirror that received its light through a pair of glass doors whose misty blue panes looked even darker against the background of the garden foliage. A mild shock brought Chéri to a halt every time he confronted his image. He couldn't comprehend that this was no longer the exact image of a twenty-four-year-old. Nor did he distinguish those precise spots where time, with imperceptible touches, defines a beautiful face's moment of perfection; and then, the moment of a more manifest beauty, which already presages a majestic decline.

As far as Chéri was concerned, there could be no misgivings about a decline for which he would have searched his features in vain. He would simply bump into a thirty-year-old Chéri, not quite recognize him, and occasionally ask himself, "What's wrong with me?" as though he felt a little ill, or badly dressed. Then he'd carry on past the parlor door and not give the question another thought.

Desmond's, a businesslike establishment, wasn't sleeping at noon, despite its long nights. A concierge was hosing down the paved court-yard; a valet was clearing the entrance steps of the elegant detritus—powdery dust, tinfoil, metal-crowned corks, gold-tipped cigarette butts, twisted drinking straws—that attested, every day, to Desmond's success. Chéri leapt across these remnants of yesterday's heavy traffic. But the smell of the interior barred his way like a taut rope. Forty couples, packed like sardines, had left this smell behind: the residue of their sweaty underclothes, cooled down now, infused with linger-ing smoke. Chéri summoned the courage to dash up the staircase, which was constricted by a massive oak handrail and balusters in the form of caryatids. Desmond hadn't squandered any funds on refresh-ing the oppressive luxury of the 1880s. Two partition walls torn down, a cold room in the basement, a well-paid jazz band: nothing more than this had proved necessary, for yet another year. "When people stop coming to dance, I'll spruce the place up to pull more people in," Desmond said. He slept on the third floor in a bedroom invaded by morning-glory frescoes and stork statuettes made of glass; he bathed in an enameled zinc tub, alongside a tiled frieze of riverbank plants; the decrepit water heater growled and wheezed like a bulldog on its last legs. But the telephone gleamed like a weapon in daily use. After bounding up the stairs, Chéri found his friend—with his lips to the chalice—appearing to imbibe the murky breath of the receiver. He cast a wayward glance down at Chéri, which barely alighted before landing again, on the ceiling cornice with its wreath of morning-glories. Desmond's golden-yellow pajamas made his night owl's face look faded. But, puffed up by profit, he'd outgrown any concern about his ugly appearance.

"Hello," said Chéri. "It's me. Your staircase stinks. Worse than a foxhole."

"If you charge twelve, you'll never get Desmond's business," Desmond was saying to the unseen party. "I have no trouble getting Pommery for that price. And, for my own cellar, I can get Pommery with no labels for eleven ... hello? Yes, labels that peeled off during the big upheaval, which proves my point. Hello ..."

"Are you coming for lunch? I have the car down below," said Chéri.

"No, and no," said Desmond.

"What?"

"No, and no. Hello? ... Sherry? ... You're playing games. I'm not a wine bar. Champagne or nothing. Don't waste your time, and don't waste mine. Hello ... It's possible. Except, at the moment, I'm all the rage ... Hello ... Two o'clock sharp ... The very best to you, monsieur."

He stretched his back, then held out a limp hand. He still looked like King Alfonso XIII of Spain. But thirty years of living, and the war, had rooted this wayward stalk of grain in fertile ground. To have survived, to have avoided combat, to have had food to eat every day, to have deceived and disguised: all these were victories he'd emerged from strong and self-confident. A sense of security and a full pocket made him less unsightly. You could be sure that when he reached sixty, he'd give the illusion of having once been viewed as a handsome man with a big nose and long legs. From his superior height, he gazed straight down at Chéri, and Chéri turned away.

"Are you this far gone? Come on, Desmond. It's noon, and you're just getting up!"

"First off, I'm already dressed," Desmond snapped back, while opening his pajama top to reveal a white silk shirt and a golden-brown bow tie. "Second, I'm not going out for lunch."

"What?" said Chéri. "What ... ? I'm at a loss for words."

"But, if you like, I can give you two fried eggs, half my ham, half my salad, my stout, my strawberries. And a coffee, no extra charge."

Chéri looked at him in a helpless rage.

"Why?"

"Business," said Desmond, in an intentionally nasal tone. "Champagne. You overheard. Ah, those wine merchants! If you don't squeeze them hard ... But I'm up to the task."

He wrung his hands and cracked his fingers with mercenary pride.

"No? Yes?"

"Yes, you rascal!"

Chéri flung his fedora in Desmond's face, but Desmond picked it off the floor and dusted it with his elbow to make it clear that the time for childish pranks was over. They had the cold eggs, the ham, some tongue, and the good, dark beer with its cream-colored foam. They hardly spoke, and Chéri, while he gazed out at the paved court-yard, was politely bored.

"What am I doing here? . . . I'm avoiding being at home, having to deal with the Fulbert-Dumonteil lamb chops." He pictured Edmée dressed in white, the baby-faced American colonel, and Arnaud, the chief of staff, in whose presence Edmée played the obedient little girl. He thought about Charlotte Peloux's epaulettes, and he was shifting a sort of inconsequential affection back onto his host, when the latter abruptly questioned him: "Do you know how much champagne they drank here last night, I mean between four o'clock yesterday afternoon and four o'clock this morning?"

"No," said Chéri.

"And do you know how many bottles came in here full and left here empty between the first of May and the fifteenth of June?"

"No," said Chéri.

"Guess a number."

"I don't know," Chéri grumbled.

"Just guess! Guess a number, pick one, come on! Say a number!"

Chéri scratched at the tablecloth, as though he were sitting for an exam. He was suffering from the heat and his own sluggishness.

"Five hundred," he said, grudgingly.

Desmond reared back in his chair. For an instant, his monocle shot a painful shaft of sunlight straight into Chéri's eye.

"Five hundred! You make me laugh."

Desmond was showing off. His only form of laughter was a kind of heaving of his shoulders. He kept sipping his coffee while he let Chéri's astonishment build, and then he put his cup down. "Three thousand, three hundred and eighty-two, my dear. And do you know how much I net from that?—"

"No," interrupted Chéri. "And I couldn't care less. Leave off. I have my mother for that kind of thing. And besides..." He got up, and added, in a hesitant voice, "And besides, money... doesn't interest me."

"How strange," said Desmond, offended. "Strange. Amusing."

"Have it your way," said Chéri. "No, believe it or not, money... money doesn't interest me... doesn't interest me anymore."

It was difficult for him to voice these simple words, and he didn't raise his head. He was pushing a crust of toast around on the rug with his foot. His awkward confession and his guarded look took him back, for a moment, to his marvelous adolescence.

Now Desmond started to pay him the critical attention a doctor shows toward his patient. "Am I dealing with a malingerer?" he wondered. Like a doctor, he used a jumble of soothing words:

"You'll get over this nice and fast. Everybody feels a bit unstuck. We don't feel like ourselves anymore. Work is a wonderful way to get things back into balance, old boy... So, you see, like me—"

"I know," Chéri butted in. "You're going to tell me I need something to keep me busy."

"Because that's what you really do want, for yourself," Desmond scoffed condescendingly. "Ah, it's such a godsend..."

He was about to go on about how elated he was to be in business, but held himself back.

"It's also a question of education. Obviously, under Léa's wing, you didn't learn about life. You don't know how to handle things, or people."

"That's what people think," said Chéri, annoyed. "But Léa knew better. The proof is, though she mistrusted me, she always consulted me before she bought or sold anything."

He thrust out his chest, proud of a time in the past when mistrust was synonymous with respect.

"You only have to get back into it—to making money," Desmond counseled. "It's a game that never goes out of fashion."

"Yes," Chéri conceded, his eyes clouding over. "Yes, for sure. I'm just waiting."

"Waiting for what?"

"I'm waiting... I mean I'm waiting for an opportunity... a better opportunity..."

"Better than what?"

"You're pestering me. An excuse, if you like, to win everything back that the war kept away from me of for so long. My inheritance, which, all things considered, is..."

"Rather considerable," Desmond suggested.

Before the war, he would have said "enormous," and in a different tone. Chéri blushed, feeling ashamed for a fleeting moment.

"Yes... my inheritance. Ah well, the little one—my wife—she takes care of it."

"Oh!" Desmond groaned, shocked.

"And she does it well, let me assure you. A profit of two hundred and sixteen thousand, the day before yesterday, from that little flurry on the Exchange. So I have reason to wonder, don't I? Where do I fit in? When I try to get involved, they tell me—"

"Who are 'they'?"

"They? My mother and my wife... They say: 'Take it easy. You're a soldier. Would you like a glass of orangeade? Why don't you run over to your shirtmaker's—he's playing you for a fool. And, on your way, pick up my necklace—they've repaired the clasp.' And so on, and so forth..."

He was getting animated, hiding his resentment as best he could, but his nostrils and his lips were twitching at the same time.

"So, should I be selling cars, should I be raising angora rabbits, should I be manufacturing luxury goods? Should I get myself hired on as a nurse, or as an accountant, at that bazaar over there, my wife's hospital?"

He strode up to the window, then wheeled around to confront Desmond: "And take orders from Dr. Arnaud, chief of staff? Should I be delivering test tubes? Should I be opening a dance hall? Can you see me as a competitor?"

He laughed, in order to make Desmond laugh. But Desmond, doubtless growing bored, kept a straight face.

"Since when have you taken to thinking about all this? You weren't thinking about these things last spring, or last winter, or before you got married."

"I didn't have time," Chéri answered, with naiveté. "We went on a trip, we started furnishing the town house, we bought cars only to see them get requisitioned. All this, leading up to the war... Before the war... before the war, I was... a rich kid, somebody with a lot of money, that's all."

"You still are."

"I still am..." Chéri echoed.

He faltered again, searching for words. "But now, things are different. People are in a frenzy, like a Saint Vitus' dance. It's the same for work, for everyday activities, for women who are 'serving their country.' And are they ever!—They're all crazy for cash... Businesswomen who make you sick of the idea of business, workers who make the idea of work disgusting..."

He lifted his uncertain gaze up at Desmond. "So is it really wrong to be rich and just go on enjoying your life?"

Desmond liked playing this role. He was making up for his former dependence. He laid a protective hand on Chéri's shoulder. "My dear boy, be rich, enjoy your life. Tell yourself that you represent a venerable aristocracy. Make the feudal barons your role model. You're a warrior."

"That's crap," said Chéri.

"Spoken like a warrior. All you need to do is let the people who really are workers go ahead and work."

"You, for example."

"Me, for example."

"It's obvious that you don't let any women get in your way, do you?"

"No," said Desmond, dryly.

In fact, he kept hidden, from everyone, a perverse predilection for his cashier-bookkeeper: a sweet-looking brunette—a little hirsute

and masculine—who wore her hair tied back and a religious medallion around her collar, and who'd admit, with a smile: "Me, I'd
commit murder for a sou. That's just how I am."

"No. It's not that! Can't you talk about anything without bringing
up 'my wife' and 'those women' right away, and, as you did just now,
'my time with Léa'... Aren't there any different topics of conversation,
now that it's 1919?"

Chéri seemed to be listening to a different sound, coming from
the far side of Desmond's voice, a sound still distant, but already
audible. "Other topics of conversation?" he repeated to himself. "Why
would there be any others?" He was daydreaming, lulled by the light
and the heat, which grew more intense as the sun rolled higher in its
course. Desmond was talking away, oblivious to the sultry atmosphere,
his complexion as pale as winter cabbage. Chéri heard the word
"chicks," and listened in.

"Yes, a whole gang of them, lots of fun. Of course, I'll introduce
you...When I say 'chicks,' it's just a casual way of talking about the
choicest specimens, exceptional...Prime game birds, my regulars,
even more refined after these past four years. Ah! My boy, when I
have the capital, what a restaurant I'll start up...Only ten tables at
most, so they'll be fighting over them...I'm putting a roof over the
courtyard...My lease covers any improvements I make, you can be
sure of that! A linoleum dance floor, with spotlights over the center...
That's it, that's the future!"

The tango trafficker was sounding off like a city founder, lifting
his arm toward the window. The word "future" jolted Chéri, who
turned to look where Desmond was pointing, high above the courtyard...He saw nothing, and he felt tired. The glaring two-o'clock
sun poured mercilessly onto the slate roof of the former stable, where
Desmond's concierge was lodged.

"What a lobby this will make, eh?" said Desmond, glowing with
enthusiasm and gesturing toward the paved courtyard. "It's coming
on, and it's coming fast!"

Chéri stared at this person who expected and received his daily bread from heaven. "And what about me?" he asked himself in frustration.

"Wait, here's my pedlar of cheap champagne," Desmond yelled. "You'd better head out. I'm going to uncork him like a bottle of Corton."

He gave Chéri's hand a squeeze. Desmond's hands had changed. In the past, they were slender and limp. Now they seemed broad, gave an impression of honesty, almost of firmness. "The war," Chéri jeered, to himself.

"Where are you off to?" asked Desmond.

He kept Chéri on the front steps long enough to show him off as an attractive customer to the champagne dealer.

"Over there," said Chéri, with a wave.

"A mystery," murmured Desmond. "Be on your way, grand sultan!"

"Oh, no," said Chéri. "It's not that."

He pictured a woman, a wet body, nakedness, a mouth ... He shuddered with vague revulsion and repeated softly, "No, it's not that," and got back into his car.

He left with a malaise he knew only too well: the agitation, the unease of never having come out with what he wanted to express, of never having met the person to whom he should have made some indefinable confession, told a secret that might have changed everything and dispelled the sense of ill omen from this afternoon of bleached paving stones, of asphalt gone oozy under the sun's downpouring rays ...

"Only two o'clock," he sighed to himself. "And this month it stays light past nine ..."

The breeze—whipped up by the speed of his open roadster—wrapped around his face like a hot, dry bedsheet; he longed for the artificial night of the blue-curtained bedroom, accompanied by the three-note tune of the garden fountain in the middle of its Italian basin.

"If I hurry through the front hall, I can get in without being noticed. They'll be just sitting down to coffee over there ..."

He could smell the refined luncheon, the lingering scents of melon and of the dessert wine that Edmée would have served after the fruit; he could see in advance Chéri's green-tinted reflection closing the mirror-backed door...

"Let's get it over with!"

Two automobiles—his wife's, and the American car—were resting under the low foliage in front of the gate. They were entrusted to a lone American chauffeur, who was asleep. Chéri steered as far as the rue de Franqueville—deserted at this hour—then walked back to his front door, which he opened without a sound. He gave his reflection a once-over in the green mirror and quietly climbed the stairs to the bedroom. It was just how he wanted it to be: blue, perfumed, devoted to rest. Everything his parched excursion had lacked was here to be found. And plenty more, because a young woman in white was powdering her face and arranging her hair in front of a tall mirrored panel. Her back was turned to Chéri, and she didn't hear him come in. This gave him enough time to study her features in the mirror. They were flushed with the heat of the day and the meal, cloaked in a remarkable combination of disarray and triumph, an air of intense emotion and scandalized victory. Now Edmée glimpsed her husband, gave no cry of surprise, turned without hesitation. She looked him over from head to foot, expecting him to be the first to speak.

Through the window, half-opened to the garden, the baritone voice of Dr. Arnaud drifted up, singing "Ay, Mari, ay Mari..."

Edmée's whole body moved toward this voice, but she resisted turning her head in the direction of the garden.

The vaguely drunken resolve in her eyes could have presaged words of grievous consequence. Either out of cowardice or disdain, Chéri called for silence by raising a finger to his lips. Then with the same peremptory finger he pointed to the staircase. Edmée obeyed and strode resolutely ahead of him. When the distance between them was at its shortest, she couldn't suppress a forward arching of her lower back and an acceleration of her pace. In Chéri, this aroused a fleeting impulse to punish her. He leaned against the handrail, serene like a cat at the top of a tree. Again, he thought of doling out punishment, of breaking things to pieces, of running away. He expected a wave of jealousy to spur him into action. Nothing came, except for a slight, everyday feeling of shame, which was easy to bear. Even so, he kept on saying to himself: "Punish her, smash it all to bits . . . But there must be something better to do . . . Yes, there must be something better . . ." Only he didn't know what that was.

Every day, whether he woke up early or late, he began a day of waiting. At first, he didn't worry about this; he assumed it to be the persistence of a morbid military mindset.

It was December 1918. He was back home, in his civilian bed, prolonging a minor convalescence from a dislocated kneecap. At dawn, he would stretch and smile. "I feel well. I expect I'll feel even better. Christmas will really be something this year!"

At Christmastime, once the truffles had been consumed and the bough of holly, soaked in eau-de-vie, had been set alight on a silver platter, Chéri sat facing a waiflike and wifely Edmée. While he took in plaudits from Charlotte, Madame La Berche, some members of the nursing staff, and an assortment of Romanian officers and athletic, barely adolescent American colonels, Chéri waited. "Ah! I wish all these people would clear out! I can't wait to breathe some fresh air and sleep with my feet warm in my comfortable bed." Two hours later, stiff as a corpse, he was waiting for sleep to come. Some cheerful winter owls were hooting from the branches, calling out to the bluish light of the half-shuttered bedroom windows. At last, he slept.

But at daybreak, in the grip again of his insatiable expectancy, he tried to sound cheerfully impatient while he waited for breakfast. "What the hell are they doing down there with the sock juice?" he shouted out. He didn't realize that his use of this crude phrase—a piece of what was called "trooper talk"—always coincided, in him, with a finicky state of mind and a sort of evasive geniality. He ate his breakfast, served by Edmée. But he sensed haste, the call of duty, in his wife's quick movements. It was only out of spite—to delay Edmée's departure and delay the resumption of waiting—that he asked for another piece of toast, a little bit of warm bread he no longer really wanted.

A Romanian lieutenant—whom Edmée employed sometimes to search for paraffin dressings and hydrophilic cotton, sometimes to lobby ministers ("What the government refuses to a Frenchman, a foreigner can always obtain!" she declared)—would fill Chéri's ear with boasting about the duties of a soldier who was all but unscathed and the heavenly purity of the Coictier Hospital. Chéri accompanied Edmée there, to see for himself. He sniffed the antiseptic odor that implacably evoked the stench of festering wounds. He recognized a comrade among the "trench foot" victims, sat down on the side of the bed, and forced himself to show common feeling the way war novels and patriotic plays teach one to do. Yet he felt keenly that, as a man who'd escaped in one piece from the war, he had neither fellows nor equals among the disabled. He saw the white flock of female nurses around him, the dark shades of burnt heads and hands above the bedsheets. An unbearable impotence weighed on him; he surprised himself by crossing an arm over his chest, out of respect, and hobbling a little. But the next moment, in spite of himself, he was filling his lungs and treading the marble floor—between the supine mummies—with a bounce in his step. He felt a reluctant reverence for Edmée, on account of her authority as a ranking angel, and her snowy whiteness. She crossed the room and touched Chéri's shoulder as she passed by. But he knew that she wanted, with this gesture of tenderness and gentle possession, to make a young nurse—a brunette, who was gazing at Chéri with the guilelessness of a cannibal—blush with envy and annoyance.

He was bored and weary, like someone who, having been taken to a gallery, grows impatient in front of the tightly spaced rows of masterpieces. Too much whiteness rained down from the ceilings, glanced off the floors, drenched the corners. He felt sorry for the stricken men who weren't getting the benefit of any shade. Noon forces wild animals to rest and take refuge, forces birds to stay quiet in the depths of the forest, but civilized man no longer follows the commands of the sun. Chéri took a few steps toward his wife. He intended to say: "Draw the curtains, set up a punkah, take the plate of noodles from that poor soul who's blinking and having trouble breathing. Have him eat when it gets dark instead . . . Give them some shade, give them some color other than this whiteness, always this white . . ." Dr. Arnaud's arrival quelled Chéri's desire to give counsel and be of service.

The doctor, with his reddish-gold hair, his belly swathed in white linen, hadn't taken three steps into the room before the ranking ascendent angel came back to earth to resume her mission as a humble handmaiden of God, flushed with faith and zeal . . . So Chéri turned toward Filipesco, who was handing out American cigarettes, and hailed him contemptuously: "You coming?" Chéri led him away, but not before waving goodbye to Edmée, Dr. Arnaud, and the nurses of both sexes, with the affable haughtiness of an official visitor. He crossed the rough gravel of the little courtyard, climbed back into his car, and allowed himself only a ten-word soliloquy: "The move is predictable. It's the chief-of-staff move." He'd never cross the threshold of the hospital again. From this day onward, Edmée would invite him only as a formal courtesy, the way one offers the roasted snipe to the vegetarians at dinner.

He was prone to reflection now, and a prey to an idleness that had been so easy before the war, so varied, but now rang like an empty, flawless wineglass. During the war, he'd withstood the military routine of inactivity, of inactivity in spite of the cold, the mud, the risks, the state of alert, even a little combat. Having been raised as a young hedonist to pursue a life of leisure, he'd watched with impunity as vulnerable, ill-prepared companions pined away from silence, loneliness, and impotence. He'd witnessed the devastating effects, on intelligent beings, of the dearth of reading material: it was comparable to being deprived of the daily dose of an intoxicant. While he—soothed by a short letter, a postcard, a thoughtfully assembled parcel—would lapse back into silence like a cat in a nocturnal garden, men who were considered his superiors would reveal that they were breaking down, as though literally starved. So he'd learned to reinforce his patience with pride, pride that depended on two or three ideas, two or three tenacious memories, richly colored like children's memories, and with his inability to imagine his own death.

Time and time again during the war, when he awoke from a long, dreamless sleep or from a rest break that had been interrupted every minute, he found himself cut loose from the present, stripped of his most recent past, and sent back to childhood—sent back to Léa. Seconds later, Edmée would reappear, in sharp outline, fully formed, and the resurrection of her image, no less than its brief banishment, would put Chéri into good humor. "This way, I have the best of both," Chéri observed. Nothing came in the mail from Léa, and he didn't write to her. But he did receive postcards signed by Ma Aldonza's contorted fingers, and cigars selected by the Baroness de La Berche. He dreamed for a while with a long, soft woolen scarf under his cheek. He loved this scarf because of its eye-blue color and the faintest trace of perfume it would emit when he was hot and tired, and he pressed himself against it in the dark. Then it lost its fragrance and its fresh suggestion of blue eyes, and he thought of it no more.

For four years, he didn't inquire about Léa. If he had, some venerable lookouts would have recorded and reported happenings he could hardly have imagined. What possible link could there be between Léa and illness, between Léa and change?

In 1918, the words "Léa's new apartment" escaped from the lips of the Baroness de La Berche and left him incredulous.

"She's moved?"

"Where have you been hiding?" the baroness snapped back. "Everybody knows. It was a nice bit of business, selling her town house to some Americans! I've seen her new apartment. It's small, but cozy. Once you sit down in there, you can't get up again."

Chéri latched on to these two words: "small, but cozy." Short on inspiration, he forced himself to picture a pink interior; threw in the enormous spice boat made of gold and steel, the spacious bedstead with its cargo of lace; and, from a sort of scudding cloud, he hung the Chaplin painting with its nacreous nipple.

When he learned that Desmond was seeking a silent partner for his dance hall, Chéri was worried and watchful. "The lowlife, he's going get Léa to loan him the money, drag her into a deal ... I'm going to phone her and warn her." However, he did nothing of the sort. Because phoning a forsaken lover is riskier than holding out your hand to an anxious enemy who's trying to catch your eye in the street.

He still waited, after the day of the surprise in front of the mirror ... after that wanton display of elation, of flushed cheeks, of confusion. He let time go by and didn't make the certainty of a complicity—still almost innocent—between his wife and the man who was singing "Ay, Mari!" any worse by putting it explicitly into words. In fact, he was feeling less burdened. He forgot, for several days, to check his wristwatch aimlessly, as he used to do when dusk was about to fall. He got into the habit of sitting out in the garden in a wicker armchair as though he'd arrived, at the end of a journey, in the garden of a hotel. He watched, amazed, as the encroaching darkness blotted out the blue of the monkshoods and replaced it with another blue into which the form of the flowers dissolved, even as the green of the mass of foliage remained distinct. The border of pink carnations turned a putrid shade of purple and sank rapidly into obscurity. Then the yellow stars of July caught fire between the branches of the narrow-leafed ash.

At his own home he tasted the pleasure felt by a passerby who stops to rest in a public square. He didn't ask himself how long he lingered there, leaning back, hands dangling. Sometimes he thought about what he called "the mirror scene," the atmosphere of the blue bedroom covertly disturbed by the appearance of a man, his movements, his flight. Under his breath, Chéri would say to himself, with deliberate and mechanical stupidity: "So, here we have a fait accompli. This is what you call a fait-accompli," putting emphasis on the *t* of the liaison.

At the beginning of July, he tried out a new roadster, which he called his "spa mobile." He took Filipesco and Desmond for rides on roads bleached white by the dry weather. But he would head back toward Paris every evening, cleaving through currents of warm and cool air that lost their scent as the city drew closer.

One day he took along the Baroness de La Berche, a virile companion. At the customs gates she gave her little felt cloche, pulled down tight, a tap with her index finger. He found her easygoing, sparing of words, good at spotting taverns shaded by wisteria and village bars that smelled of the cellar and wine-soaked sand. Motionless, in silence, they covered some two hundred miles; they removed the bit from their teeth only to smoke and to feed. The next day Chéri issued a terse invitation to Camille de La Berche—"Shall we saddle up, Baroness?"—and took her out for a second run.

The high-class convertible penetrated the verdant countryside, then returned to Paris in the evening, like a child's toy reeled in at the end of a string. Without taking his eyes off the road, Chéri could make out to his right the profile of the old woman with the face of a man: noble, like the countenance of an elderly coachman from a respectable house. He was amazed to find that she was respectable because she was unaffected, and he began to grasp dimly—being alone with her, for the first time, away from town—that a woman endowed with sexual deviance can bear it bravely, with a certain grandeur, like a convict on her way to the gallows.

Since the war, she'd no longer indulged in her wickedness. The hospital put her back in her place, that is to say, among the males, who were just young enough, just subdued enough by grief, for her to live peacefully in their midst and forget about her extinct femininity.

Secretly, Chéri observed his companion's large nose, her graying, shaggy upper lip, her beady peasant's eyes, which wandered indifferently over the ripe grainfields and mown pastures.

For the first time, he felt himself drawn toward the venerable Camille by an impulse that resembled friendship, a feeling of commonality. "She's alone. When she isn't with her soldiers, or my mother, she's alone. She, too... Aside from her pipe and her glass of wine, she's alone."

On their way back to Paris they stopped at a "country inn" where there was no ice to be had; where rosebushes fried by the sun were expiring, attached to shafts of stone columns and old baptismal fonts set out as lawn ornaments. A nearby woods sheltered this powdery precinct from the breeze, and a compact, cherry-red cloud stood sentinel at the top of the sky.

The baroness emptied her stubby brierroot pipe on the ear of a marble satyr.

"It'll be hot in Paris tonight."

Chéri nodded in agreement and lifted his head toward the cherry-red cloud. Pink reflections settled on his white cheeks and dimpled chin, like the patches of rouge that give an actor's face a radiant glow.

"Yes," he said.

"Oh—you know what, if it tempts you, let's not go back until tomorrow morning. I'd need only a minute to buy some soap and a toothbrush...We'd give your wife a call. We could set sail at four in the morning, when it's cool and fresh..."

Chéri got up impulsively.

"No. No. I can't."

"You can't? Come on now!"

Below him, he saw the small mannish eyes and the fleshy, trembling shoulders.

"I didn't think it still had such a hold on you," she said. "But, so long as it does..."

"What?"

Heavy, robust, she stood up and gave him a sharp slap on the shoulder.

"Yes. Yes. You go scampering around during the day, but you head back to your hole in the ground every night. Ah! You're really stuck!"

He looked at her coldly. He already liked her less.

"Nothing escapes your notice, Baroness. I'm bringing the car around for you now. In two hours, we'll be at your door."

Chéri never forgot their nocturnal trip back: the redness that lingered, mournfully, in the west; the scent of pasturelands; the feathered moths entrapped in the headlights' beams. A block of black made thicker by the dark, the baroness stayed watchful by his side.

He drove carefully. When he slowed down at the bends, the cool air of the straightaways changed to warm. He had confidence in his sharp eyesight and quick reflexes, but he was preoccupied, in spite of himself, with the strange, massive woman sitting motionless to his right, and he experienced a sort of terror, a nervous disturbance that brought him within inches of colliding with an unlit farm cart. It was then that a fleshy palm lightly touched his forearm. "Pay attention, my dear boy."

He paid no attention, to be sure, to either her gesture or her tone of distress. But nothing accounted for the emotion that ensued, or this knot, this hard lump in his throat. "I'm an idiot, I'm an idiot," he kept repeating to himself. He slowed down and diverted himself with the broken shafts, the golden zigzags, the peacock fans that danced around taillights for a moment or two through the tears that were filling his eyes.

"She said it had a hold on me, that I was really stuck. If she could see us, Edmée and me . . . How long have we been sleeping side by side like brothers?" He tried to count: three weeks, maybe more? "What's even funnier is that Edmée doesn't ask for a thing. She's all smiles when she wakes up." In his own mind, he always used the word "funny" when he wanted to avoid the word "sad." "An old married couple. That's what we are, an old married couple . . . madame and her chief of staff, monsieur and . . . his car. Anyway, old Camille said I was stuck. Stuck. Stuck. If I ever take her out again . . ."

He did take her out again, because July turned Paris into an inferno. But neither Edmée nor Chéri complained about the heat wave. Chéri would come back in the evening, well-behaved, distracted, the backs of his hands and the lower half of his face tanned walnut-brown. He would walk around naked between the bathroom and Edmée's boudoir.

"You must have cooked today, you poor Parisians!" Chéri taunted.

A little pale and depleted, Edmée straightened her pretty slave girl's back and denied she was tired. "Oh well, not all that bad, believe it or not. The air was fresher than yesterday. My office over there stays cool, you know. Anyway, we don't have time to think about it. My dear little twenty-two-year-old, who was doing so well . . ."

"Ah, yes?"

"Yes. Dr. Arnaud doesn't like the way he looks."

She never hesitated to push the name of the chief of staff forward, the way one advances a winning piece on a chessboard. But Chéri didn't frown. So Edmée kept her eyes on the naked man; his bare skin was tinted a delicate green by reflections from the blue curtains. He passed back and forth in front of her: there for the taking, pristine, trailing his fragrant aura, already out of reach. The very confidence of this naked body, incomparable, haughty, left Edmée languishing in a state of vaguely vindictive immobility. This naked body . . . At this moment, she could only have demanded it in a voice from which the cry of urgency was missing; in the considerate voice of a submissive partner. An arm covered with fine gold down, an ardent mouth under a golden moustache: these held her attention now. Protective, demure, self-assured as a lover who has designs on a virgin inaccessible to everyone else, she contemplated Chéri.

They began talking again, about vacations, departure dates. Their responses were casual, mundane.

"The war hasn't changed Deauville enough. And, what a mob . . ." Chéri sighed.

"There's nowhere to eat anymore. Reorganizing the hotel industry is a tough proposition!" Edmée declared.

Around the 14th of July, over lunch, Charlotte Peloux announced a successful "venture in loan hedging," and lamented out loud that Léa had shared equally in the profits. Chéri raised his head in astonishment.

"So you mean you still see her?"

Charlotte Peloux bathed her son in a loving gaze as cloying as aged port wine and called on her daughter-in-law to back her up. "A question like that . . . a question like that . . . it's like somebody who's been mustard-gassed. Don't you think? Like somebody who's been gassed. It makes me worry, sometimes. I've never stopped seeing her, my dear. Why would I have stopped seeing her?"

"Yes, why?" Edmée chimed in.

He looked at the two women and found that their benevolence had a strange aftertaste.

"It's just that you never talk about her..." he began, naively.

"Me!" barked Charlotte. "Listen here... No, listen... Edmée, do you hear him? In fact, it's all a tribute to his feelings for you. He's managed to completely forget everything that isn't you."

Edmée smiled without answering, lowered her head, and, plucking at it with two fingers, lifted the lace that bordered the décolletage of her dress. Her movement led Chéri's eyes toward her bodice. He could see that her nipples and their mauve areolae—like two matching bruises—were showing through the yellow linen. He shuddered, and realized from his shudder that Edmée's graceful body, in its most immodest details, her impeccable bearing, the whole of this young woman next to him—unfaithful and freely available—no longer aroused in him anything but a distinct repugnance. "Shake it off! Shake it off!" But he was flogging a dead horse. And he heard Charlotte pouring out, in a nasal stream:

"Just the other day I was saying, right in front of you, that when it comes to a car I'd prefer a taxi, *a taxi*, to Léa's decrepit Renault. And then, even the day before yesterday... no, it was yesterday, I was saying, when I was talking about Léa, that if you're going to keep a male servant when you're a single woman, you might as well have a gigolo. And Camille, when she was with me the other evening, said that she regretted she'd had a second barrel of Quart-de-Chaume sent on to Léa instead of keeping it for herself... Seeing as I've complimented you on your fidelity, I'm going to reproach you for your ingratitude. Léa deserved better from you. Edmée would be the first to acknowledge that!"

"The second," Edmée corrected.

"I didn't hear any of it," said Chéri.

He was gorging on hard, pink July cherries and tossing some, under the lowered awning, to the sparrows in the garden. Overwatered, it was steaming like a hot spring. Edmée, inert, was dwelling on Chéri's last words: "I didn't hear any of it." He certainly hadn't lied, yet his offhand manner, his false childishness as he squeezed a cherry pit between his fingers and took aim, with his left eye closed, at a songbird, spoke what were almost audible words to Edmée. "What was he thinking about, when he wasn't hearing anything?"

Before the war, she would have suspected another woman. A month earlier, on the day after the mirror scene, she would have feared reprisals: some sort of savage cruelty, a bite on the nose. But no... nothing... He went on living harmlessly, roaming about, untroubled in his freedom like a prisoner in the recesses of his cell, chaste like an animal imported from the antipodes that doesn't even try to seek out a female in our hemisphere.

"Is he sick?" He'd been getting enough sleep, and eating however he liked, which is to say, fussily. He would sniff at meats with suspicion, being partial to fruits and fresh eggs. No nervous tic marred the fine equilibrium of his features, and he drank more water than champagne. "No, he's not sick. And yet, he has . . . something. Something I'd be able to guess, no doubt, if I were still in love with him. But . . ." Again, she lifted the lace of her décolletage and inhaled the warmth, the scent rising from her bosom. Lowering her head, she saw the matching mauve and pink medallions of her breasts appear through the cloth. She blushed with sensual pleasure and pledged this fragrance, these mauve shadows, to the redheaded man, skillful and patronizing, whom she would be meeting again in an hour.

"They've been talking about Léa every day, right in front of me, and I haven't noticed. So, does this mean I've forgotten her? I have forgotten her. But what does it mean, to forget? If I think about Léa, I can see her, clearly, I remember the sound of her voice, the perfume she used to spray herself with and rub in, all wet, with her big hands."

He tightened his nostrils and lifted his mouth toward his nose, in a scowl of delectation.

"Fred, you just made a horrible face, you were the spitting image of the fox that Angot brought back from the trenches."

They were getting through the least difficult part of their day, after they'd woken up and eaten breakfast. Revived by their morning shower, they listened with gratitude as a heavy rain fell, three months ahead of season, tearing off the leaves of Paris's false autumn and flattening the petunias. On this particular morning, they didn't bother to look for an excuse for their stubborn decision to stay in the city for the summer. Hadn't Charlotte Peloux, the day before, relieved them of any embarrassment by declaring: "We're the real Parisians! The true and the pure! Along with the concierges, we can say we've really enjoyed the first postwar summer in Paris!"?

"Fred, are you in love with that suit? You never take it off anymore. Don't you realize it's out of style?"

Chéri waved his hand in the direction of Edmée's voice, a gesture that demanded silence and begged that no one should distract him while he was dedicated to an exceptionally cerebral task.

"I'd like to know if I've forgotten her. But what does it mean, to forget? After I haven't seen her for a year..." He felt a little shock of awakening—a start—and realized his memory was blanking out the war years. Then he counted them, and for a minute, he was mute with astonishment.

"Fred, will I ever be able to get you to leave your razor in the bathroom, instead of bringing it in here?"

He turned around, listlessly. Nearly naked and still damp, he bared his chest, silvery with patches of talc.

"What was that?"

His distant-sounding voice made her laugh.

"Fred, you look like a badly frosted cake! A cake that looks unwell... Next year, we won't be so silly. We'll have an estate out in the country."

"You want an estate?"

"Yes. Not this morning, obviously..."

She was pinning up her hair, pointing with her chin toward the curtain of rain cascading down, without wind or thunder, from a gray storm cloud.

"But maybe next year... Right?"

"It's a thought. Yes, it's a thought."

He was putting her off, politely, in order to go back into his state of astonishment. "I really thought it had been only a year since I'd seen her. I wasn't thinking of the war. So it's been one, two, three, four, five years since I've seen her. One, two, three, four... But, if that's so, doesn't it mean I had forgotten her? No, because they've been talking about her right in front of me, and I haven't jumped up and shouted: 'Hold on, that must be true, but what's all this about Léa?' Five years... How old was she in 1914?"

He counted again, and came up with an implausible number. "Wouldn't that make her almost sixty by now? What a ridiculous idea..."

"The important thing would be," Edmée went on, "not to make the wrong choice. A pretty part of the country. Let's see, there's—"

"Normandy," Chéri finished her sentence, distractedly.

"Yes, Normandy... Do you know much about Normandy?"

"No... Not exactly... It's green. There are lindens... ponds..."

He closed his eyes, as if dazed.

"Where do you mean? Which part of Normandy?"

"Artificial ponds, fresh cream, strawberries, pheasants..."

"So you know a lot about Normandy! What a place! All of that, and what else besides?"

He sounded as though he was reading out a description while he was leaning toward the circular mirror. This was where he habitually checked, after his ablutions, that his cheeks and his chin were nice and smooth. He continued, passive and hesitant. "Pheasants... the moon on the floorboards, and a big, big red rug thrown down on a lane..."

He didn't finish his sentence. He rocked back and forth unsteadily and slipped on the rug. The side of the bed broke his fall midway. The unmade sheets cushioned his dizzy head; his suntan, layered over his pallor, tinted his face an ivory green.

Almost the instant he fell, and without a sound, Edmée dropped to the ground and cradled his lolling head in her hand. She held a vial of smelling salts under his bloodless nostrils. But two shaky arms pushed her away.

"Leave me alone...You can see I'm dying."

However, he wasn't dying, and his hand stayed faintly warm between Edmée's fingers. He'd spoken in a murmur, with the suave theatricality of suicidal youngsters who for a brief moment court, and then slip away from, death.

He half parted his lips over his sparkling teeth. He was breathing regularly. But he was in no hurry to come completely back to life. He was taking refuge, behind his eyelids and his lashes, in the heart of the green domain he'd conjured up just before he swooned: a level expanse, rich in strawberry vines and honeybees; lily ponds bordered with banks of warm stone...When he did revive, he kept his eyes shut. "If I open them, Edmée will see everything I'm looking at..."

She stayed leaning forward with one knee bent. She was ministering to him efficiently, professionally. With a free hand, she reached for a magazine and used it to fan the air around his lolling forehead. She whispered insignificant but necessary words.

"It's the storm...Relax...No, don't get up. Wait while I slide a pillow under you..."

He sat up, smiled, thanked her with a squeeze of his hand. A thirst for lemons, for vinegar, made his throat feel parched. The ringing of the telephone pulled Edmée away.

"Yes...Yes...What's that? I know very well it's ten o'clock. Yes. What?"

From the peremptory tone of the answers, Chéri realized it was someone calling from the hospital.

"Yes, of course, I'm coming. What? In..."

She gave Chéri a quick glance to gauge how far he'd come back to life.

"In twenty-five minutes. Thanks. See you soon."

She opened both sides of the double glass door, and a few gentle drops of rain entered the room, along with a stale smell of river.

"Do you feel better, Fred? What came over you? Nothing to do with your heart, I hope? You must be low on phosphates. On account of our ridiculously hot summer. But what can you expect..."

She glanced furtively at the telephone, as if it were a witness.

Chéri stood up without any obvious effort.

"Get going, darling. You'll be late for work. I feel completely fine."

"A sip of rum toddy? A little hot tea?"

"Don't worry about me...You've been very kind. Yes, a little tea. Ask them for it on your way out."

Five minutes later, she left, after giving him a look she thought showed nothing but concern. But it was a look that sought in vain for a truth, for an explanation of an inexplicable state of affairs. As if the sound of the closing door had unshackled him, Chéri stretched his limbs, felt unburdened, cold, and empty. He sped toward the window, saw his wife cross the front garden, with her head bowed, in the rain. "She looks guilty from behind," he declared, "she's always looked guilty from behind. From the front, she looks like a fine little woman. But her back tells a different story. My fainting spell made her lose a good half hour. But let's get back to the case at hand, as my mother would say. When I got married, Léa was fifty-one (at the very least! according to Madame Peloux). So by now she must be fifty-eight, maybe even sixty...The same as General Courbat? Come on!...It's just a joke!"

He tried to conjure the image of a sixty-year-old Léa, with the white moustache and sunken cheeks of an aged general and a stance like that of a superannuated cab horse.

"It's the funniest thing imaginable..."

Madame Peloux's arrival found Chéri lost in his state of distraction, pale, standing still while he looked down on the rain-soaked garden, chewing on a burnt-out cigarette. He didn't bat an eyelid as his mother came in.

"Here you are, off to an early start, my dear Mama," he said.

"And you, who look like you woke up on the wrong side of the bed," she shot back.

"A mere illusion. Do you have a good excuse for being up and about, at least?"

She raised her eyes and shrugged her shoulders at the ceiling. The brim of a little leather cap, sporty and impish, covered her forehead.

"My poor dear," she sighed, "if you knew what I have on the go at the moment . . . If you knew what a monumental project . . ."

He gave his mother's face a searching look and saw the deep furrows—like double chevrons—around her mouth; and the soft, compact swelling of her double chin, whose ebb and flow concealed and then revealed the collar of her raincoat. He felt the weight of the quivering pouches of her lower eyelids, while he kept repeating to himself: "Fifty-eight . . . sixty . . ."

"Do you know what it is, the project I'm putting all my energy into? Do you?"

She waited a moment, then opened her big eyes, ringed with black pencil, even wider. "I'm resurrecting the thermal baths at Passy. The Passy baths. Yes, naturally, it means nothing to you. The hot springs are right there, under rue Raynouard, just two steps away. They're lying in wait, they only need to be revived. Very potent waters. If we pull it off, it will mean the end of the spas in the Alps—Uriage, maybe even Mont-Dore—wouldn't that be something! I already have guarantees of support from twenty-seven Swiss doctors. Edmée and I have been working on the Paris city council . . . Which, by the way, is why I'm here, but I must have missed your wife by a minute or two . . . What's the matter with you? Are you listening to me at all?"

He was stubbornly trying to light his damp cigarette. He gave it up and tossed it onto the balcony, where big drops of rain were splashing skyward like grasshoppers. He looked his mother up and down, sternly.

"I am listening to you," he said. "And I know what you're going to say before you even say it. I know all about this business of yours. It has different names: scheming, trickery, bribes, founder's shares, American hedging deals, dried beans, and so on . . . Do you think I've been deaf and blind for the past year? You're a bunch of mean, nasty women. That's all there is to it. I don't hold it against you."

He stopped talking and sat down, rubbing, as was his wont, the pair of tiny matching scars below his right breast. He was gazing at the verdant, rain-soaked garden. Across his slackened features, a battle was underway between weariness and the vitality of youth. The former was hollowing his cheeks, darkening the sockets of his eyes, while the latter was still present in the ravishing curve and fleshy firmness of his lips, in the downy wings around his nostrils, in the black luxuriousness of his hair.

"Ah well," Charlotte Peloux said at last. "I get it! Sanctimony roosts where it can. It seems I gave birth to a moral guardian."

He neither spoke nor stirred.

"And from what lofty place do you pass judgement on this poor, corrupted world? From the height of your integrity, no doubt?"

Trussed up like a knight in a leather jerkin, she was at the top of her form, and ready for a fight. But Chéri appeared to be done with battles of any kind.

"Of my integrity... It could be. If I'd tried to find the right word, I wouldn't have found that one. You're the one who's come up with it. Let's stick with 'integrity.'"

She said nothing in return, leaving her counterattack for later. She stayed quiet in order to focus all her attention on the strange appearance of her son. He had his elbows on his knees and was spreading them apart, while tightly gripping his hands. He kept looking at the garden, beaten down by the lashing rain. After a minute, without turning to her, he said with a sigh, "Do you think this is any kind of a life?"

Without missing a beat, she asked, "Whose life?"

He raised his arms, then let them drop.

"My life. Your life. Everything around us."

Madame Peloux paused for a moment. Then she threw off her leather jacket, lit a cigarette, and sat down.

"Are you bored?"

Seduced by the unaccustomed sweetness in her voice—it sounded airy and solicitous—he became genuine, almost trusting.

"Bored? No, not bored. Why would you think I'm bored? I'm a bit... how can I put it: I'm a bit concerned, that's all."

"About what?"

"About everything. About me, even about you."

"You can see I'm taken aback."

"Me too. These people . . . this year . . . this peace . . ."

He spread his fingers apart, as though they'd felt stuck together or tangled in a lock of hair.

"You say that the way people used to say 'this war' . . ."

She placed a hand on his shoulder, and lowered her voice in a tone of empathy. "What's troubling you?"

He couldn't stand the probing pressure of this hand. He stood up and paced around, erratically.

"What's troubling me is that everybody's rotten to the core. No," he begged, when he saw an air of affected superiority on her maternal countenance. "No, don't start up again. No, present company is not excluded. No, I don't see us living in an age of glory, with a new dawn here, a miraculous rebirth there. No, I'm not angry, I don't love you any less, and I don't have liver disease. But I do know I've reached the end of my tether."

He paced around, cracking his knuckles, inhaling the faintly sweet-smelling mist produced by the heavy rain as it struck the balcony. Charlotte Peloux tossed aside her hat and her red gloves, investing the gesture with the character of a peace offering.

"Explain yourself, dear. We're all alone."

She smoothed back her thinning, boyishly cut, hennaed hair. Her sulfur-yellow dress hugged her tightly, like a sheet of canvas wrapped around a wine cask. "A woman . . . She was a woman . . . Fifty-eight . . . sixty . . ." Chéri was lost in reflection. Charlotte turned to him with her lovely velvet eyes, full of a maternal coquettishness whose feminine power he'd long since forgotten. Caught suddenly in his mother's gaze, he glimpsed the danger, the difficulty of the explanation she was coaxing him to make. But he felt slack and empty, preoccupied with what he lacked. At the same time, the hope of upsetting her drove him on.

"Yes," he said, in answer to himself. "You have your hedging schemes, your pasta imports, your civic awards. You make jokes about the chamber of commerce and the law courts. That murderess, Madame Caillaux, fascinates you. So do the Passy hot springs. For Edmée, it's her warehouse full of wounded soldiers and her chief of staff. Desmond—he plays around with dance halls, the wine trade, pimping. Filipesco, he filches cigars from the Americans and the hospitals, then sells them in the nightclubs. Jean de Pouzac, he plays the stock market ... And that says it all ... What a motley crew ... What a ..."

"You're forgetting about Landru, the guy who killed seven women," Charlotte slipped in.

He gave her a cheerful wink, a silent tribute to the malicious sense of humor that made the faded champion seem younger than her years.

"Landru doesn't count. That sort of case was common before the war. There's nothing unusual about Landru. But the rest of them ... Well ... to be blunt, they're a bunch of lowlifes, and ... and that's not to my liking. There you have it."

"Blunt, yes, but not very clear," Charlotte said, a moment later. "You do a good job of describing us. Notice I'm not saying that you're wrong. I do gain some advantages from my failings, and nothing scares me. But none of this explains what you're trying to get at."

Chéri rocked awkwardly in his seat. He was knotting his eyebrows and creasing his forehead, as though he was trying to stop the wind from tearing off his hat.

"What I'm trying to get at ... I don't know. I wish people weren't rotters ... that they were more than just rotters. Or else I wish I could simply ignore them."

He was manifesting such a lack of confidence, such a need to give in to his malaise, that Charlotte tried to cheer him up.

"But why do you pay them any notice?"

"Ah, that's it ... That's right. Precisely."

He smiled at her—a smile of resignation—and she noticed how much less youthful her son's face looked when he smiled. "We should feed him bad news, nonstop, she thought. Either that, or drive him mad. Cheerfulness doesn't suit him." Through a puff of smoke, she came out with her own bland vacuity.

"You hadn't noticed any of this before?"

He raised his head abruptly.

"Before? Before what?"

"Before the war, of course."

"Ah, yes..." he murmured, downcast. "No, before the war, obviously... But before the war I saw all of this differently."

"Why?"

This one word left him speechless.

"I'll tell you why," Charlotte mocked, "it's because you've gone straight!"

"You wouldn't want to admit, by any chance, that I've simply stayed the same?"

"No, no. Let's not get mixed up!"

Her cheeks flushed, she was arguing the point with the intensity of a soothsayer.

"Anyway, your way of life before the war—I'm putting myself in the shoes of narrow-minded people who see only the surface of things, understand! That sort of existence... Anyway, there's a name for it!"

"If you like," Chéri conceded. "And so?"

"Well, it suggests a... a way of looking at things. You saw existence through the eyes of a gigolo."

"It's quite possible," said Chéri, with indifference. "What of it? Do you see anything wrong with that?"

"Certainly not," Charlotte objected, with childlike simplicity. "But don't you agree, there's a time for everything?"

"Yes..."

He sighed profoundly, his head raised toward the sky, which was shrouded with cloud and rain. He continued: "Yes, there's a time to be young and a time to be not so young. There's a time to be happy... Do you think I needed you to be able to figure that out?"

All at once, she became agitated and stalked back and forth across the room, showing her plump bottom squeezed into her dress. Thick-set and nimble, like a pudgy little canine, she came back and planted herself in front of her son.

"All right, darling. You're well on your way, I fear, to some kind of foolishness."

"And what would that be?"

"Oh, there aren't so many possibilities. A monastery. Or a desert island. Or love."

Chéri smiled in amazement. "Love? You want me to ... Love with ..."

He cocked his chin toward Edmée's boudoir, and Charlotte's eyes glittered.

"Who's saying anything about her?"

He laughed, and his instinct of survival made him go back to talking crudely. "In a minute you'll be offering me some American broad!"

She defended herself with a histrionic start. "Some American broad? Absolutely! And why not one of those rubber dolls they make for sailors, too?"

He approved of this chauvinistic disdain coming from a professional. Since childhood, he'd known that a Frenchwoman doesn't debase herself by living with a foreigner, as long as she takes advantage of him, or he brings her to ruin. He knew, by heart, the catalogue of insulting epithets that a native Parisian courtesan draws on in denigrating a fallen woman from another country. But he turned his mother's offer down without irony. Charlotte drew back her short arms and projected her lower lip, like a physician who admits to being at a loss.

"I'm not proposing you work ..." she ventured, discreetly.

With a shrug of his shoulders, Chéri dismissed her unwelcome suggestion. "To work," he repeated, "to work would mean associating with the lot of them ... You don't work on your own unless you're a postcard painter or a seamstress ... Poor, dear mother, you don't get it: if men disgust me, women leave me cold. The truth is, I can't stand the sight of women anymore, either," he concluded, bravely.

"My God!" Charlotte shrieked.

She pressed her hands together as if she were facing a fallen horse. But her son enjoined her to silence with a wave. She felt admiration for the virile authority of this beautiful young man who'd just revealed his own peculiar form of impotence.

"Chéri! ... My dear boy!"

He looked at her with a mild, vacant expression, vaguely pleading. She gazed deeply into those wide eyes. Maybe their pure whites, long lashes, and suppressed emotion exaggerated their brightness. She wanted to delve down, through these sumptuous portals, to an inscrutable heart, a heart that had first begun to beat, long ago, next to her own. Chéri seemed not to resist and to delight in being hypnotically probed. Charlotte had already seen her son ill, irritable, elusive. She'd never seen him wretched. This sight induced in her a rare exaltation: the swoon that throws a woman at a man's feet when she dreams of turning him—the desperate stranger—into the dependent stranger; in other words, when she dreams of making him forget his despair.

"Listen, Chéri..." she murmured, very softly. "Listen... You should... Wait, come on now, at least let me speak—"

He cut her off with a furious shake of his head, and she stopped insisting. She broke their protracted, mutual gaze, picked up her coat, put on her leather cap, and made her way toward the door. But as she passed by the table, she stopped and casually picked up the telephone.

"May I, Chéri?"

He nodded his consent, and she started emitting her nasal tones, like a clarinet:

"Hello...hello...Hello...Passy 29-29. Double 29, young lady. Hello...Is that you, Léa? But of course it's me. What awful weather, eh?...Don't go on about it! Yes, very well. Everybody's very well. What are you up to today? Not budging? Ah! That's the Léa I know and love, the great hedonist! Me? Oh you know! I'm not my own mistress anymore....Oh! But no, it's not about that anymore, it's something completely different! A hugely ambitious enterprise... Ah, no, not over the telephone!...You'll be at home all day? Good. That makes it easy. Thanks. See you soon, Léa dear!"

She set the receiver down, keeping only her convex back turned toward her son. While she walked away, she inhaled blue smoke and ejected it in jets. Then she vanished, along with her cloud, like a sorceress who's accomplished her mission.

He climbed, at a measured pace, the single flight of stairs that led to Léa's apartment. At six in the evening, after a rain, rue Raynouard rang loud with bird calls and children's shouts, like a playground at a boarding school. The entry lobby, with its thick mirrors, hand-buffed stairway, and blue carpeting; the elevator cage, adorned with as much lacquer and gold as a pasha's palanquin: he cast a cold eye on all of this and didn't even register surprise. On the landing, he felt like the patient whose pain suddenly disappears as he approaches the dentist's door. He came close to turning around. But the thought that he might feel compelled to return dissuaded him, and he rang with a determined finger. A young housemaid, a brunette—wearing a butterfly bow of sheer linen over her close-cropped hair—took her time opening the door. Chéri, faced with an unfamiliar visage, lost his last chance of feeling any emotion.

"Is madame in?"

The young housemaid eyed him with admiration, unsure of what to do.

"I don't know, monsieur ... Was monsieur expected?"

"Of course." He spoke with his former harshness.

She left him standing there and disappeared. In the semidarkness, he scouted with his unadjusted eyes and hypersensitive nose. There was no blond perfume in the air, and a cheap, pine-scented resin crackled in an electric burner. Chéri felt put out, like someone who's come to the wrong floor. But a big innocent laugh on a low, descending scale rang out, muffled by a heavy curtain, and plunged the uninvited visitor into a vortex of memories.

"If monsieur would like to pass through to the salon ..."

He followed the white butterfly bow, while repeating to himself: "Léa's not alone ... She's laughing ... She's not alone ... As long as it's not my mother ..." Daylight tinged with pink greeted him from inside a doorway, and he stood there waiting for the realm prefigured by this dawning to reopen again at last.

A woman was writing, with her back turned, sitting at a secretaire. Chéri made out broad shoulders, and a grainy roll at the base of the neck underneath a vigorous growth of thick gray hair, cut like his mother's. "Well, I was right, she's not alone. But who can that old woman be?"

"Write the address down for me too, and the name of the masseur. You know…me and names…" said an unfamiliar voice.

A seated woman dressed in black had just spoken, and Chéri felt an inward stirring of anticipation. "So, now…where is Léa?"

The gray-haired woman turned around, and Chéri absorbed the shock of her blue eyes head-on.

"What? Good lord! My dear, is it you?"

He came forward, as if in a dream, and kissed a hand.

"Princess Cheniaguine—Monsieur Frédéric Peloux."

Chéri kissed another hand and sat down.

"Is he…?" asked the lady in black, talking about him in the third person as openly as if he were deaf.

The big, benign laugh rang out again, and Chéri tried to locate its source…there, here, anywhere else…anywhere but from the throat of this gray-haired woman…

"Oh, no! He's not. Or, more precisely, he isn't anymore! Come on, Valérie, what are you getting at?"

She wasn't monstrous, but vast, invested with a generous development of every part of her body. The thick flesh on her upper arms, as fat as thighs, kept them from resting at her sides. The plain skirt and the long, nondescript jacket—half-unbuttoned to reveal a pleated jabot—proclaimed the usual abdication and withdrawal from femininity, and a sort of sexless dignity.

Léa stayed standing between Chéri and the window. Her substantial mass, almost blocklike, didn't dismay him at first. When she moved to take a seat, she revealed her outlines, and he started pleading with her mentally, as if she were an armed madman. Her complexion was red—a slightly overripe red, since she'd come to disdain powder—and she laughed with a mouth full of gold. In short: a healthy, mature woman with wide jowls and a double chin, capable of bearing her burden of flesh, liberated from struts and stays.

"So, tell me, darling, where have you come from in such a state? You're not looking your best, are you?"

She held a box of cigarettes out to Chéri, and he was horrified to find her manner so direct and jovial, like an old man's. She was calling him "darling," and he looked away as though she'd said something indecent. But he pleaded with himself to be patient, in the vague hope that this first impression would give way to a radiant revival.

The two women were observing him calmly, sparing him neither their goodwill nor their curiosity.

"There's a bit of Hernandez in him," said Valérie Cheniaguine.

"Oh, no, I don't agree," Léa objected. "Maybe ten years ago . . . but even then! Hernandez had a stronger jaw."

"Who's that?" Chéri forced himself to ask.

"A Peruvian, who died in a car accident, something like six months ago," said Léa. "He was with Maximilienne. She was grief-stricken."

"Even if she did find ways of consoling herself," said Valérie.

"Same as anyone would have," said Léa. "Would you really have wanted her to die of it?"

She laughed again, and her bright blue eyes disappeared behind her broad, uplifted cheeks. Chéri turned toward the woman in black: a sturdy brunette, ordinary and feline, like countless women from the south. She was dressed with such meticulous good taste that it seemed like a form of disguise. Valérie wore the timeless uniform of foreign princesses and their ladies-in-waiting: a tailored suit jacket and skirt of middling cut, black, with tight armholes, and a sleeveless, sheer cambric blouse, a bit constricting at the level of the breasts. The pearl buttons, the renowned necklace, the upright, whalebone collar: everything, like the name she legitimately bore, was worthy of a princess. In the same royal fashion, she sported everyday hose, walking shoes, and costly gloves embroidered in black and white.

She was looking at Chéri as though he were a piece of furniture: attentively, and without courtesy. In a loud voice, she returned to her critical comparison.

"Yes, I'm telling you, there's something of Hernandez. But to listen to Maximilienne, Hernandez never existed, now that she has a firm hold on her famous Amérigo. And there's more! There's more! I speak with full knowledge of the facts: I saw him myself, her Amérigo.

I've just come back from Deauville. I saw them there, the two of them."

"No! Do tell!"

Léa sat down, filling an armchair entirely. She had a new habit of tossing back her head of thick gray hair. With each of these movements, Chéri could see the lower part of her face—like Louis XVI's—quiver for a moment. Ostensibly, she was paying attention to Valérie. But more than once, Chéri caught a flutter of her narrowed blue gaze as it tried to catch her unexpected visitor's eye.

"So, here's the thing." Valérie started telling the tale. "She'd hidden him in a villa in some godforsaken place, far away from Deauville. But this didn't meet Amérigo's requirements—you get my drift, monsieur! He complained to Maximilienne. She was piqued. 'Ah! So that's how it is? You want people to see you? Well, then: they will see you!' And she phoned and reserved a table for the following evening at the Normandy. An hour later, everybody knew about it, and I booked a table for myself along with Becq d'Ambez and Zahita. And we were saying to ourselves: 'So, we'll get to see this human marvel!' At nine o'clock sharp, in walks Maximilienne, all decked out in white and pearls, and Amérigo... Ah! My dear, what a disappointment! Tall, yes. That we expected. But rather too tall. You know my opinion of men who are too tall: I'm still waiting for someone to show me one, just one, who's well built! The eyes, yes, the eyes, I don't object to the eyes. But, from here to here, look, from here to here, there was something about the cheeks that was too round—something a bit silly—and the ears were tacked on a little too low... In short, a disappointment!... And there was a stiffness in the back."

"You're exaggerating," said Léa. "The cheeks, as for the cheeks, they're not so bad. And from here to here, the form's fine, really, it's well bred; the brows, the bridge of the nose, the eyes, they're fine! I grant you, his chin won't take long to get puffy. And his feet are too small—the most ridiculous thing for a boy that tall."

"On that, I don't agree with you. But I did notice that the thigh's too long, compared to the lower part of the leg, from here to here."

They were coolly debating, weighing up and scrutinizing the forequarters and hindquarters of a prize piece of horseflesh.

"Connoisseurs of meat on the hoof," thought Chéri. "They would have done a good job in the army Supply Corps."

"When it comes to proportions," Léa went on, "no one will ever come close to Chéri...You see, Chéri, you've come at the right moment. Go ahead and blush! Valérie, if you could remember Chéri, just six, seven years ago..."

"But of course I remember him. And monsieur hasn't changed that much after all this time...You were really proud of him!"

"No," said Léa.

"You weren't proud of him?"

"No," said Léa evenly. "I loved him."

In one motion, she swung her imposing bulk and rested her cheery gaze, free of any ulterior motive, on Chéri.

"It's true I loved you. And loved you well."

Abashed and ashamed, he lowered his eyes before these two women, while the bulkier one was affirming with equanimity that she and he had been lovers. At the same time, the sound of Léa's voice—almost masculine, voluptuous—besieged his memory with an agony he could hardly bear.

"You see, Valérie, how ridiculous a man looks when you remind him of something to do with an affair from the past? Silly boy, I'm glad to remember what we had. I'm quite happy with my past. I'm quite happy with my present. I don't regret what I used to have, and I don't miss what I don't have anymore. Am I wrong, darling?"

He let out a cry like someone whose toes have been crushed.

"But no! Of course not! On the contrary!"

"It's nice that you've remained good friends," said Valérie.

Chéri waited for Léa to explain that this was the first time in five years that he'd set foot in her home, but she only laughed unaffectedly and gave a knowing wink. His agitation was increasing. He didn't know how to object, how to cry out that he wasn't trying to regain the affection of this huge woman, who dressed like an elderly cellist;

and that, if he had known, he would never have climbed the stairs, never have crossed the threshold, never have trod the carpet, never have curled up in the feathered armchair in the depths of which he was now lying impotent and mute...

"Ah well, I'm off," said Valérie. "I don't want to wait for rush hour on the metro. Not on your life."

She got up, turned, and faced the bright daylight that was kind to her Roman features. They were so solidly formed that almost sixty years had barely touched them, and were enhanced, in the old-fashioned style, with white powder applied evenly over both cheeks and a smooth, almost blackish rouge on her lips.

"You're on your way home?" Léa asked.

"Yes, I am. And what will my little rascal get up to, once she's left to her own devices?"

"Are you still happy with your new apartment?"

"A dream! Especially since I had the iron bars put in the windows. And a steel grille over a fanlight I hadn't noticed at first, in the pantry. So, along with my entry buzzer and burglar alarm... Ugh! It was high time for me to feel at a bit more secure."

"And your town house?"

"All taken care of. On the market. And the paintings stored away. At eighteen hundred francs a month, my little mezzanine's a treasure. No more servants lurking about and looking like hired assassins. You remember those two footmen I had?... They still give me the shivers."

"You really did find it depressing, didn't you."

"You'd have to have lived through it yourself to have any idea, my dear... Monsieur, a pleasure... Don't get up, Léa."

She wrapped them both in her silky, savage gaze and left the room. Chéri watched her move away and reach the front door, but didn't dare follow in her tracks. He stayed frozen, almost annihilated by the conversation between these two women who'd spoken of him in the past tense as though he were a dead man. But Léa was already starting up again and breaking into laughter. "Princess Cheniaguine! Sixty million! And a widow! And she isn't happy! If that's what it means to live the good life...well, really...no!"

Her hand, raised in exclamation, smacked her thigh as if it were the rump of a mare.

"What's the matter with her?"

"She's scared. Just scared. She's a woman who doesn't know how to handle money. Cheniaguine left her everything. But he might have done more harm by giving it than he would have done by taking it away. Did you hear her?"

She let herself sink into the hollow of the plush armchair. Chéri abhorred the soft sigh the cushion made underneath her huge backside. She ran the tip of her finger along a groove in the wooden molding of the arm, blew on a patch of dust, and her face darkened. "Ah! Nothing's the same anymore, even when it comes to servants, eh?"

He felt drained. The skin around his mouth was stiff, as if he'd been exposed to a severe chill. He was holding back a terrible surge of bitterness and entreaty, the urge to cry out: "Stop! Come back to life! Drop this masquerade! I know you're in there somewhere, because I can hear your voice! Break out of it, come back brand-new, freshly hennaed and powdered; put on your lace-up corset again, your blue dress with the fine ruffles, your prairie-land scent that I'm trying in vain to find in your new home ... Leave it all behind, come with me through rain-soaked Passy, past its flocks of birds and packs of dogs, all the way to avenue Bugeaud, where Ernest must be polishing the brass on your front gate ..." He shut his eyes, utterly exhausted.

"My dear, I'm going to give you some good advice: you should have your urine tested. Your complexion, the pinched look around your lips, I know what they mean: you're not taking care of your kidneys."

Chéri reopened his eyes, filled them with the sight of the serene disaster facing him, and said, heroically, "Do you think so? It's quite possible."

"There's no doubt about it. And you're too thin ... They may say the best fighting cocks are the scrawny ones, but you could do with another ten pounds ... on balance."

"Pass them over," he said, with a smile.

But his cheeks felt strangely stiff and resistant to his smile, as if his skin had aged.

Léa broke into her happy laugh, the same laugh that would have greeted some glaring impertinence from the "bratty nursling" in days gone by. At the sound of this deep, full-throated laugh, Chéri experienced a delight he wouldn't have been able to endure for long.

"Oh! It wouldn't do me any harm! I've put some on, eh? Look here ... and here ... Can you believe it?"

She lit a cigarette, blew twin jets of smoke through her nostrils, and shrugged. "It comes with age!"

The words took flight from her lips with a lightness that restored to Chéri a sort of extravagant hope. "Yes, it's a joke. In no time, she's going to show her real self to me ..." He fixed her with a gaze that she appeared, briefly, to understand.

"I've changed, eh, little one? Fortunately, it doesn't matter. But you seem, I don't know ... down for the count, as we used to say. Eh?"

He didn't like this new, halting "eh?" that punctuated Léa's sentences. But he braced himself for each interrogation, and with each he restrained an impulse whose motive and aim he didn't want to recognize.

"I'm not asking if you have any troubles at home. First of all, it's none of my business. And second, your wife, I know her as well as if I'd raised her myself."

He was listening to her, but not attentively. Most of all he noticed, when she wasn't smiling or laughing, that she no longer conformed to a definite sex. In spite of her enormous breasts and massive rear end, she'd made the transition, by virtue of her age, to an altogether easygoing virility.

"And I know she's very capable—that wife of yours—of satisfying a man."

He couldn't conceal an inward laugh, and Léa promptly continued, "I said *a* man. I didn't say *any* man. Here you are, at my place, out of the blue. I can't imagine you've turned up for the sake of my beautiful eyes, eh?"

She let them rest on Chéri, her "beautiful eyes": reduced in size, riddled with blood vessels, mocking, neither cruel nor kind, certainly knowing and glowing, but ... Where was the healthy sheen that used to bathe their whites in azure? Where their contour, rounded like a fruit, like a breast, like a hemisphere, and blue, like a land fed by many a river?

With a comical sneer, he said, "Pooh!...The great detective!"

He was amazed to find himself sitting in a carefree posture, his legs crossed, like a handsome young blade who wasn't minding his manners. Amazed because, in his mind's eye, he was observing his distraught alter ego down on his knees, arms waving, chest bared, wailing incoherently.

"I'm no more stupid than the next woman. But you have to admit, you haven't put me to much of a test today."

She inflated her chest, spreading her double chin over her collar; and the alter ego, down on his knees, bowed his head as if he were being beaten to death.

"You look exactly like someone who's suffering from the sickness of the times. Let me speak!...You're just like the rest of your fellow soldiers: you're looking for your heavenly reward, eh, the heaven we owed you after the war? Your victory march, your being able to feel young again, your beautiful women...We owed you everything, we promised you everything, it was all so well deserved...And what is it you find? Nothing but a pleasant little life. So now you indulge in nostalgia, lethargy, disappointment, neurasthenia...Am I wrong?"

"No," said Chéri.

Because he'd have cut off his little finger to make her stop talking.

"Ah!" Léa went on, raising her voice. "You're not the only one, are you! How many have I seen, since the war ended, boys just like you...?"

"Really? Where?" Chéri broke in.

The abruptness of the interruption, its aggressive tone, left Léa's benign lyricism hanging in the air. She withdrew her hand.

"But there's no shortage of them, my dear. Are you still proud of yourself, all the same? Did you think you were the only one who finds the taste of peacetime disappointing? Think again!"

She gave a low laugh and tossed her gray locks playfully around a meaningful smile, like an expert judge of wine.

"Does it make you proud to go on wanting to be the only one like you!"

She pulled back a little, sharpened her gaze, and concluded, with what could have been vindictiveness, "You were unique...but only for a while."

Behind the vague but telling insult, Chéri felt her femininity return, and he sat upright, happy at the prospect of feeling less pain. But Léa was already becoming kind again.

"But you didn't come here to be told that. Did you decide on the spur of the moment?"

"Yes," said Chéri.

He would have preferred this "yes" to have been the last word between them on the subject. He was wary; his eyes were wandering all over Léa. He picked a wafer off a plate and put it down again, convinced that, if he took a bite, gritty cinders of pinkish brick would fill his mouth. Léa noticed his movement and the painful way he tried to gulp back his saliva.

"Oh! Oh! Are we a bit on edge? Pouting like a little pussycat with rings under its eyes. What a lovely sight!"

He closed his eyes and meekly submitted to hearing her without seeing her.

"Listen, darling, I know a bistro on Gobelins..."

He reopened his eyes, earnestly hoping she was going mad and that, consequently, he could forgive her both her physical deterioration and her erratic old woman's ways.

"Yes, I know a bistro...Don't interrupt! The thing is, we need to get there before the Clermont-Tonnerres and the Corpechots declare it to be chic, and the cook gets replaced by a chef. It's the country-woman herself who's doing the cooking now, and, mmm, darling..."

She raised her fingers to her mouth in a kiss of approval. Chéri shifted his gaze toward the window, where the shadow of a branch was whipping through the sun's rays at even intervals, like a blade of grass bobbed by the steady rippling of a stream.

"What a strange conversation..." he risked, his voice cracking.

"No more strange than your being here *chez moi*," Léa shot back, sharply.

He signaled with a wave that he wanted peace—only peace—and

not a lot of talk; even silence . . . He sensed this aging woman's renewed powers and resilient appetite, and he was beating a retreat. Léa's hot blood was already rising, violet, to her grainy neck and her ears. "She has the neck of an old hen," Chéri noted, with the bloodless and cruel satisfaction he used to feel in days gone by.

"It's true, what I said!" Léa hurled, in high temper. "You show up here looking like Fantômas, and I'm trying to find a way to work things out . . . I do know you pretty well, after all . . ."

He smiled at her, dejectedly. "How could she possibly know me? People smarter than her, even than me . . ."

"A certain kind of melancholy, my dear, and disillusionment, they come from the stomach. Yes, yes, laugh if you like!"

He wasn't laughing, but she could have thought he was.

"Romanticism, nervous breakdowns, disgust with life: it's the stomach. All of this: it's the stomach. Even love! If you were honest, you'd admit that there's well-fed love, and there's badly fed love. All the rest is just stuff they write in books. If I were a good writer or a good talker, my dear, I'd have plenty to say on the subject . . . Oh! Naturally, I wouldn't invent anything, but at least I'd know what I was talking about. Which would be a welcome change from writers nowadays."

Something worse than this culinary philosophy was causing Chéri to grimace: an affectation, a fake sense of ease, a studied sprightliness. He suspected that Léa was playing the jovial epicurean, the same way a fat actor in the theater plays "good-natured" roles because he has a potbelly. As if defiant, she rubbed her shiny nose, blotched with vermilion, with the back of her index finger, and thrust her chest out with the help of the two flaps of her long jacket. In doing so, she displayed herself to Chéri with excessive smugness. She even ran her hand through her stiff gray hair and gave it a toss.

"Does it look good on me, short hair?"

He deigned to respond only with a mute look of dissent, the way one brushes off a tiresome argument.

"So, you were saying, there's a bistro on avenue des Gobelins . . . ?"

Following suit, she responded with a knowing, unvoiced "no," and he could tell, by the twitching of her nostrils, that he'd finally started to annoy her a little. An animal wariness was reviving in him, sooth-ing his anxiety, resharpening his instincts. Up until now they'd been thrown into disarray. He aimed—getting past her unapologetic bulk, her graying curls, and her friarly good cheer—to communicate with the hidden creature to whom he was returning as though to the scene of his crime. A feral, delving instinct kept him circling around the buried treasure. "How did it happen that she got old? Suddenly, one morning? Or little by little? And this load of fat that makes armchairs creak? Is it some grief that's turned her into this and unsexed her? What grief? Is it because of me?"

But he posed these questions only to himself, in silence.

"She's angry. She's coming closer to understanding what I want. She's going to tell me…"

He saw her get up, walk around, gather up some papers on the dropped leaf of the writing desk. He noted that she was holding herself more upright now than when he first came in, and as he fol-lowed her with his gaze she straightened up even more. He resigned himself to the fact that she was truly enormous. There were no curves visible between her underarms and her hips. Before she turned back toward Chéri, she tightened a white silk scarf around her neck, in spite of the heat. He heard her breathing deeply. Then she swung around to face him again, with the relaxed rhythm of a heavy animal, and smiled at him.

"I think I've received you very badly. It's impolite to welcome somebody by giving them advice, especially useless advice."

A string of pearls, which Chéri recognized, popped out from a fold in the white scarf, coiled downward, and gleamed in the sunlight.

Captive underneath the pearls' ethereal surfaces, the seven colors of the rainbow played like occult flames inside each of the precious spheres. Chéri recognized the pitted pearl, the slightly ovoid pearl, and the biggest pearl, which stood out for its matchless shade of pink.

"They…they haven't changed! They, and me, we haven't changed."

"And you still have your pearls," he said.

The stupidity of this statement surprised her, and she seemed to want to interpret it literally.

"Yes, I was able to hold on to them, in spite of the war. Do you think I would have, or should have, been able to sell them? Why would I have sold them?"

"Or 'for whom?'" he said in jest, but his tone was weary.

She didn't restrain herself from taking a rapid glance at the writing desk and its scattered papers. Now Chéri, in his turn, wanted to interpret her glance, and he related it to a yellowed visiting card with the portrait of a bewildered-looking, callow little serviceman ... He pondered, with haughty disdain, the image he conjured up. "This doesn't matter to me." A moment later he added, "But what does matter to me, here?"

The unease he'd brought along was spreading outside him, amplified by the sinking of the sun, the cries of hungry swallows on the chase, and the ember-colored shafts passing through the curtains. This incandescent pink ... he remembered that Léa carried it everywhere she went, the way the sea, when the tide goes out, bears away earthy scents of flocks and hay.

They didn't talk for a while, rescued by the sound, drifting in from outside, of a lively children's song, to which they seemed to listen. Léa was still standing. Erect, massive, she was raising her incurable chin, and a sort of malaise was being translated through the rapid batting of her eyelids.

"Am I holding you up? Do you need to go out? Do you want to get dressed?"

His questions were abrupt, and they forced Léa to look at Chéri.

"To get dressed? And in what, milord, would you like me to get dressed? I am dressed—and that's the end of it."

She laughed her incomparable laugh, which began high and cascaded down, at equal intervals, to a low register reserved for sobs and amorous moaning. Chéri unconsciously raised his hand in entreaty.

"Dressed for living, I'm telling you! In things that are easy, comfortable. Smocks, fine lingerie, and this uniform on top: this is me decked out. Prepared for dinner at Montagné's just as well as at Monsieur Bobette's, ready for the cinema, for bridge, and a walk in the woods."

"And for the lover you're not mentioning?"

"Oh! darling!"

She blushed unabashedly behind her chronic, arthritic redness, and Chéri, after enjoying the craven satisfaction of having come out with a few injurious words, was seized with shame and regret in the face of her girlish reaction.

"I was trying to make a joke," he said clumsily. "Have I shocked you?"

"Hardly. But, you know, I've never been partial to a certain brand of vulgarity, or to jokes that fall flat."

She was making an effort to talk calmly, but her face revealed that she was wounded, and its coarse surface trembled with a disturbance that could have been an expression of modesty.

"My God, what if she's getting ready to weep..." He foresaw disaster: tears covering these cheeks hollowed out by a single, deep crease on either side of her mouth, eyelids reddened by the salt of her tears... He said, all in a rush, "Oh, no. Come on now! What a thought! I didn't want...come on now, Léa—"

She gave a start, and he realized that he hadn't yet called her by her name. Proud, as in the past, of her self-mastery, she gently interrupted.

"I don't hold it against you, dear. But since you're here for just a few minutes, don't leave me with anything sordid."

He was touched neither by her gentle manner nor by her words, which he found inappropriately sensitive.

"Either she's lying, or this is who she really has become. Peace and quiet, innocence, and what else? It suits her like a nose ring. Peace of mind, good grub, the flicks... She's lying, she's lying, she's lying! She's trying to make me believe it's easy, even enjoyable, to turn into an old woman... Let her tell that to other people! Let her tell them her fibs about what a good life she has, about the bistro with its country cooking. But not me! I was born surrounded by fifty-year-old beauties, electric massagers, and smoothing creams! Not me, who's seen all of my painted pixies fighting over the suggestion of a wrinkle, tearing each other to pieces over a gigolo!"

"Believe it or not," she added, "I'm no longer used to your way of going quiet. Seeing you sitting there, I feel every second that you have something to tell me."

Still on her feet, separated from Chéri by a side table holding the port wine glasses, she made no attempt to avoid his harsh scrutiny. But certain, barely visible signs were flickering across her face. And in between the flaps of her long jacket Chéri could detect the muscular effort she was making to pull in the weight of her potbelly.

"I wonder how many times she put her corset on, took it off, then bravely put it on again, before she gave it up for good?... How many mornings did she change the shade of her face powder, rub her cheeks with a new kind of rouge, massage her neck with cold cream and a chunk of ice wrapped in a handkerchief, before she resigned herself to having her cheeks shine like patent leather?"

She might only have been trembling, imperceptibly, with impatience. But because of this trembling he kept on expecting—stubbornly, unconsciously—a miracle of emergence, a metamorphosis...

"Why don't you say something?" Léa pressed.

She was losing her composure, bit by bit, in spite of her resolve. With one hand, she was toying with her string of heavy pearls, twisting and untwisting their timeless, luminous nacre—veiled by an indescribable mist—around her long, faded, carefully manicured fingers.

"Maybe it's just that she's afraid of me," Chéri mused. "A man who doesn't say anything, as I'm doing now—he's always a bit of a lunatic. She's thinking about Valérie Cheniaguine's fears. If I raised my arms, would she scream bloody murder? Oh, my poor Nounoune..."

He was afraid of saying this name out loud, and he talked in order to prevent himself from revealing a sincere emotion, however fleeting.

"What must you think of me?" he asked.

"That depends," Léa answered, circumspect. "Right now, you strike me as the type that leaves a box of cakes on the hall table on his way in, thinking, 'There'll be other chances to offer this,' and picks it up again on his way out."

Lulled by the sound of their voices, she was thinking like the Léa of old, perspicacious and shrewd, in the way peasants can be shrewd. Chéri stood up and shifted the table that separated them, so that he was bathed—full in the face—by the bright late-afternoon light passing through the bay window with its pink drapery. At her ease, Léa could read in his features—which were almost unaltered, but would all be imminently under assault—the cumulative effect of the days and the years. A deterioration as hidden as this was capable of eliciting her pity, of stirring up memories, of wresting from her the word, the gesture, that would make Chéri's head spin in humility. Exposing himself to the sunlight—his eyes lowered, as though he were asleep—he ran the ultimate risk of a final affront, a final entreaty, a final homage...

Nothing happened, and he reopened his eyes. Once more, he had to accept the true picture: at a safe distance, his well-fleshed former lover was showing him a measure of goodwill with her wary, narrowed blue eyes. Disillusioned, distraught, he tried to find her anywhere in this room where she was nowhere to be found. "Where is she? Where is she? This one's hiding her from me. I'm getting on her nerves. She's thinking—while she's waiting for me to leave—that all these memories are just a nuisance, that this apparition from the past...But anyway, what if I did call out to her to come to my rescue, did ask her to let me have Léa back..." Inside himself, his kneeling alter ego was still flinching, like a body being drained of its blood...With an effort he felt utterly incapable of making, Chéri extricated himself from his tortured mirror image.

"I'll be on my way," he said out loud. And then added, in a tone of trite refinement: "And I'll take my box of cakes with me."

Léa's overflowing bosom rose with a sigh of relief.

"As you wish, my dear. But you know, I'm always at your disposal, if you're ever feeling troubled."

He sensed the resentment behind her false benevolence. The enormous, fleshy edifice, crowned with a silvery thatch, had produced, once more, a feminine sound; had rung, all of a piece, with penetrating harmony. But the ghostly apparition—reduced to his phantom-like sensitivity—needed, in spite of himself, to vanish into thin air.

"Certainly," Chéri replied. "I thank you."

From now on, he knew, without fail or false airs, how he ought to take his leave, and the appropriate words flowed from him effortlessly, like an incantation.

"You know why I came here today...Why today instead of yesterday?...I should have come a long time ago...But you forgive me..."

"Naturally," said Léa.

"I'm even more mixed-up than I was before the war, you understand, so—"

"I understand, I understand."

Because she was cutting him off, he thought she was in a hurry to see him go. But a few more words passed between them during Chéri's retreat; there was the sound of a table being bumped; a patch of daylight, in a contrasting blue, that poured through a window open to the courtyard; a large hand studded with rings that rose to Chéri's lips; one of Léa's laughs that halted halfway in its habitual descent, the way the spray of a fountain, broken off at its height, cascades as a string of pearls...Like the bridge that connects two dreams, the stairway passed under Chéri's feet, and he found his way back to rue Reynouard...which he didn't recognize.

He did notice that the pink sky was being reflected by the stream in the gutter—which was still swollen with rain—and off the blue backs of the swallows that were swooping level with the ground; and, because the evening air was cooling down and the memory he'd taken away with him was shrinking, like a traitor, into the inmost depths of his being—there to assume its definitive power and scale—he believed he'd forgotten all about it, and he felt happy.

Only one old woman, who coughed heavily over a crème de menthe, disturbed the peace of this barroom, where the hum of the place de l'Opéra died down as though muffled by a dense layer of air impervious to the resounding turbulence outside. Chéri ordered a champagne cocktail and wiped his hairline. He'd acquired this fastidious habit long ago, when, as a little boy, he used to hear the music of feminine voices trading pearls of wisdom with biblical solemnity: "If you want real cucumber milk, make it yourself... Don't rub your face when it's drenched with sweat, it goes back inside your skin and eats it away..."

The silence of the uncrowded bar created an illusion of freshness. Chéri didn't immediately see a couple, leaning their heads close together over a table, who were lost in indecipherable whispering. A minute or two later, he did take notice of the unknown man and woman, because their murmuring allowed a few hissing consonants to escape and their exaggerated expressions made their faces stand out: the faces of two impoverished bellhops, overworked and long-suffering.

He took two draughts of his champagne cocktail, threw his head back against the yellow velvet of the banquette, and felt the burden of thought—which had been draining him of energy for the past two weeks—deliciously melt away. His heavy mood hadn't followed him over the threshold of the old-fashioned bar—with its reddish interior, garlands of gilt rosettes, and decorative rustic chimney—where the washroom attendant, half-glimpsed in her realm of faience tiles, was draping her white hair forward under a green lamp while she darned linens, counting her stitches.

A passerby came in, didn't set foot in the yellow lounge, drank standing up at the bar—as if trying to be discreet—and left without saying a word. Only the toothpaste smell of the crème de menthe offended Chéri's nostrils; he frowned toward the indistinct old woman at the table next to him. Under a soft, black, battered hat, he glimpsed a timeworn face, accented here and there with heavy powder, wrinkles, kohl, blisters—all jumbled up, like the keys, handkerchief, and coins you've thrust pell-mell into a pocket. An aged, vulgar face, all in all, and unexceptional in its vulgarity, showing hardly any wild or abject indifference. She coughed, opened her handbag, gave her nose a cursory wipe, and set the blackish reticule back on the marble table-top. Her bag resembled her hat; cut from the same black taffeta, kneaded and threadbare.

Chéri followed her movements with exaggerated distaste. For the past two weeks, he'd been suffering, beyond reason, from everything feminine and old. He thought about leaving because of the reticule sprawled on the table; he wanted to turn his eyes away, but didn't, his attention held by a little twinkling arabesque, an unexpected glint coming from the folds of the bag. His curiosity surprised him, but, thirty seconds later, he was still looking at the twinkling spot and had utterly ceased wondering what it might be. He emerged from his stupor with a triumphant, involuntary start that restored free play to his breathing and his thoughts.

"I know! It's two intertwined 'L's!"

He enjoyed a moment of sweet relief, something like the feeling of having arrived safely at the end of a journey. He really did forget about the close-cropped nape, the vigorous head of gray hair, the long, nondescript jacket buttoned over a potbelly, and the innocent peals of contralto laughter: all the thoughts that had been dogging him so tenaciously and robbing him, for the past two weeks, of the desire to eat and the freedom to be alone.

"This is too good to last," he thought. In fact, he did summon the courage to bring himself back to reality, looked again at the offending object, and rhymed off the precise details. "The pair of initials Léa had designed for her doeskin change purse, in tiny gems, and then, later on, for her golden tortoiseshell toiletry set, and her stationery!"

He didn't admit the possibility, even for a moment, that the monogram on the bag could belong to any other name, and smiled ironically. "Some other people might think so! But you can't teach me anything about this kind of coincidence. Today, I come across this purse by chance; tomorrow, my wife will hire one of Léa's former valets, again by chance; and from then on, I won't be able to go into a restaurant, a cinema, or a tobacco shop without encountering Léa everywhere I turn. It's my fault, I have no excuse. All I had to do was let her be."

He put some bills down next to his glass and stood up before he called out to the barman. He turned his back to the old woman while he slid between their two tables, sucked in his stomach like a tomcat squeezing under a door, contained himself with such adroitness that the hem of his jacket barely brushed the glass of crème de menthe, mouthed "Pardon me" under his breath, made a dash for the glass door—to get to the threshold of breathable air—and heard, to his horror, without being the least surprised, someone call out "Chéri!"

Steeling himself for the all too predictable shock, he turned around and failed to recognize, in the old wreck, anything he could put a name to. But he didn't try to escape for a second time, knowing that everything would now be revealed.

"You don't recognize me? No? And how would you recognize me? That war, it aged more women than it killed men, you might say. Still, I can't complain. I didn't risk losing anyone in the war... Eh, Chéri...?"

She laughed. And now he did recognize her, realizing that what he'd taken for decrepitude was mostly poverty and profound indifference. Sitting up straight, laughing, she didn't look any older than sixty, which she probably was, and her hand, which reached out for Chéri's, wasn't that of a trembling grandmother at all.

"La Copine..." Chéri murmured, in a tone almost of admiration.

"So, you're glad to see me?"

"Oh, yes...!"

He wasn't lying. He was gradually calming down, thinking, "It's only her... Poor little la Copine... and I was afraid..."

"Would you drink something, Copine?"

"Just a whiskey soda, pretty one. Haven't you stayed handsome, though!"

He swallowed down the bitter compliment, which she tossed to him from the placid seashore of her old age.

"And decorated too," she added, out of pure politeness. "Oh! I knew about your medal, you know! We all knew about it."

This ambiguous "we" failed to coax a smile from Chéri, and la Copine thought she'd shocked him.

"When I say 'we,' I'm talking about the women who were your real friends, Camille de La Berche, Léa, Rita, me... You better believe it wasn't Charlotte who told me. I don't exist for her. But you can be just as sure she doesn't exist for me."

She gravely extended a wan hand, long deprived of sunlight, across the table.

"You see, from now on Charlotte won't be anything more to me than the woman who managed to have poor little Rita held under arrest for twenty-four hours... Poor Rita, who never even knew a word of German. Was it her fault, was it Rita's fault, that she was Swiss?"

"I know, I know, I've heard the story," Chéri interrupted, abruptly.

La Copine lifted her huge, dark, unctuous eyes, full of an inveterate complicity and a compassion that was always misplaced.

"Poor kid," she sighed. "I understand you. Forgive me. Ah! You've had your own cross to bear!"

He gave her a questioning look, unused as he was to the superlatives that always gave la Copine's vocabulary a funereal richness. He was afraid she might go on about the war. But she wasn't thinking about the war. Maybe she'd never thought about it, because concerns about the war affect only two generations. She explained herself: "Yes, I'm saying that a mother like yours is a heavy cross to bear, for a son like you, a child who lived a life beyond reproach before your marriage, and afterwards! A peaceful child, who didn't flit from one affair to the next, and managed to keep his inheritance intact!"

She shook her head. And now his memory of her began to revive little by little: a common prostitute, with a big, ravaged face, one who'd grown old without dignity and free from disease, who'd smoked opium and then given it up—opium, the drug that's merciful to those who are unworthy of it—with impunity.

"You don't smoke anymore?" Chéri asked, suddenly.

She raised her pale and neglected hand.

"You'd better believe it! That sort of nonsense, it's all very well when you aren't on your own. Back when I would do things to impress the kids, yes... You remember how you used to come around, nights? Ah! You really liked it... 'My dear Copine,' you used to say to me, 'one more little pipe, nice and strong!'"

He took in this humble flattery from the old courtesan, who lied—the better to dote on him—without batting an eye. He smiled with a knowing look and searched—in the shadow cast by the faded hat onto the neck wrapped in black tulle—for a string of big artificial pearls.

In small mouthfuls, he mechanically drank the whiskey the barman had mistakenly served him. He wasn't fond of liquor, but tonight it gave him pleasure and the ability to laugh with ease; it relieved the harsh feeling of unpolished surfaces and coarse fabrics; and he listened, with benevolence, to this old woman for whom the present had no meaning. They were meeting again on the other side of an era with no purpose, in the wake of so many untimely, early deaths. La Copine threw Chéri a line, a sort of aerial footbridge made from the names of indestructible old men and women who'd either faced up to the struggle or been left frozen in their final form, never to change again. She recounted, in minute detail, a failed venture in 1913 and a fraud uncovered in the month of August 1914, and something wavered in her voice when she spoke of la Loupiote dying—"during the week of your wedding, my dear! Do you see the coincidence? The hand of fate lies upon us, does it not!"—after four years of pure, untroubled friendship...

"We'd quarrel all day long, my dear, but only in front of other people. Because, you see, it convinced them that we were a couple. If we hadn't had our shouting matches, who'd have believed it? So we went at each other...like a pair of hellcats! And the others would laugh, 'Ah, what sweethearts!' My dear, I'm going to tell you a story that will keep you glued to your seat: you must have heard about it, the supposed will of Massau..."

"Which Massau?" Chéri murmured, full of languor.

"Oh, come on, Massau Gérault, he's the only one you know! The will—so-called—that he'd left in the hands of Louise Mac-Millar... It was 1909, and at the time I'm talking to you about, I belonged to Gérault's pack, his pack of 'faithful hounds.' There were five of us he was keeping boarded down there at Nice, every night at the Belle-Meunière. And, you know, we only had eyes for you on the Promenade, all dressed in white like an English baby, and Léa all in white too... Ah, what a couple! A miracle straight out of the hands of the Creator!

Gérault would tease Léa, stretching out his words: 'You're too y-o-u-n-g, g-i-r-l, and too stuck-up. I'll take you on in fifteen or twenty years...' And such a man as that had to let go of this world... His funeral was bathed in real tears, tears shed by a whole multitude... So, now, I should finish telling you the story of the will..."

A flood of incidents, and a tide of tired-out regrets and trivial resurrections whipped up with the skill of a dirge-singer, swept over Chéri. He leaned toward la Copine, who leaned symmetrically toward him; she lowered her tone for the dramatic parts, let out an abrupt cry or a laugh, and he could see in a mirror how much the two of them resembled the whispering couple who'd preceded them. He got up, feeling the need to change their appearance. The barman imitated his movement, but at a distance, like a well-mannered dog when its master is drawing a visit to its close.

"Ah, yes..." said la Copine. "Very well, I'll tell you the rest another time."

"After the next war," Chéri smiled. "Tell me, those two letters there... Yes, that monogram in little gems. It's not yours, is it, Copine?"

He gestured at the black bag with the tip of his index finger, pointing forward while his body backed away, as though the bag were alive.

"You don't miss a thing," la Copine said, with admiration. "But yes. Can you believe it—she gave it to me. She said, 'They're too feminine for me now, trinkets like these.' She said, 'What do I want with all this folderol of mirrors and powders, me with my big fat policeman's face?' She made me laugh..."

To interrupt la Copine, Chéri pushed across the change from his one-hundred-franc note: "For your taxi, Copine."

They went out through the side door and onto the pavement. The dimmed radiance of the streetlamps made Chéri realize that the night was almost at an end.

"You don't have your car?"

"My car? No. I'm on foot, it does me good."

"Is your wife staying out in the country?"

"No, her hospital keeps her in Paris."

La Copine gave her invertebrate hat a shake.

"I know. She's a woman with a big heart. She's been put forward for the Legion of Honor. I heard that from the baroness."

"What?"

"Wait, hail that one for me, my dear, the one with its windows closed … And Charlotte's going to great lengths, she knows people in Clemenceau's circle. It will make up a little for the episode with Rita … A little … not a lot. She's as black as sin, Charlotte is, my dear."

He bundled her into a taxi, where she blended with the shadows and ceased to exist. As soon as she stopped talking, he found it hard to believe that he'd run into her. He took in his surroundings, slowly inhaling the nocturnal haze that would lead to another blazing hot day. He believed instead, in the way you believe something in a dream, that he was going to wake up at home—surrounded by the gardens that were watered every evening, by the scent of Spanish honeysuckle and the calls of birds—lying up against the slender hips of his young wife. But la Copine's voice rose from the depths of the taxi: "Two hundred and fourteen, avenue de Villiers! Remember my address, Chéri! And, you know, I often dine at Girafe, on avenue de Wagram, in case you're ever looking for me … Right? Just in case you're ever looking for me …"

"She must be joking," Chéri thought, lengthening his stride. "Looking for her? Thanks a lot. If I ever see her again, I'll head off in another direction."

Cooler and calmer now, he walked effortlessly and didn't leave the embankments until he reached the place de l'Alma. From there he went by taxi back to avenue Henri-Martin. A muted glow, coppery red, was already staining the east, looking more like a setting sun than a summer's dawn. Not a single cloud obscured the sky, but a high, chalky canopy, immobilized by its own weight, blanketed Paris. Any minute now it would take on the hues of the conflagration, the somber intensity of red-hot metal; because at sunrise a heat wave drains cities and their suburbs of the moist pinks, floral mauves, and dewy blues that bathe the verdant regions where plant life thrives in profusion.

Nothing was stirring in the town house when Chéri turned the diminutive key in the lock. The tiled vestibule still smelled a little of last night's dinner, and the boughs of mock orange, bunched in white vases tall enough to hide a man, loaded the atmosphere with their noxious, unbearable scent. An unfamiliar gray cat shot out, kept its distance on the short walkway, and coldly measured the intruder.

"Come, pussy," Chéri called, softly.

The cat looked him up and down in an insulting manner, without yielding an inch, and it occurred to Chéri that no animal—dog, horse, or cat—had ever shown him any sympathy. He could hear, from fifteen years ago, the raspy voice of Aldonza, who'd warned: "People who animals don't like are cursed!" But when the cat—wide awake now—started rolling a spiny green chestnut with its two front paws, Chéri smiled and climbed the stairs to the bedroom.

It was blue and dimly lit, like a night scene on the stage, and the dawn stopped short at the balcony, which was decked out with trellis roses and geraniums tied up with raffia. Edmée was sleeping, her bare arms and feet outside the light blanket. She was lying on her side, with her head bent forward and one finger tucked behind her pearl necklace. In the half-light, she looked more like a woman deep in thought than a woman asleep. Her frizzy hair had strayed across her cheek, and Chéri didn't hear her breathing.

"She's at rest," thought Chéri. "She's dreaming of Dr. Arnaud, or her Legion of Honor, or her Royal Dutch shares. She's pretty. Oh, so pretty! Carry on! Two or three more hours of sleep and you'll get to see him again, your Dr. Arnaud. It's not so bad, really. You'll meet up on the avenue d'Italie, in that lovely hole-in-the-wall that stinks of phenol. You'll say to him, 'Yes, Doctor, no, Doctor,' like a little girl. You'll look earnest, you'll toss around some temperatures—37.4 degrees, 38.9 degrees, and so on—and he'll hold your little paw smelling of antiseptic in his big hand smelling of coal tar. You're lucky, my dear girl, to have some romance in your life! I won't be the one who takes it away from you, not me ... I wish I had some too ..."

Suddenly, Edmée woke up, with a movement so brisk that Chéri lost his breath, like a man cut off rudely in mid-sentence.

"It's you! It's you! ... How come it's you?"

"If you were expecting somebody else, please accept my apologies," said Chéri, smiling.

"Oh, that's clever!"

She sat up in bed and tossed back her hair.

"What time is it? Are you just getting up? Ah, no! You haven't come to bed yet ... you're just getting home ... Oh, Fred! What have you been up to again?"

"'Again' is a compliment ... If you had any idea what I was really doing ..."

Gone were the days when she would plead, with her hands covering her ears: "No! No! Don't say a thing, don't tell!" But Chéri, more quickly than she, had moved beyond the playful and mischievous stage when, coming home at daybreak, he could routinely torment a woman in tears, as though it were an everyday occurrence, and then pull her along with him into a sleep of reconciled combatants. No more caprices ... No more betrayals ... Nothing more, now, than this unavowable chastity ...

He kicked off his dusty shoes, turned his pale face—a face used to concealing everything but his willingness to conceal—in his wife's direction, and sat down on the cambric and lace bedcovers.

"Smell me!" he said. "See? I've been drinking whiskey."

She brought their two lovely mouths close together.

"Whiskey ..." she repeated, dreamily. "Whiskey ... Why?"

A less sophisticated woman would have asked, "With whom?" and Chéri took note of this finesse. He showed that he knew how to play the game, by responding, "With a girlfriend. And would you like the whole truth?"

She smiled, lit up now by the rising sun, which was gradually bringing her into bolder relief as it reached the side of the bed, then the mirror, then a painting on the wall, then the gold of a fish swirling in a water-filled crystal sphere.

"Not all of it, Fred, not all of it! A half-truth, a truth for an ungodly hour ..."

Meanwhile, she was pondering, almost certain that neither love nor lust was pulling Chéri away from her. She surrendered a limp body into Chéri's arms. But he felt a hard, clenched hand, stiffened with wariness, on his shoulder.

"The truth is," he continued, "I don't know her name. But I gave her ... hold on a second ... eighty-three francs."

"Just like that, right away? The first time you met her? How princely of you."

She pretended to yawn and sank listlessly back into the hollow of the bed, as if she didn't expect any answer; he felt pity for her—briefly, for a few seconds—until a bright, horizontal sunbeam sharpened her almost naked form lying next to him; and then his pity evaporated.

"She ... she's beautiful. It's not fair."

Leaning back, she half opened her eyes to him and parted her lips. He saw the glint of the explicit, narrowed glance—so decidedly unfeminine—that a woman aims at her pleasure-giver; and, in his abstinent state, which he couldn't avow, he felt violated. He answered, haughtily, with a different sort of glance—withdrawn, complicated— the glance of the man who forbears. He didn't want to pull away and only raised his head toward the golden sunlight, the garden soaked by the water sprinkler, and the blackbirds weaving a vocal arabesque over the repetitive chirping of sparrows. On his blue, unshaven cheeks, Edmée could see the marks of protracted fatigue and a perceptible loss of weight. She noticed the dubious condition of his genteel hands, his nails, which hadn't been properly scrubbed since yesterday, and the gray-brown stain, in the form of a spearhead, that ran along a lower eyelid and into the corner of his eye. She concluded that this beautiful young man—half-undressed and shoeless— displayed all the specific and peculiar forms of physical deterioration typical of someone who's been arrested and has spent a night in jail. He hadn't become unsightly; rather, he'd been diminished, through a mysterious process of stripping away that put Edmée in a position of authority. She gave up making any voluptuous advances, sat up, and placed a hand on Chéri's forehead.

"Ill?"

He slowly withdrew his attention from the garden, and turned back to Edmée. "What?... But no, there's nothing wrong with me, except that I'm sleepy. So sleepy, I can't even manage to get into bed, if you can believe it."

He smiled, exposing his pallid inner lips and his dry, coral-red gums. But, above all, his smile exposed a sadness that sought no cure, a sadness as unassuming as a pauper's malady. Edmée came close to questioning him clinically, then thought better of it.

"Get into bed," she ordered, making room for him.

"Into bed? Is there some water? You have no idea how filthy I am!"

He still had the strength to grab a carafe, take some gulps, and throw off his jacket. Then he collapsed onto the bed like a ton of bricks and stopped moving altogether, drained by fatigue.

For a while, she contemplated the half-dressed stranger who lay in drug-induced oblivion beside her. Her examination proceeded from his bluish lips to his sunken eyelids, and from an outflung hand to his forehead, which kept his singular secret sealed. She braced herself, as if the sleeper had caught her off guard, and composed her features. She got up quietly. Before she drew the curtains away from the dazzling window, she threw a silk spread over his sprawling body to hide its disarray—he looked like a burglar knocked out cold—and left his beautiful, constricted face uncovered so that it could shine. She carefully drew the fabric over a dangling hand, feeling a little pious disgust, as though she'd concealed a weapon that might have fired a lethal shot.

He didn't move a muscle. For the time being, he was holed up in an impregnable lair; besides, the hospital had taught Edmée professional moves—not so much gentle as assured—that could reach their target without disturbing the surrounding area. She didn't get back into bed, but savored—seated half-naked—the surpassing freshness of the hour when the sun revives the wind. The long curtains were billowing in and out in time with the breeze, casting lighter and darker azure shadows over Chéri's sleeping body.

Edmée wasn't thinking, as she watched him, of the wounded and the dead whose rustic hands she'd clasped together on top of coarse cotton sheets. None of the wounded racked with nightmares, none of the dead bore any resemblance to Chéri, whom sleep, repose, and silence imbued with an inhuman otherness.

Extreme beauty elicits no sympathy; it doesn't belong to any homeland; it only grows more austere with time. Wisdom born of experience, which bears the responsibility of enhancing human grandeur by gradually wearing it down, respected in Chéri an admirable edifice dedicated to instinct. What power could love—with its Machiavellian maneuvers, its selfish self-denials, its brutalities—hold over this inviolable bearer of light and his unstudied majesty?

Edmée readily focused her mind on acquiring degrading, profitable truths. But at the same time, the deep and omnivorous hunger shared by those women who, by birth or inclination, are destined to make the most out of love, kept on growing inside her. Endowed with patience and frequently perceptive, she was blind to the fact that the feminine appetite to possess tends to emasculate every living conquest and can reduce a male, magnificent but less powerful, to the duties of a courtesan. Her parvenue's good sense had no intention of renouncing the riches—money, security, domestic despotism, marriage—acquired in so few years, and made doubly delicious by the war.

She looked at the exhausted body, closed in on itself and seemingly abandoned.

"It's Chéri," she kept repeating to herself, "here he is, Chéri... How insignificant he is, Chéri!" She shrugged a shoulder and added, "So, this is their Chéri..." while working herself up to feel scorn for the supine man. She summoned memories of conjugal nights, of languorous mornings of pleasure and sunshine, and—for this sublime corpse draped in floral silk and cooled by the curtains' wings—she came up with only a cold, vindictive tribute; because, more and more, he treated her with disdain. She raised a hand to one of her small upturned breasts, set low on her slender torso, and squeezed this supple fruit, as if she were calling the most tempting part of her youthful body to bear witness to the injustice of her abandonment.

"What he needs for himself is definitely something different... What he needs..."

But she strove in vain to think scornful and abusive thoughts.

Even a woman loses her desire and power to scorn a man who's suffering completely on his own; and if he's free from her control, she tends inwardly to place him on a pedestal.

Edmée felt suddenly fed up with this spectacle, which the curtain's shadows, the sleeper's pallor, and the whiteness of the bed were coloring in the romantic shades of night and death. She jumped to her feet, full of vim and vigor, but resistant to mounting any emotional offensive around the unmade bed, around the traitor, the runaway taking refuge in his sleep, in his distasteful, mute unwellness. She was neither aroused nor regretful. Her heart beat faster and her pearl-white cheeks flushed only when she pictured the ginger-haired, fiery man she called "dear sir" and "chief" in tones of playful formality. Arnaud's soft, weighty hand; his laugh; the sparks that sunlight, or the operating room lamp, ignited in his red moustache; and the white surgeon's coat, put on and taken off only inside the hospital, like an intimate garment that never leaves a lovers' tryst ... Edmée rose up as though ready for a dance.

"That's it, yes, that's it ... !"

With a shake of her head and a toss of her hair, she strode to the bathroom without turning back.

Uninspired in design and middling in size, the dining room depended for its sense of luxury on a yellow wall hanging streaked with purple and green. The gray-and-white stucco of the walls reflected too much brightness back at the assembled guests, who were already robbed of any shade by the electric light pouring down mercilessly from the ceiling.

A constellation of crystal shimmered with every movement of Edmée's beaded dress. For the family dinner, Madame Peloux was still wearing her leather-buttoned suit, and Camille de La Berche her nurse's headdress, which made her the spitting image of a hirsute Dante Alighieri. Because of the heat, the women were staying mum, and Chéri's silence was habitual. A hot bath followed by a cold shower had triumphed over his fatigue, but the powerful light ricocheting off his cheekbones betrayed his sunken cheeks. He kept his eyes down, so that the shadow of his lashes hid his lower lids.

"Chéri looks sixteen tonight," the baroness boomed, out of nowhere, in her basso profundo.

No one answered her. Chéri bowed his chest forward slightly in acknowledgement.

"It's been a long while," the baroness went on, "since I've seen the outline of his face so drawn."

Edmée frowned imperceptibly.

"I've seen it this way. But only during the war."

"It's true, it's true," Charlotte Peloux piped up in agreement. "My God, did he look shattered at Vesoul in 1916! My dear Edmée," she continued, abruptly changing tack, "I saw somebody you know today, and it looks as if *everything*'s going very well."

Edmée blushed in a submissive manner that didn't suit her, and Chéri raised his eyes to ask, "Who did you see? And what's going well?"

"Trousellier's pension. My little amputee, the one who lost his right arm. He got out of hospital on the twentieth of June. Your mother has taken up his case with the ministry."

Edmée hadn't missed a beat, and she bathed him in her calm, golden gaze. Even so, he knew she was lying.

"It's a matter of his Medal of Honor. After all, he deserves it, poor kid ..."

She was lying to him in front of these two women, who knew she was lying.

"What if I smashed the carafe to pieces in the midst of all this?"

But he didn't budge. From what depth of passion could he have drawn the impulse that squares the shoulders and guides the hand?

"Abzac is leaving us in a week," Madame de La Berche carried on.

"That's not for certain," Edmée started up again, with intensity. "Dr. Arnaud doesn't agree that we should let him take off like that on his new leg ... He'd be free to do all sorts of risky things, and then there's the possibility of gangrene ... Dr. Arnaud is too well aware of how that sort of rashness, during the whole duration of the war—"

Chéri looked at her, and she halted in mid-sentence, for no apparent reason. She was waving a long-stemmed rose like a fan. When someone passed her a dish, she shook her head, then set her elbows down on the table. Dressed in white, with her shoulders bare, even while she was motionless she couldn't conceal the inner satisfaction, the high degree of self-regard that defined her. Something repulsive radiated from her smooth outlines. An immodest glow showed her for what she was: a woman who craved status, but had so far known only success.

"Edmée," Chéri decided, "is a woman who should never have lived past twenty. Look how she's already starting to resemble her mother."

The next moment, the resemblance had disappeared. There was nothing obvious about Edmée that connected her to Marie-Laure. Edmée could lay claim to only one facet of the poisonous beauty—red hair, pale complexion, brazen temperament—that Marie-Laure had used as a snare throughout her career: the brazen temperament. Edmée took care not to shock anyone, but she did shock all the same. Like an overly stylish outfit or a second-rate racehorse, she offended beings who were endowed—by their essential nature or their lack of education—with an instinctive delicacy. The servants and Chéri dreaded in Edmée what they sensed was more vulgar than themselves.

Taking her cue from Edmée, who lit a cigarette, the Baroness de La Berche took her time grilling the tip of a cigar and smoked it with sensual delight. Her white nurse's veil, with its red cross above her forehead, draped down to her virile shoulders. She looked like one of those solemn men who, when Christmas Eve celebrations are coming to a close, put on Phrygian caps, women's headscarves, and feathered, cylindrical military hats made of tissue paper. Charlotte undid the braided leather buttons of her jacket and reached out for the box of Abdulla cigarettes; and the butler, mindful of the customs of this inner circle, rolled a magician's table—full of mysteries, false drawer bottoms, liqueurs in silver flasks—within arm's length of Chéri. The butler then left the room, and the yellow wall lost the long shadow of the venerable wooden-faced, white-haired Italian.

"He really is well bred, that Giacomo," said the Baroness de La Berche. "And I know whereof I speak."

Madame Peloux shrugged her shoulders, a movement that, for quite some time now, no longer unsettled her breasts. Her bosom filled a frilly white silk blouse to overflowing; her close-cropped hair, still abundant, smoldered somber red above her big, ominous eyes; she had the handsome brows of a member of the revolutionary National Convention.

"He has the breeding of all the old, white-haired Italians. To look at them, you'd think every one of them was a private secretary to the pope. They write out your menu in Latin, and the next thing you know, you swing open a door and find them molesting a seven-year-old girl."

Chéri welcomed this stream of venom like a timely downpour. His mother's malice cleared away the storm clouds, made the air breathable again. Lately, he'd enjoyed seeing the Charlotte of old, the one who, from her balcony, would label a graceful passerby a "cheap hussy," and who, in response to Chéri's question—"You know her?"— would shoot back, "No, but I probably should, the tramp!" In a confused way, he'd recently begun to develop a taste for Charlotte's superior vitality; in a confused way, preferred her to the other two women at the table. But he didn't know that this preference, this bias, might be what's called filial love. He laughed, applauded Madame Peloux for being once more in sparkling form, the woman he'd known, despised, feared, disparaged. For a moment, Madame Peloux assumed her authentic character in her son's eyes. In other words, he took her true measure, appreciated her for being fiery, rapacious, calculating, and impulsive all at once, like a powerful financier, and capable, like a comic actor, of revelling in cruelty. "A scourge, yes," he thought, "but no more than that. A scourge, but not a stranger . . ." In the high forehead of the revolutionary, he recognized the same sort of blue-black indentations that, on his own forehead, made the pallor of his skin and the blue-black of his hair stand out.

"She is my mother," he thought. "No one's ever told me that I look like her, but I do look like her." The "stranger" sitting across from him glowed with the milky, veiled radiance of a pearl... Chéri heard the name of the Duchess of Camastra boomed out in the baroness's basso profundo, and on the stranger's face he saw a momentary flicker of cruelty, like the serpent of fire that suddenly reignites the shape of a charred vine shoot inside a bed of ashes. But Edmée didn't open her mouth and didn't join in the concert of barrack-room curses the baroness was heaping on a rival clinic.

"People say there's a problem over there with an experimental drug... Two fatalities in two days from injections. I don't think they're free from blame!" said Madame de La Berche, laughing heartily.

"You're imagining things," Edmée corrected her dryly. "That's an old rumor from Janson de Sailly that's being trotted out again."

"Where there's smoke, there's fire," Charlotte sighed benignly. "Chéri, are you tired?"

He was wasted with fatigue, and he admired the resilience of these three women whom hard work, the Parisian summer, and their daily hustle and bustle didn't knock out of action.

"The heat," he said, tersely.

Edmée's gaze intersected his, but she made no comment, and didn't contradict him.

"Pooh-pooh-pooh," Charlotte hummed. "The heat... But of course. Pooh-pooh-pooh."

Her gaze, fastened on Chéri's, overflowed with complicity, with affectionate blackmail. As usual, she knew everything. Whisperings in the kitchen, tidings from concierges... Maybe even Léa herself, taking pleasure in a feminine fib, in one last triumph, had told Charlotte... The Baroness de La Berche let out a little whinnying snigger, and the shadow of her large priestly nose fell across the lower part of her face.

"In the name of God!" Chéri swore.

His chair toppled behind him, and Edmée stood up right away, on guard. She didn't express the least surprise. Charlotte Peloux and the Baroness de La Berche braced themselves too, but in the old-fashioned way, hands at their skirts as though ready to gather them up and flee. Chéri, leaning forward with both his fists on the table, was breathing heavily, tossing his head left and right like an animal trapped in a net.

"You, to start with, you . . ." he stammered.

He brandished his arm toward Charlotte. She'd seen plenty of men in this state before, and the threat, coming from her own son, in front of witnesses, sharpened her resolve.

"What? what? what?" she yelped. "You're insulting me? A wretched little boy, a wretched little boy, who, if I wanted to talk—"

The crystal vibrated to her piercing voice, but an even shriller voice cut her off. "Leave him alone!" Edmée shrieked.

The silence following three such abrupt outbursts was deafening. Chéri, who'd regained his physical composure, shook himself, then smiled through his greenish pallor.

"I beg your pardon, Madame Peloux," he said, trying to make light of it.

She was already indulging him with benign looks and gestures, like a champion boxer who rests at ease at the end of a round.

"Ah! You *are* hot-blooded, aren't you!"

"He's a warrior," said the baroness, while squeezing Edmée's hand. "I bid you goodbye, Chéri, my foxhole awaits me."

She turned down a ride in Charlotte's car, preferring to return home on foot. Her height, her white nurse's veil, and the glowing tip of her cigar would discourage even the worst night prowlers along avenue Henri-Martin. Edmée accompanied the two old women to the front door: an exceptional courtesy that enabled Chéri to take the measure of his wife's suspicions, and of her peacemaking diplomacy.

He drank some slow mouthfuls of cold water and stood, reflecting, under a downpour of electric light, tasting the extent of his terrible isolation.

"She protected me," he kept repeating. "She protected me, but not out of love. She protected me the way she protects the garden from blackbirds, her supply of sugar from the light-fingered nurses, her wine from the servants. She must know I've been to rue Raynouard, that I came back from there and haven't gone back there again. She hasn't said a word, and maybe she doesn't care, either way. She protected me, because my mother couldn't be allowed to go on talking... She protected me, but not out of love."

He heard Edmée's voice from the garden. From a distance, she was trying to gauge Chéri's state of mind.

"Do you want to go up right away, Fred? You're not taking it too hard?"

Her head appeared in the half-opened doorway, and he laughed bitterly to himself. "She's being so cautious..."

She saw his smile and carried on more firmly.

"Come on, Fred. I think I'm almost as done in as you are. The way I let myself go a minute ago proves it...but I've just apologized to your mother."

She turned off some of the harsh lighting, then gathered a few roses that were lying on the tablecloth and plunged them into the jug of water. Her body, her hands, the roses, her head inclined inside a mist of frizzy hair smoothed a little by the warmth: everything about her could enchant a man.

"I said *a* man. I didn't say *any* man." Léa's voice resounded insidiously in Chéri's ears.

"I can do anything to her," he thought, following Edmée with his eyes. "She won't complain, she won't ask for a divorce, I have nothing to fear from her, not even love. It's only up to me, really, to find peace of mind."

But at the same time he recoiled with an unspeakable aversion from the idea of living as a couple in a household devoid of love. His illegitimate childhood, his drawn-out adolescence as a ward, had taught him that—in a world that appeared unbridled—there was a code of conduct almost as strict as bourgeois prejudice. Chéri had learned that love is tied up with money, betrayals, crimes, and cowardly surrenders. But now he was leaving behind the old dictates and rejecting the tacit forms of deference. So he let the tender hand slip away from his sleeve. And while he walked beside Edmée toward the bedroom, which would be the scene of neither reproaches nor endearments, he was convulsed with shame, and he blushed at their monstrous pact.

He found himself outside, in street clothes, almost unaware that he'd put on a light raincoat and a fedora. He left behind an entry hall filled with a mist of suspended tobacco smoke, the strong perfume of women and flowers, and the toxic, bitter almond scent of cherry brandy. He was leaving the company of Edmée, Dr. Arnaud, the Filipescos, the Atkinses, and the Kelekian girls, two young socialites who, after volunteering as truck drivers during the war, now cared only for cigars, automobiles, and the companionship of garage mechanics. He was abandoning Desmond (flanked on one side by a real estate agent, on the other by an undersecretary of state), a poet-amputee, and Charlotte Peloux. A fashionable young couple—up, no doubt, on all the latest trends—had seemed virtuous and avid while they dined. They wore knowing looks, as though in shocked, naive, and eager expectation that Chéri would dance stark naked, or that Charlotte and the undersecretary would copulate on the entry hall rug.

Chéri was departing with the awareness that he'd conducted himself stoically and without fault, aside from a sudden disconnection from the present, a disconcerting onset of apathy during the meal. In any case, this stupor had lasted for only a moment, unmeasurable as a dream. Now he was getting away from all the strangers who were crowding his house, and his footsteps made a muffled sound, like padded paws, on the sanded pathway. The silver-gray of his outfit merged with the fog that had descended over the Bois. A few evening strollers envied this young man in a hurry who wasn't going anywhere.

The image of his crowded house kept pursuing him. He still heard the voices, held the memory of the faces and the laughter, and above all, the shapes of the mouths. An old man had talked about war, a woman about politics. He also remembered the new intimacy between Desmond and Edmée, and the interest she took in a building site . . . "Desmond . . . what a husband for my wife . . ." And then the dancing...Charlotte Peloux available to tango...Chéri quickened his pace.

A humid night, presaging autumn, was shrouding the full moon with haze. In place of the lunar disk, a big halo appeared, ringed by a pale rainbow. This milky orb faded at times, smothered by puffs of scudding clouds. The scent of September was emanating from leaves that had fallen during the scorching heat of midsummer.

"It's nice out," thought Chéri.

Feeling tired, he sat down on an inviting bench but didn't linger there for long. An invisible female companion came to join him, but he refused to make room for her. A gray-haired companion, wearing a long jacket, irrepressibly gay...Chéri turned his head in the direction of the La Muette gardens in Picardie, as though he could hear, from that far away, the cymbals of the jazz band.

It wasn't time yet to go back to the blue bedroom. The two high society girls might still be up there, smoking fine cigars, sitting side-saddle on the blue velvet bedcover while entertaining the real estate agent with anecdotes about lady quartermasters.

"Ah, a nice hotel room, a nice, pink bedroom, very ordinary and very pink..." But wouldn't that bedroom cease to be ordinary the instant the lamp was turned off and the pitch dark permitted the entrance—heavy-footed and lighthearted—of the long, nondescript jacket and the thick gray hair? He smiled at the female intruder because he'd passed beyond the stage of being afraid. "No matter where... she'll be just as loyal. But I don't want to live with these people anymore."

Day by day, hour by hour, he was becoming more contemptuous and inflexible. He was already passing harsh judgements on the minor heroes in the columns of the daily papers and on the young war widows who were clamoring—like burn victims thirsting for fresh water—for new husbands. His intransigence extended to the realm of finance, but he was blind to this profound change in himself. "All of that scheming, during dinner, about ships and rawhides...How distasteful! And they talk about those things out loud..." But nothing in the world would have induced him to reveal publicly that he was turning into a person out of step with his peers. Prudently, he kept quiet about this, as he did about everything else. When he'd accused Charlotte Peloux of having sold off, for no good reason, a few tons' worth of sugar stocks from his inheritance, hadn't she reminded him, in so many words, of the time when Chéri had flippantly demanded: "Léa, hand me five louis d'or so I can go and get cigarettes."

"Ah," he sighed, "those women will never understand ... That wasn't the same thing at all."

This was his reverie while he sat—bareheaded, with his hair wet—almost incorporeal in the mist. A feminine shadow passed close by him, on the run. The racing pace, the grinding sound of her feet as they dug into the gravel, bespoke haste and anxiety. The woman's shadow flew toward the shadow of a man who'd come to meet her and swooped down on her, breast to breast, as though he'd just been run through by a cannon ball.

"Those two are meeting in secret," thought Chéri. "Who are they deceiving? Everybody deceives. But me ..." He didn't finish his sentence. Instead, he stood up and made a grimace that signified, deep down: "Me, I'm pure." An indistinct light, shining on stagnant regions that had been imperceptible until now, was beginning to teach him that purity and solitude are one and the same affliction.

As it got darker, he felt the cold. Having spent many an hour aimlessly awake, he'd learned that each phase of the night has a different flavor and that midnight is mild compared to the period just before dawn.

"Winter will come on fast," he thought, while lengthening his stride. "We won't be done with this endless summer a minute too soon. Next winter, I want ... Come on ... what I want, next winter ..." His effort to foresee the future failed almost immediately, and he came to a halt, his head lowered, like a horse that catches sight of a steep climb in the distance.

"Next winter, it'll be my wife, my mother, and Ma La Berche, all over again. Along with Whatsit, Whoosit, and Thingamabob. That whole crowd. Nothing for me anymore ..."

He paused to watch a mass of low clouds passing over the Bois.

They were an indefinable shade of pink. A gust of wind beat them down, grabbed them by their tufts of fog, twisted them, and dragged them over the open stretches before carrying them off to the moon... Chéri stood and gazed. He was familiar with these otherworldly, luminous displays in the night, which people who sleep assume to be pitch-dark.

The half-obscured apparition of a flat, wide moon, in the midst of fast-moving puffs of cloud—which it seemed to be pursuing and tearing to pieces—failed to draw Chéri away from a distracting calculation: he was summing up—in years, months, days, and hours— a precious time, forever lost.

"If only I'd held on to her that day when I went to see her before the war, there would have been three, four more good years, hundreds and hundreds of days and nights won and set aside for love." A word as strong as this didn't make him falter...

"Hundreds of days. A life—a real life. Life the way it was before. Life with my worst enemy, as she used to say... My own worst enemy, who forgave me everything and let me get away with nothing..." He was squeezing his past to infuse one last drop of juice into his barren present; reviving, inventing, if need be, his ideal, princely adolescence shaped and steered by two big, vigorous, womanly hands, tender, poised to dole out punishment. His protracted, exotic, sheltered adolescence, through which sensual pleasures flowed like pauses in a song... Indulgences, tantrums, childish cruelties, unconscious fidelity... He threw his head back toward the mother-of-pearl halo that filled the top of the sky and cried softly: "It's all over! I'm thirty years old!"

He hurried back, cursing himself in time with his brisk footsteps: "Imbecile! The worst thing isn't her age, it's mine. For her, everything's probably finished, but for me..."

He quietly opened the door to his finally silent house and encountered once more the nauseating stale odor of the company who'd drunk, eaten, and danced inside. The vestibule mirror across from the door brought him face to face again with the lean young man with firm cheekbones, a sad and beautiful upper lip—a little blue with dark, unshaven growth—and big, tragic, reluctant eyes. In short, the young man who, inexplicably, had ceased to be twenty-four.

"...for me," Chéri completed his sentence, "I'm sure everything's been said and done."

"You get that what I need is a quiet place ... Nothing big: a bachelor's apartment, a pied-à-terre."

"I'm not a child," la Copine chided. She raised her inconsolable eyes toward the garlanded ceiling. "Something a little dreamy, a place for a little bit of adventure and a few soothing caresses for a man who's down at heart ... You'd better believe I understand! Any preference?"

Chéri frowned.

"Preference? For what?"

"You don't get me, my dear boy. A preference for a particular part of town?"

"Ah, no ... No preference. Someplace quiet."

La Copine nodded her big conspiratorial head.

"I see, I see. Something in my style—the style of my apartment. You know where I live?"

"Yes."

"No, you know nothing about it. I was certain you wouldn't write it down. Two hundred and fourteen, avenue de Villiers. It's neither beautiful nor grand. But you aren't looking for a bachelor's apartment in order to get noticed."

"No."

"I got mine thanks to an arrangement with my landlady. A rare jewel of a woman, by the way—married, or she might as well be. A dove with periwinkle eyes, but fate has left its mark on her forehead. And I've already read in her cards that she does everything to excess, and that—"

"Right. You said a minute ago, you know of a pied-à-terre ..."

"A pied-à-terre, yes, but unworthy of you."

"You think so?"

"For you... for the two of you!"

La Copine muted her suggestive laugh with a shot of whiskey that smelled like damp horse tack and made Chéri queasy. He tolerated her banter about imaginary conquests because he saw, on her grainy neck, a string of big false pearls that he thought he recognized. Any surviving reminder of the past brought him to a standstill on a road he was sliding down imperceptibly, and during these pauses he rested at ease.

"Ah!" sighed la Copine. "I'd like to get a good look at her going by! What a couple!... I don't know her, but I can picture you together!... Naturally, you'll want to furnish it?"

"What?"

"Your apartment, of course!"

Perplexed, he gazed at la Copine. Furniture...what furniture? He'd dreamt of only one thing: to possess a retreat whose door opened and closed for him alone, someplace unknown to Edmée, to Charlotte, to anybody else...

"Will you furnish it traditional style, or modern? That belle Serrano draped her whole ground floor in nothing but Spanish shawls. But that's an eccentricity. Anyway, you're old enough to know what you want..."

He wasn't listening to much of what she said. He was caught up in the effort of imagining a prospective hideaway: cozy, warm, and dark. Meanwhile—like a girl in days of old—he was sipping a red currant cordial, here inside the red-hued, outmoded, unchanging bar. It was exactly the same as it had been when Chéri—as a young lad— had sucked his first champagne cocktail from the end of a straw. Even the bartender hadn't changed. And if the woman sitting across from Chéri was withered, at least he'd never known her when she was beautiful, or young...

"My mother, my wife, the people they mix with, all of them are on the move; they live for change...My mother could become a banker, and Edmée a member of the city council. But me..."

He made haste to go back to thinking about his future refuge. Though its location wasn't yet known, it would be hidden away, cozy, warm, and—

"Mine's done up Algerian style," la Copine carried on. "No longer in fashion, but I don't care, especially since all the furniture's borrowed. I've thrown in some souvenirs, photos of good times, photos you'd be sure to recognize, along with la Loupiote's portrait ... Come for a visit, I'd enjoy it."

"I'd like to. Let's go!"

From the doorway of the bar, he hailed a taxi.

"You mean you don't have your car? Why don't you have your car? It's absolutely amazing that people who own cars never use them."

She gathered up her faded black skirt, fastened the cord of her lorgnette to the clasp of her purse, dropped a glove, and endured the glances of the passersby with disdainful indifference. At her side, Chéri was the recipient of insulting smiles and the sympathetic wonder of a young woman who cried out: "My Lord, what a waste!"

In the cab, he patiently and sleepily put up with the old lady's chatter. Besides, she was telling him soothing stories: the one about the diminutive dog that held up all the traffic returning to town from the races in 1897; the one about Ma La Berche abducting a young bride on her wedding day in 1893 ...

"Here we are. Open the car door for me, Chéri, it's stiff. I'm warning you, there isn't much light in the front hall or, as you can see, here at the entrance ... But it's a ground floor apartment, right? ... Hold on a moment."

Standing in the dark, he waited. He could hear the noise of a bunch of keys, the huffing and puffing of the wheezy, aged creature with the voice of a beleaguered servant.

"I'm turning on some lights ... Anyway, you're going to find yourself in familiar surroundings. Of course, I have electricity ... May I present to you my small sitting room, which is also my large sitting room."

He went in and, without being able to see a thing, politely praised a low-ceilinged room with vaguely garnet-colored walls coated with the fumes of innumerable cigars and cigarettes. Instinctively, he looked for the window, which was blinded with shutters and drapes.

"Can't you see in here? You aren't an old night owl like la Copine... Hold on, I'm turning on the ceiling lights."

"Don't bother. I'm just stepping in for a minute, and..."

Turned toward the brightest wall, which was covered in little framed pictures and photos pinned with four thumbtacks, he fell silent, and la Copine began to laugh.

"Didn't I say you'd find yourself in familiar surroundings! I was sure you'd enjoy it. You don't have it, that one?"

"That one" was a very large photo portrait, retouched with watercolors, now almost entirely faded. Blue eyes, a laughing mouth, a blond chignon; an air of peaceful, armed victory. Tall in stature, in... a First Empire corselet, her legs visible through the gauzy fabric, legs that seemed to go on forever, rounded at the thighs, tapered at the knees, legs that... And a cabaret singer's hat, a hat with only one flap raised, held up like a single sail to the wind.

"She never gave you that one, I bet? A goddess, and a pixie to boot! She walked on air! And yes, it really is her! This big photo, in my opinion it's the most beautiful, but I'm just as fond of some other ones. Look, that little one, for example, it's much more recent. Isn't it gorgeous?"

A snapshot, fastened with a rusty hairpin, showed the dark figure of a woman in a sunny garden.

"It's the navy blue dress, and the hat with the seagulls," Chéri said to himself.

"Me, I'm all for portraits that flatter," la Copine went on. "A portrait like this one. Come on now, tell the truth: doesn't it make you want to press your hands together and believe in God?"

A crude and ingratiating artist's brush had licked across the captivating "portrait-postcard," lengthening the neck, slightly narrowing the sitter's mouth. But the nose—just aquiline enough—the delectable nose with its imperious nostrils; but the innocent crease, the velvety furrow that divided the upper lip below the nose: these remained untouched, authentic, treated with respect by the photographer himself...

"Can you believe she wanted to burn it all, on the pretext that nobody's interested anymore in knowing how she used to look? My blood rose, I screamed to high heaven, and she gave them all to me, the same day she made me a present of the handbag with her initials."

"Who's this guy, up here, with her?"

"What? What are you saying? What's the matter..? Hold on while I take off my hat.

"I'm asking you who this guy is, here... Come on, hurry up."

"My God, how you're rushing me... Here? It's Bacciocchi, of course! Naturally, you can hardly recognize him, he dates back to two rounds before you."

"Two what?"

"After Bacciocchi she had Septfons, and then, no, wait, Septfons, that was before... Septfons, Bacciocchi, Spéleïeff, and then you. These checkered pants, eh... They're funny, these old-fashioned men's clothes."

"And this photo here, when was this one taken?"

He took a step back, because la Copine was leaning forward next to him, bareheaded, and her magpie's nest of matted hair smelled like a wig.

"This one, this was her outfit for the Drags in... in 1888 or '89. Yes, the year of the Exposition. You have to take your hat off to this one, my dear. They don't make beauties like this anymore."

"Pooh... I don't find her breathtaking."

La Copine pressed her hands together. Without her hat on, she had grown visibly older. Her hair, dyed a shade of greenish black, lay over a bare, butter-yellow forehead.

"Not breathtaking! That waist that you could fit inside your hands! That neck like a dove's! And take a look at the dress! All in sky-blue silk chiffon, with drawstrings, and cords of rosebuds sewn to the ends of the drawstrings, and a hat to match! And the little purse, matching too, looped to the waist—what we used to call an 'alms purse'... Ah, what a beauty! We never saw débuts like hers again. A dawning, a very sunbeam of love!"

"Débuts, where?"

She gave Chéri a gentle shove.

"Oh, come on! How you make me laugh! Hard times must be easy to take with you around!"

He turned toward the opposite wall, hiding his stiffened face. He appeared to be aware still of several Léas, one of them inhaling a draft from an artificial rose, another bent over a book with a Gothic clasp, exposing her broad nape and smooth collar, circular and white like the bole of a birch tree.

"Ah well, I'm off," he said, like Valérie Cheniaguine.

"What, you're leaving? And my dining room? And my bedroom? Give them a quick look, my handsome boy. See if they're anything like what you want for your bachelor apartment?"

"Ah, yes!... Listen, not today, because..."

He cast a mistrustful glance toward the bastion wall of portraits and lowered his voice.

"I'm meeting someone. But I'll come back...tomorrow. Probably tomorrow, before dinner."

"All right. So, I can go ahead?"

"Go ahead?"

"With the apartment?"

"Yes, right. See what turns up. And...thanks."

"My word, what sort of times are we living in?...Young people, old people, it's only a matter of who'll turn out to be the most disgusting...Two 'rounds' before me...And débuts, according to that old spider, dazzling débuts!...And all of it right out in the open. No, really, what a world..."

He realized he was keeping up an athletic walking pace and running out of breath. At the same time, a distant thunderstorm—that wouldn't break over Paris—was stemming the breeze behind a bank of violet cloud like a wall against the sky. On the fortifications along boulevard Berthier, under trees stripped of their leaves by the mid-summer heat, a scattered crowd of Parisians in espadrilles and half-naked children wearing red jerseys seemed to be bracing for a rising tide to rush toward them from Levallois-Perret. Chéri sat down on a bench, unaware that his physical powers—mysteriously sapped since he'd been squandering them in late-night vigils and neglecting to exercise and nourish his body—were likely to betray him at any moment.

"Two rounds! Really! Two rounds before me! And after me, how many more? And, if you add them all up, including me, how many altogether?"

In his mind's eye, he could see, at the side of a Léa dressed in blue and wearing a hat adorned with seagulls, a tall, broad-shouldered Spéleïeff convulsed with laughter. He remembered how, when he was a little boy, a sad Léa—red-faced from crying—would stroke his hair while she called him "naughty seed of a man."

Léa's lover ... Léa's new crush ... Familiar phrases of no consequence, as ordinary as weather forecasts, as odds at the Auteuil racetrack, as household thefts. "Are you coming, kid?" Spéleïeff would say to Chéri. "We're going to drink port at Armenonville while we wait for Léa to join us. I can't drag her out of the sack this morning ..."

"She has a gorgeous new little Bacciocchi!" Madame Peloux announced to her son, who was fourteen or fifteen years old at the time ...

But, being both unspoiled and corrupted at once, accustomed to lovemaking, blinded by the manifest presence of lovemaking, at that age Chéri talked love in the manner of children who've learned all the words of a language—clean or dirty—as purely musical sounds coming from nowhere. No living or pleasurable image emerged from the shadow of that towering Spéleïeff, barely arisen from Léa's bed. And, that "gorgeous little Bacciocchi," what difference was there between him and a "an absolutely stunning boy from Peking"?

Neither portraits nor letters, nor stories imparted by the only pair of lips that could have told the truth ever penetrated the confines of the Eden where Léa and Chéri coexisted for years. Almost nothing in Chéri dated from before Léa—so how could he have cared about anything that had ripened, grieved, or enriched his lover before his time?

A blond child with fat knees leaned his crossed arms onto the bench next to Chéri. They looked at each other with identical expressions of invaded privacy, since Chéri treated all children like strangers. This one let his pale blue eyes linger on Chéri's for a long time. Chéri saw a sort of indescribable smile rise up, full of scorn, from the small, anemic mouth to the flaxen gaze. Then the child turned around, gathered some toys from the dusty earth, and started playing at the foot of the bench, excluding Chéri from this realm. So Chéri got up and left.

Half an hour later, he was submerged in lukewarm, fragrant bathwater clouded with a milky perfume. He was delighting in a sense of luxury and well-being, in the creamy soap suds, and in the muted noises of the household, as if he deserved all these on account of an exceptional act of bravery, or was savoring them for the very last time.

His wife came home, humming. She stopped humming when she caught sight of him, but didn't do enough to conceal her mute astonishment at finding Chéri here, *chez lui*, wearing a bathrobe. He asked, without irony, "Am I bothering you?"

"Not at all, Fred."

She took off her daytime clothes with a youthful abandon that cared nothing for notions of propriety or impropriety. Her rush to get naked and into the bath diverted Chéri's train of thought.

"How I've forgotten about her," he reflected, as he studied her sinuous slave-girl's back with its hidden vertebrae, while she bent down to unlace her shoes.

She didn't talk to him. She moved about unconcerned, like a woman who feels she's alone. And he could see the child again, playing in the dust at his feet just a few minutes ago, the child who was determined not to pay him any attention.

"Tell me…"

Edmée raised her forehead and lifted her half-bare, supple body in surprise.

"What would you say if we had a child?"

"Fred! What on earth are you thinking?"

It was almost a cry of terror, and now Edmée was holding a linen scarf tight against her bosom with one hand while her other hand groped for the first kimono she could find. Chéri couldn't stop himself from laughing.

"You want my revolver?... I'm not here to attack you, you know."

"Why do you laugh?" she asked, quietly. "You should never laugh."

"I rarely laugh. But tell me, why—we're so settled here, the two of us—tell me ... is it so unbearable for you, this idea that we might have had ... that we could have a child?"

"Yes, it is," she said, cruelly, and her unexpected frankness seemed hurtful even to herself.

She kept her eyes on her husband, who was leaning back in a low armchair, and she murmured distinctly so that he'd be able to hear: "A child ... So that he can look like you ... You times two ... you times two in a woman's single existence?... No ... Oh, no!"

He started to make a gesture that she misinterpreted.

"No, please, I beg of you ... That's all. I won't say another word. Let's leave everything the way it is. All we have to do is be a bit careful and carry on ... I'm not asking you for anything."

"That's all you need?"

Her only response was a look that went along with her captive woman's nudity, a look full of helpless outrage and wretched complaint. Her freshly powdered cheeks, her youthful, rouged mouth, the faint halo around her brown eyes, the subtle and studied affectation of her whole face: all of these were in stark contrast to the disarray of her body, which was naked except for the bunched-up silk dressing gown she was pressing against her breasts.

"I can't satisfy her anymore," Chéri was thinking, "but I can still make her suffer. She isn't completely unfaithful to me. But I, even though I'm not deceiving her, I've abandoned her."

With her back turned to him, Edmée was getting dressed. She'd recovered her freedom of movement, her mendacious air of indulgence. Now a pale pink dress hid the woman who was wrapping a final layer of fabric ever so tightly around her neck, as though she were dressing a wound.

She'd regained her resilient willpower, her desire to live, to rule, the prodigious, feminine capacity for happiness. Chéri looked at her again with disdain, but a moment arose when the evening light, passing through the delicate pink dress, defined the form of a young woman who no longer resembled the naked, wounded victim; a form reaching for the sky, full of energy, her back arched like a snake that's poised to strike.

"I can still hurt her, but how quickly she gets over it . . . Even here, I'm neither needed nor expected . . . She's left me behind, and she's headed somewhere else. As la Copine would say, I was my wife's first round . . . My turn to do the same, if I were able to. But I can't. And, what's more, would I want to, even if I could? Edmée hasn't stumbled . . . she hasn't tripped over that thing that leaves you stunned after only one encounter . . . Spéleïeff used to say that some horses, after a certain kind of fall, even if they haven't broken any limbs, you would put down right there in front of the obstacle, rather than force them to jump . . . I've run into one of those unlucky obstacles."

He was still searching for slightly gruesome sporting analogies that could have put his decline and illness down to an accident. But his hours of sleep—which he started too early—and his dreams—those of an exhausted man—were filled with visions of sweetness, of sky-blue drawstrings and reminiscences drawn from ageless literature that finds its way across the well-trodden thresholds of houses of ill repute: verse and prose dedicated to faithfulness, to lovers whom death cannot part; works in verse and prose that worn-out courtesans and adolescents—equals in credulity and exaltation—imbibe . . .

"So, she says to me, 'I know where this is coming from. It's Charlotte who's made trouble for me, again.' 'It serves you right,' I say to her, 'you just have to stop seeing Charlotte as much as you do, and stop telling her all your secrets.' She answers, 'I'm more accustomed to being with Charlotte than with Spéleïeff, and I've known her a lot longer. Believe me, I'd miss Charlotte, Neuilly, bezique, and the kid more than I'd miss Spéleïeff. You can never really change who you are as a person.' 'All the same,' I say to her, 'it costs you plenty to put garment or the embroidered flowers. But an ignominious, regal attitude marked all his features with their true character. He seemed to be burning with the desire to harm and destroy, and the photograph thrown by his hand had flown like a blade. The fine, hard bones in his cheeks twitched with the rhythmic contractions of his jaw. Where he lay in the shadows, glints of white and black light played across his eyes, like moonbeams caught by the crest of the tide at night...

But while he was alone, he sank his head into the cushion and closed his eyes.

"Lord!" la Copine exclaimed when she came back in, "you'll never look more beautiful, even when you're dead! I've made some fresh coffee. You want some? It has an aroma that sends you to the Isles of the Blessed."

"Yes. Two lumps."

He talked curtly to her, and she obeyed with a sweetness that concealed, perhaps, a deep, submissive pleasure.

"You ate hardly anything for dinner?"

"I ate enough."

He drank his coffee without sitting up, resting on one elbow. An oriental curtain hung like a canopy from the ceiling above the divan. It cast its shade over an ivory, enameled Chéri clad in costly silks, lying on an old, threadbare, dust-laden blanket.

La Copine set out, on a brass tabletop, the coffee, an opium lamp capped with its glass chimney, two pipes, the pot of opium paste, the silver snuffbox filled with cocaine, and a flask whose firmly inserted cork didn't really contain the chill and treacherous volatility of the ether. To these she added a tarot deck, a case holding poker cards and chips, and a pair of eyeglasses. Then she sat down, with the solemn solicitude of a nurse.

"I've already told you," Chéri growled, "that I'm not interested in all this business."

She raised both of her horribly white hands in protest. She used to say that, when she was at home, she would assume a "Charlotte Corday style," with her hair down and big white linen scarves tied your trust in Charlotte.' And then she says, 'Oh well, if something's worth it, you have to pay the price.' You remember her that way, always big-hearted and generous, but never a pushover. And the next thing I know, she's putting on a dress for the racetrack, and she tells me she's going with a gigolo…"

"With me!" Chéri cried, with acid in his voice. "Am I right? Maybe?"

"I'm not disagreeing with you. I'm just telling you things the way they happened. A white dress, made of white Chinese silk, very exotic, hemmed with real, blue Chinese embroidery, the same dress you see here in the photo taken at the track. And nothing will rid me of the idea that the man's shoulder you see behind her is yours."

"Bring it to me," Chéri ordered.

The old woman got up, removed the rusty thumbtacks that pinned the photo to the wall, and brought the picture over to Chéri. Lying on the Algerian divan, he lifted his tousled head and gave the snapshot no more than a passing glance before tossing it across the room.

"Did you ever see me wear a collar that flared out at the back, or a morning coat for the races? Enough of this, enough. Let's change the subject! I don't find this one amusing."

She emitted a "tut, tut!" of mild disapproval, bent down on her stiff knees to pick up the photo card, and opened the door that led to the vestibule.

"Where are you going?" Chéri cried.

"I hear the water for my coffee boiling. I'm going to pour it."

"Good. But come back right away!"

The sounds of worn-out taffeta and heelless slippers accompanied her out of the room. Alone now, Chéri rested the nape of his neck against the cushion, which was covered in heavy woven fabric with Tunisian designs. In place of his usual jacket and vest, he was wearing a new dazzling Japanese robe embroidered with pink wisteria on an amethyst background. A cigarette he'd smoked for too long was drying out his lips, and his fanned-out hair was touching his eyebrows and half-covering his forehead.

There was no ambiguity about him wearing either the feminine over her dusty mourning dress. In this mode she bore a striking re-semblance—elevated and lowly at once—to many a heroine of the Salpêtrière Hospital.

"It doesn't matter, Chéri. I brought it out just in case. And it makes me happy to see all of my paraphernalia lying here, right in front of me, in good order. The arsenal of dreams! The ammunition of de-lirium, the golden gate of illusions!"

She nodded her elongated head and lifted her sympathetic eyes—like those of a grandmother who spends her fortune on children's toys—to the ceiling. But her guest didn't reach out for any of the potions. A sort of respectability concerning his physical being persisted in him, and his contempt for drugs went hand in hand with his aver-sion for brothels.

For days now—he wasn't keeping count—he'd been coming reg-ularly to this dark hole, watched over by this subservient Fate. He doled out money without courtesy or discussion, for meals, coffee, and liqueurs provided by la Copine, and for his personal supply of cigarettes, ice, fruits, and cordials. He'd assigned his helot to purchase the sumptuous Japanese robe, perfumes, and finely milled soaps. Less mercenary than intoxicated with complicity, she devoted herself to Chéri with a zeal that matched her missionary spirit of times gone by: the indulgent, guilty urge to undress and bathe the virgin girl, to heat and stretch the pearl-like pill of opium, to pour out the alcohol or the ether. She was thwarted in her vocation, because her singular guest didn't bring along any female companions, drank fruit cordials, and, while he was stretched out on the old divan, simply commanded: "Talk."

She talked, and believed that she talked in any way she pleased. But he was steering her, sometimes brutally, sometimes subtly down a slow and muddy stream of memories. She talked like a dressmaker's assistant, with the persistence, the dulling monotony of women who apply themselves to tedious, sedentary tasks. But she never sewed, thereby revealing the aristocratic indifference of a former prostitute. While she talked, she would pin a fold over a tear or a stain, carry on reading a spread of tarot cards, or play a game of solitaire. She would put on gloves to grind the coffee bought by the maid but had no qualms about handling cards that were blackened with filth.

She talked, and Chéri listened to the numbing voice, to the dampened sound of dragging feet. In the run-down abode, he lay magnificently robed. His keeper didn't dare to ask questions. It was enough for her to recognize, in his total withdrawal, the signs of monomania. She was serving a strange sick man, but a sick man nonetheless. To be on the safe side, and as though it were an obligation, she summoned a very pretty young woman, childlike and professionally merry. Chéri didn't pay her any more attention than he would have paid to a little dog, and he said to la Copine, "Are we done with these social niceties?"

She didn't allow herself to be scolded twice, and he never had the need to enjoin her to secrecy. One day, she came close to discovering the plain and simple truth. She suggested to Chéri that he might enjoy the company of one or two of the women friends he'd shared good times with in the past, for example Léa. He didn't bat an eye.

"Nobody. Or else I'll look for a different hole."

A fortnight went by, as funereal and regular as life in a monastery. This didn't weigh on either of the two nocturnal recluses. During the day, la Copine would go out to enjoy her frivolous old-lady pastimes: poker and whiskey parties, illicit gambling, mindless chitchat, lunches of country cooking in the stifling obscurity of a Limousin or Normandy cabaret ... Chéri would arrive with the first shadows of night, sometimes soaked to the skin with rain. She recognized the slamming of the taxi door and no longer asked, "But why do you never have your car?"

He would leave after midnight, usually before dawn. During his long watches on the Algerian divan, la Copine would sometimes see him tremble in his sleep and then freeze for a few moments, his neck stretched to one side as though he were caught in a trap. Ignoring her own need for rest, she wouldn't go to sleep until after he left. Once, before dawn, when he was refilling his pockets piece by piece—his house key on its chain, his billfold, his small, flat revolver, his handkerchief, his green-gold cigarette case—she risked asking, "Doesn't your wife wonder why you come home so late?"

Chéri raised his long eyebrows over his dilated, insomniac eyes. "No. Why? She knows I'm not doing anything wrong."

"It's true. You're as predictable as a child. Are you coming tonight?"

"I don't know. I'll see. Assume I am coming for sure."

He cast another glance at all the fair-haired napes, all the blue eyes that adorned one wall of his asylum, and went on his way, only to come back faithfully some twelve hours later.

When he did coax la Copine to talk of Léa, by roundabout ways he believed to be astute, he made her skip over the licentious bits that slowed the story down. "Faster, faster ..." He barely pronounced the words; only their whistling *s*'s cut into and abridged the monologue. All he wanted to hear were benign reminiscences, purely descriptive celebrations ... He demanded of the chronicler a documentary observance of the truth, and he went over these details with a vengeance. He memorized dates, colors, the names of fabrics, places, dressmakers.

"Poplin, what's that?" he asked rapid-fire.

"Poplin? It's a cloth made of silk and wool. Fine to the touch, you know, it doesn't cling—"

"Right. And mohair? You said 'white mohair.'"

"Mohair, it's like alpaca, but it tends to sag more, you see? Léa didn't like to wear linen in the summer, she claimed it was only good for underwear and handkerchiefs ... She had lingerie fit for a queen, I'm sure you still remember it, and at the time that photo was taken ... yes, the beauty with the muscular legs ... we didn't wear formfitting underwear then like we do today. It was all ruffles and ruffles, like foam, like snow, and long panties, my dear, that would make you swoon, with white Chantilly lace on the sides, and black Chantilly in the middle, can you imagine what that looked like! ... Can you picture it?"

"Sickening," Chéri thought. "Sickening. Black Chantilly in the middle. A woman doesn't wear black Chantilly lace for herself alone. Who was she with when she wore that? Who was it for?"

He could picture again the movement Léa would make when he

came into the bathroom or the boudoir, how she would furtively wrap herself in her gandoura. He could picture again the innocent self-assurance of her pink body lying naked in the bathtub, veiled by milky water clouded with essential oils...

"But they had to be for other men, long panties made of Chantilly lace..."

He kicked one of the carpet-covered cushions, stuffed with straw, to the ground.

"Are you too warm, Chéri?"

"No. Let me have a look at that photograph, the big framed one... Swivel the shade of your table lamp. More... there!"

Casting off his usual restraint, he studied, with his penetrating gaze, details that were new to him, almost refreshing.

"A high waistband with cameos," he thought. "Never saw that on her. And tall lace-up sandals, Roman-style. Is she wearing tights? No, of course not, her toes are bare. Sickening."

"In whose house was she wearing this outfit?"

"I can't really remember... One evening at her place, I think, with our regular crowd... Or at Molier's..."

Looking disdainful and put out, he handed the photo back at arm's length. He left shortly thereafter, under a sky that was overcast yet again, and passed through a late night smelling of woodsmoke and washhouses.

He was visibly changing but barely realized it. Through eating and sleeping so little, through walking and smoking so much, he was losing weight, trading his formerly manifest vigor for a lightness, an impression of youthfulness that daylight revealed to be false. When he was at home, he did as he pleased. He put up with or fled from guests at meals, from people passing through who knew nothing about him except for his name and his beauty—which was being turned, little by little, into stone, and reshaped, as if by a sculptor's ruthless chisel—and the inconceivable ease with which he ignored the presence of visitors.

In this way, until the last days of October, he bore his quiet and carefully managed despair. He was overcome with hilarity, one after-noon, when he surprised his wife recoiling from him reflexively. All of a sudden, he lit up with merriment, like someone who's immune to feeling. "She thinks I've gone crazy. What luck!"

His merriment was short-lived. He reflected that, between a scoun-drel and a crazy man, the scoundrel was the better bet. Edmée would have been scared by the crazy man, but wouldn't she have stood her ground, bitten her lip, swallowed her tears, in order to win back the scoundrel?

"They don't even think I'm a scoundrel anymore," he thought, bitterly. "It's because I'm not, anymore. Ah! how she harmed me, the woman I left ... All the same, other men left her, and she left other men ... What sort of life is Bacciochi leading now, for example, or Septfons, Spéleïeff, all the others? ... But what do all the others have in common with me? ... She used to call me 'petit bourgeois' because I'd count the bottles in her cellar. Petit bourgeois, faithful man, love of my life: these are my names, these are my real names, and she, who was glazed over with tears when I left, it's she, Léa, who'd rather live like an old woman than be with me, it's she who counts with her fingers, by the fireside. 'I had Thingy, Whatsit, Chéri, So-and-so ...' I thought she was mine. I didn't realize I was only one of her string of lovers. Is there anybody I can face, now, without shame?"

Inured to gymnastics of self-composure, he strove to withstand the capricious onslaught, like a possessed man worthy of his demon. Haughty, dispassionate, he'd hold a lit match firmly in his hand and glance sideways at his mother, who he could tell was being watchful. Once he'd lit his cigarette, it wouldn't have taken much for him to strut about before an invisible audience, to have scoffed "So what?" at his tormentors. The inscrutable strength born of dissimulation and resistance was arising, painfully, in his innermost being, and he could taste the extremity of his alienation. He foresaw, obscurely, that a paroxysm can be exploited like a reprieve and can offer the guidance that clarity of mind denies. As a child, Chéri would often turn a genuine outburst of anger into a calculated state of annoyance. Today, he was already close to the point where, having reached an actual crisis, he would rely on it to bring everything to a close...

A September afternoon—scoured by blustery winds and leaves sailing level with the ground; an afternoon of blue crevasses in the sky and scattered drops of rain—beckoned Chéri back to his dark refuge, to his servant in a black robe with a white medallion on her chest, like an alley cat. He felt light on his feet, eager for confidences with a hint of sweetness like an arbutus berry, and, like it, armed with thorns. Already, he was reciting words and phrases that had a healing quality, however poorly defined: "Her initials embroidered with her own hair on her lingerie, my dear, with golden hair from her own head... something out of a fairy tale! And have I told you how her masseuse would pluck the hairs from her calves, one by one..."

He stepped back from the window and turned around. Charlotte, seated, surveyed her son from head to foot; on the restless surfaces of her large, watery eyes he could see convex gleams forming, gleams that shifted—crystalline and huge—and dropped away from her golden-brown irises, to turn, no doubt, into mist on her flushed, fiery cheeks... Chéri felt touched and buoyed up. "How kind she is! She's crying for my sake!"

An hour later, he found his old accomplice at her post. But she was wearing a sort of priest's hat wrapped in black oilskin, and she held out a sheet of blue paper to Chéri. He pushed it away.

"What's this?... I don't have time. Tell me what it says."

La Copine looked up at him, at a loss.

"It's my mother."

"Your mother? Are you kidding?"

She made an effort to look offended.

"I'm not kidding at all. Honor to the ancestors! She's dead." And she added, as though it were an excuse, "She was eighty-three."

"My condolences. Are you going out?"

"No, I'm leaving."

"For where?"

"For Tarascon, and from there, on a little branch line that takes me—"

"For how long?"

"Four or five days ... at least ... There's the notary to see about the will, because my youngest sister—"

He exploded, with his arms raised skyward, "And now there's a sister! Why not four children too?"

He heard his own voice, surprisingly loud and high-pitched, and regained his self-control.

"All right, good. What do you want me to do with everything here? Get going, go ..."

"I was just about to leave you a note, I'm catching the seven-thirty."

"Catch the seven-thirty."

"My sister doesn't mention the time of the service in the wire, she only tells me about the burial. It's so hot down there, they'll be forced to do it quickly. It's only the paperwork that will tie me up. When it comes to the formalities, you're never in charge."

"Of course, of course."

He was pacing from the doorway to the wall of photographs, and back from the wall to the doorway. In the corridor, he bumped into a sagging travel bag. The coffee pot and two cups were steaming on the table.

"I made you some coffee, just in case."

"Thanks."

They drank standing up, as if they were in a train station, and the chill sensation of departure caught at Chéri's throat; he hid the fact that his teeth were chattering.

"So, goodbye, my dear," said la Copine. "Rest assured, I'll hurry back."

"Goodbye. Have a good trip."

They clasped hands, but she didn't dare to kiss him.

"Won't you spend a little time here?"

"No, no."

"Take the key."

"Why?"

"You're at home here. You have your routine. I've told Maria to come at five every day, to start a fire and make coffee. You should take my key."

With a limp hand, he took hold of a key that looked enormous to him. If he'd been outdoors, he'd have thrown it away or returned it to the concierge.

On their way out of the vestibule and onto the sidewalk, the old woman, bolder now, filled his ears with the kind of advice she would have dispensed to a twelve-year-old.

"The switch for the electricity is on your left as you come in. The kettle's always sitting on the gas burner in the kitchen, all you have to do is light a match under it ... I've told Maria to leave your Japanese robe folded on the corner of the divan, and your cigarettes in their usual place."

Chéri nodded "yes, yes," with the untroubled and courageous air that students feign on their first day back at school. And once he was left alone, he didn't deride his servant with the dyed hair; her, who knew how much a man without hope values his last privileges and enjoyments.

The following morning, he awoke from an indecipherable dream, in the midst of which passersby were crowding and pressing forward, all of them in the same direction. He knew them all, even though he could see only their backs. As they went by, he named his mother, Léa (conspicuously naked and out of breath), Desmond, la Copine, Maudru Junior ... Edmée was the only one to turn around and smile, with a little, sardonic smile, like a marten's. "But it's the marten that Ragut caught in the Vosges!" Chéri cried out in his dream, and this realization gave him an inordinate amount of pleasure. Then he named and counted again the people who were running in the same direction, and he thought: "There's one missing ... There's one missing ..." No longer dreaming, but still not fully awake, it dawned on him that he himself was the missing one. "I'm going back there ..." But, as though he were an insect struggling with its many legs to get free from some flypaper, he saw a bar of blue grow wide between his eyes, and then he emerged into a real existence where he was squandering his powers and wasting his time. He stretched out his legs and bathed them in the coolness underneath the sheets. "Edmée's been up for a while."

Looking down from the bedroom window, he was surprised to see a new planting of yellow chamomile and heliotropes; he recalled only the summer garden, blue and pink. He rang the bell, and its sound summoned an unfamiliar chambermaid, whom he challenged.

"Where is Henriette?"

"I'm her replacement, monsieur."

"Since when?"

"But ... it's been a month ..."

"Ah!" he breathed, as if to say "That explains it!"

"Where is madame?"

"Madame is on her way, monsieur, she's ready to go out."

Edmée did indeed come in, looking alert, but she paused for a moment on the threshold in a way that made Chéri laugh inside. He treated himself to the pleasure of alarming his wife a little more, by crying out "But it's Ragut's marten!" and her lovely chestnut-brown eyes wavered for a moment under his gaze.

"Fred, I ..."

"Yes, you're going out. I didn't hear you get up?"

She blushed ever so slightly.

"Nothing special about that. I've been sleeping so badly the last few nights, I've had the divan made up, in the boudoir ... You aren't doing anything unusual today, are you?"

"Yes, I am," he said, darkly.

"Is it serious?"

"Very serious."

He waited for a moment and then added, on a lighter note, "I'm going to have my hair cut."

"But you'll be having lunch here?"

"No, I'll grab a bite in town, I've made an appointment at Gustave's for a quarter past two. The regular barber is sick."

The lie blossomed effortlessly, polite and childlike, from his lips.

Because he was lying, his mouth rounded into a kiss and pouted flirtatiously, like it did when he was a boy. Edmée looked at him with a sort of masculine indulgence.

"You're looking well this morning, Fred . . . I'm off."

"You're catching the seven-thirty?"

She stared at him in alarm, then left so precipitously that he was still laughing about it when she closed the behind her.

"Ah, that feels good," he sighed. "How easy it is to laugh when you no longer expect anything of anyone . . ." In this way, while he got dressed, he imagined a kind of monasticism, and the little, insincere tune he hummed through closed lips kept him company like a mindless nun.

He went down into a city he'd forgotten. The throng threw off his paradoxical state of equilibrium, which called for crystal-clear emptiness and predictable pain. From a mirror on the rue Royale, his reflection caught him full in the face, from head to foot, just as the noonday sun was breaking through some rain clouds, and Chéri felt no connection with this novel, raw image mounted against a background of shopgirls and newsboys surrounded by jade necklaces and silver fox stoles. He thought that a certain internal fluttering he was experiencing, which he likened to a grain of lead jumping around inside a plastic ball, must be due to his being famished, and he took refuge in a restaurant.

Shaded from the sunlight, with his back to the windows of the terrace, he dined on choice oysters, fish, and fruits. Some young women seated nearby, unconcerned by his presence, afforded him a relief comparable to having a bouquet of chilled violets applied to one's closed eyelids. But the sudden aroma of coffee reminded Chéri of the necessity of getting up, of keeping the appointment that this aroma of fresh coffee set for him. Before he complied, he did go to his hairdresser's, held out his hands to be manicured, and, while a pair of skilled palms substituted their will for his, he glided through an interlude of incalculable repose.

The enormous key took up his whole pocket. "I won't go, I won't go . . ." To the rhythm of this refrain, repeated incessantly, cleansed of all meaning, he arrived at avenue de Villiers without difficulty. His clumsiness as he groped around for the keyhole and the grinding of the key inside the lock made his heart race for a moment, but an invigorating warmth in the vestibule calmed his nerves.

He made his way forward cautiously, master of this empire a few square feet in extent, which he possessed but didn't really know. On the table, the well-schooled housemaid had laid out the useless daily arsenal, and the embers of the fire were dying under a velvet blanket of hot ashes around an earthenware coffee pot. Methodically, Chéri removed from his pockets and lined up his cigarette case, the heavy key, the little key, the flat revolver, his wallet, his handkerchief, and his watch. But when he'd put on his Japanese robe he didn't stretch out on the divan. He opened the doors and inspected the cupboards, with the silent curiosity of a cat. Despite its feminine touches, a makeshift washroom offended his peculiar prudishness and made him back away. The bedroom—it, too, draped in that sad shade of red that settles around the lives of people in decline—was taken up mainly by the bed and smelled of old unmarried men and eau de cologne. Chéri came back into the sitting room. He lit the two wall sconces and the ribbon-and-bow chandelier. He listened to the faint sounds coming from the house, and, being alone for the first time in the shabby abode, tried to feel for himself the presence of those, departed or transient, who'd lived in it. He thought he heard and recognized a familiar tread, with its sound of threadbare slippers or an aged animal's paws, then shook his head.

"It's not her. She won't be back here for eight days. And when she is back, what more will I have in this world?...I'll have..."

In his head, he listened to the voice of la Copine, the tired-out voice of a rootless vagabond: "And so, I should finish the story about the run-in at the racetrack, between Léa and old man Mortier. Old man Mortier thought that a little publicity in *Gil Blas* would get him everything he wanted from Léa. Oh, là là my dearies! What a comeuppance! She took herself out to Longchamp, all dressed in blue, like a dream, cool and collected in her victoria drawn by two piebald mares..."

He raised his head toward the partition wall where, facing him, so many blue eyes were smiling, so many luscious necks were puffing out proudly above impassive bosoms.

"That's what I'll have. That's all I'll have. It's true that it might be a lot. It was a great stroke of luck that I met up with her again, here, on this wall. But now that I have met up with her again, all I can do is lose her. I'm still fixed, like her, with these rusty tacks, with these crooked pins. How long with this hold? Not long. And then—I know myself, I'm in dread of a stronger, irresistible need. I might cry out, all at once: 'I want her! I must have her! Right away!' And then what will I do?"

He pushed the divan toward the wall of pictures and lay down. When he was lying in this position, the Léas with their eyes lowered seemed to take an interest in him. "But it's no more than a look they have, I'm sure of it. And so, when you sent me on my way, what did you figure I'd be left with, after you, my Nounoune? Your generosity didn't cost you dearly, you knew what a Chéri amounted to, you weren't risking much. But for you to have been born so long before me, and for me to have loved you above and beyond all other women, for that we've paid a heavy price: look at you, you're worn out, and you find it consoling, when it's such a disgrace. And I . . . I, when other people say: 'There was the war,' I can say: 'There was Léa. Léa, the war . . .' I really did believe I wasn't thinking about either of them anymore, but it's both of them that have cast me out of the times we live in. From now on, I won't take up any more than half a place, anywhere . . ."

He pulled the table toward him to check his watch.

"Five thirty. The old woman won't be back here for eight days . . . And this is the first day. What if she dies en route?"

He shifted a little on the divan, smoked, and poured a cup of lukewarm coffee.

"Eight days. Even so, I shouldn't spend too much time thinking about it. Eight days from now . . . what story will she tell me? I know the one about the Drags off by heart, the one about the run-in at Longchamp, the one about her final showdown with Léa—and, once I've heard all of them, over and over again, what will come next? . . .

Nothing. In eight days, this old woman—I'm already waiting for her, as if she were was coming to give me an injection—this old woman will be back here, and . . . and she'll bring me nothing."

He turned a pleading gaze toward his favorite portrait. Already, the lifelike image inspired in him nothing more than diminished feelings of grievance, of ecstasy, of anxious anticipation. He tossed back and forth on the rug-covered divan, and, in spite of himself, mimicked the muscular contractions of a man who wants to jump off a height but doesn't dare.

He worked himself up to moan aloud and say repeatedly, "Nounoune, my Nounoune . . ." to make himself believe he'd reached a state of exaltation. But he felt ashamed and fell silent, because he knew he had no need of exaltation to lift the small, flat revolver off the table. Without raising himself, he tried to find a favorable position, ended up stretched out on top of his folded right arm, which held the weapon, then pressed his ear against the end of the barrel wedged between the cushions. Right away, his arm started to go numb, and he knew if he didn't hurry, his tingling fingers would refuse to obey. So he did hurry, and emitted a few stifled groans of complaint over the task, because his right arm, crushed under his body, was bothering him, and he knew nothing more of life past a pressure of his index finger on a little protrusion of finely ridged steel.

TRANSLATOR'S ACKNOWLEDGMENTS

EDWIN Frank embraced this project with enthusiasm and edited my draft translations with discernment.

Sara Kramer has perspicaciously overseen every stage of production.

Once again, I'm indebted to Isabelle Génin, maître de conférences at the Sorbonne Nouvelle—Paris 3, for her invaluable support. Edmund White read and responded to numerous passages and offered scores of insightful suggestions. Susan Stewart generously read and provided astute commentary on both of the novels, as did Linda Archibald.

My gratitude goes out as well to Tim Brook, Wendell Block, Peter Sakuls, Mark Silverman, JoAnne McFarland, Chris Harries, and David Friend.

Shortly after I began to translate *Chéri*, I read Judith Thurman's inspired biography of Colette, *Secrets of the Flesh*. I was delighted (and humbled) when Judith offered to review my draft translations, and overjoyed when she agreed to write the introduction to this volume. Her commendation is a signal honor.

OTHER NEW YORK REVIEW CLASSICS

For a complete list of titles, visit www.nyrb.com.